CO-STAR

HOLLYWOOD LIVES

AVA OLSEN

"I can live without money, but I cannot live without love." - Judy Garland

FOREWORD

Please note that Tate often calls Reed, "Ree" (the 'd' is deliberately left out)

CHAPTER 1

TATE

TEN YEARS AGO

"Are you going to throw up?"

I was startled by the blunt question as I stared at the stern-faced casting agent.

What the fuck?

I vigorously shook my head. "No, of course not."

Sure, this was only my third audition since I'd arrived in LA two weeks ago, but I wasn't about to blow it by puking on this chance. This chance being the agent in front of me, one Charlene Tilden, a middle-aged woman with silver hair and a blue gaze so pale, it was like staring into the eyes of a ghost.

"Are you sure?" she asked. "You look grey."

"It's the lighting."

I glanced up at the florescent lights that polluted the ceiling.

"Your name again?"

"Tate Aduma."

"Nice. Your own or a stage name?"

"Mine."

The one I'd changed before I left home.

Joshua Tate Hanratty was dead and buried.

"Your headshots suck," Charlene announced in her booming voice. "They don't do you justice at all. Get better ones if you want to find work in this town."

"I'll certainly do that. Thank you, ma'am."

"And lose the southern accent. The role is for a cop who's from Chicago. Talk faster."

"I didn't know the audition had already started."

"It has."

"Okay."

I guess I had a lot to learn about the movie business.

She glanced at my portfolio and then back at me. I struggled not to flinch or look away.

"It says here you're twenty. You look older."

No fucking kidding.

Inside, I felt close to fifty.

The things I'd endured to date were not fit to discuss.

Outside was a different matter.

When I turned seventeen, I hit a growth spurt. I went from a gangly, rail thin boy to a six-three man with a square jaw, and a beard that any mountain man would envy.

The changes in my body changed my life. Day by day, I was able to take back my power, and three years later, I was here.

I'd survived.

"It's the facial hair," I replied as I rubbed my face.

I'd shaved three hours ago, but the stubble was already growing in fast and thick.

"No. It's your eyes. You've had a shit life."

Who the fuck was this woman? An agent or a goddamn psychic?

Now I was really starting to sweat, and it had nothing to do with the audition.

"Let's get on with it," she sighed. "Page 4 of the script, paragraph five. Barry, read it out with him. Go."

I stared at the camera that was set up in between Charlene and her assistant, Barry. He held the script in his hand and yawned.

Tough crowd.

You can do this.

No. I *will* do this. No can or would or should or anything else but success.

Confidence.

I was going to get this fucking role. I could feel it in my bones. I was launching myself into the Hollywood stratosphere, no matter what.

And nothing, not even this intimidating casting agent, was gonna stop me.

The role, as Charlene mentioned, was for a cop. One who just discovered that his partner was on the take. There was an ensuing confrontation. A shootout was set to occur.

The role was a perfect fit for me.

I'd experienced plenty of violence in my life. Enough to summon an anger so intense it would burn this fucking warehouse down.

And score me this role.

I took a deep breath and went for it.

"I said put the fucking gun down," I bit out, each word lower and deadlier than the last.

"You're really not going to shoot me, are you? You wouldn't. I'm your fucking partner." Barry read off the script.

"You're a dirty cop, that's what you are! A traitor to your oath and to me. Now I'm done talking to you. Either put the gun down or I swear to God, I'm gonna shoot."

"You won't. You can't," Barry scoffed.

"I fucking will!" I roared.

"I got a wife at home. Are you really going to do that to her? Make Jenny a widow?"

"Damn right. Not only that, I'm gonna console your wife. Poor, beautiful Jenny. So young, all alone, and fragile now that her lying, thieving husband is gone. But I'm here. I'm a real man. One that doesn't screw up. But I'll be damn ready to screw her."

"You son of a—*Bang, the sound of a gun goes off,*" Barry muttered in a monotone voice. "Cut scene."

I glanced at Charlene, hoping, wondering, but she said… nothing.

She just stared at me with those creepy eyes of hers, like she could see right into my soul.

I hoped to hell this audition was over.

"Thank you, Tate," Charlene finally replied. "This script is so cheesy you could grate it and serve it over pasta. But, surprisingly, your performance was not horrible."

I barked out a laugh. Couldn't help it. My nerves had finally let loose.

"I'm not sure what that means," I replied as I placed my hands on my hips.

"Of course, you don't. You're so green, you've got okra growing out of your ears."

I ignored her attempt at an insult. "How did I really do?"

Charlene scoffed but I noticed the smirk on her face. "You're a cocky SOB, aren't you? You've got movie star looks and a dark charisma that's very enticing. Because of all that, I'll let your comment go. This time. But don't ask that question in an audition ever again. Not if you want anyone in this business to take you seriously. Understood?"

"Yes, ma'am."

She shook her head. "I really want to dislike you, Tate, but I can taste your ambition. It's nearly choking me from across the room. And I know raw talent when I see it. Here's my card."

Charlene held out her hand and I reached for the black card with gold lettering.

Swear to God, I heard music in my head. I felt like I'd been handed the keys to heaven.

"I'll be in touch this week about the role. Since you don't have representation yet, I'm going to refer you to someone I know. They may or may not be trustworthy—it's hard to tell in this town—but they get their clients in for the big auditions."

"Thanks, that's generous of you."

"I doubt you'll be saying that in a year's time."

For someone who made her money in this business, she sounded like she hated it. It was strange. She was strange. But she saw something in me, so I let her sarcasm go.

I pocketed the card, feeling it burn a hole in my jeans.

"Wait in the hallway. I'm going to make a call."

"Thanks."

I nodded at Barry—who looked at me like I was a piece of shit he'd stepped on—and then headed out to the hallway to wait as instructed.

It was really happening. Fucking hell, it was happening.

I'd made a good first impression. No, maybe not that.

Memorable.

Memorable was always better than good.

As I walked out of the room, I noticed three guys standing around, waiting for their turn.

Fuck, talk about competition. One man was more beautiful than the next. Then I mentally chastised myself for thinking that way at all.

Making it big wasn't just about looks. It was about presence.

And I got the casting agent's card, that had to count for something.

My eyes landed on the last guy standing, the blond leaning against the wall. He was laughing and gesturing with his hands at something the other two were saying. And he looked so relaxed, so completely at ease, that I was instantly irritated.

I had giant pit stains on my white t-shirt, never mind the

hunger in my belly that was now making itself known. I barely had enough money to pay for my ticket to LA and my lodging for the next three months, never mind three meals a day. Or deodorant.

You're here. You're making it happen. Focus on that.

I walked down the hallway, ignoring the pretty boys, and stood as far away from them as I could.

Apparently, that was no deterrent to the blond, who sidled up to me about two seconds after my back hit the exposed brick wall.

"Hey."

I turned towards the husky voice and was sucked in, without awareness, by the greenest eyes I'd ever seen in my life.

If that agent considered me movie star handsome, she didn't know shit.

My protective wall engaged as this guy, just shy of my height and standing in my personal space, stared at me. With a messy mop of wavy hair, pouty pink lips, and a nose that had never been broken (not in anger, anyway), he was pretty in a way that made my teeth ache.

I viciously reminded myself that I hated sweets.

"I'm Reed," he announced as he held out his hand.

Instead of taking it, I stared back at him. At those electric eyes that were made for movie cameras.

All my southern instincts screamed at me about minding my manners, but I ignored them—and his hand. I was in California now, and I would do whatever the fuck I wanted.

And I did not want to tempt fate by touching him.

"Reed Larkin," he repeated. "I've never seen you here before. You new in town?"

His voice was smooth, just like him. With no trace of any discernible accent and with a hint of a raspy undertone, he belonged not just in the movies, but on audio too.

Red carpet worthy for sure.

You are too.

"Fresh off the bus from Doncaster, Alabama," I replied with an extra twang to my speech, hoping that my act would push him away.

No such luck.

Reed shook his head. "Never heard of it."

"Not surprised. It's a dump. I'm never going back."

"That bad?"

If only he could see the scars on my lower back. Once I got my big break, and had money in the bank, the first person I was going to see was a plastic surgeon.

"Let's just say I'm really fucking happy to be in LA. Acting is my dream. One that I'm going to make come true."

Reed smiled at me, and it was like looking directly into the sun.

I shouldn't, but I couldn't look away.

Strange.

"I've been here just over eight months," Reed replied. "I'm from upstate New York. Not a shithole town, but a small one, so there's not much going on either. And LA? It's fucking wild, man. The party scene is next level. Thank fuck I just turned twenty-one."

"I'm here to find work and to make it big. I don't give much thought to partying," I replied, crossing my arms.

Reed looked me up and down and I struggled not to fidget.

"You've got the tall, dark, and handsome bit down just fine. How did your audition go?"

"She's referring me to a rep since I don't have an agent yet."

"Charlene did that for you? Fuck, you must be good."

"I am."

"Ooh, cocky and broody. I'm intrigued," Reed chuckled as he elbowed me.

I shook my head. *Broody?* Jesus Christ.

"You got a place to stay?" he asked.

"Not yet." I shook my head. "I just got here two weeks ago. I have a room at a hostel."

"I've got a two-bedroom that I share with one roommate, but he's moving out. If you can put in $500 a month, the second bedroom is yours."

"I'll think about it. Let's trade numbers."

His offer wasn't the cheapest, but he looked nicely dressed and I assumed his place was the same. And even if I thought Reed was over the top—kinda like an eager blond Labrador— I did need some friends in this town. And a safe place to sleep.

He looked harmless but I never made assumptions.

Mistakes like that could be deadly.

"You got another audition after this?" I asked.

He leaned in again, his shoulder rubbing against mine. I did my best to slowly step away.

"Nope. Just lick me."

"Excuse me?" I snapped.

I was louder than I realized, and the other guys turned and glared at me.

Reed threw his head back and laughed. That honeyed rasp of his was something else.

"I'm going to Lick Me, it's a club. A gay club in West Hollywood."

"A… gay club?"

I squeaked like a ten-year-old, no joke. Gone was the voice my drama teacher once described as a 'velvet baritone'.

"Yeah, gay clubs are the best. And I'm not just saying that because I'm gay. The parties are freaking incredible."

Reed was so open about it, like there it was. Here he was. Out and proud. No big deal. Was everyone in LA so relaxed about revealing their sexuality to strangers?

"I'm not gay," I blurted out.

I'd been telling that lie since I was thirteen years old. No sense in changing now. Not when I was so close to my dream of making it as an actor.

I was going to have money, and fame, and everything I could get out of this life. And that hellhole where I grew up, the nightmare that was my childhood, it was all in my rear-view mirror.

Where it would stay.

The Hollywood movie machine was still operating in a hetero world. A world I was used to acting in. It was perfect fit.

"Okay, that's cool. You still wanna come with?" Reed asked. "There's dancing and strong, cheap drinks. Wait, how old are you? I forgot to ask."

"Twenty."

He elbowed me again. "It shouldn't be a problem getting you in. You look older than I do."

I should've been insulted but he was smiling so hard I couldn't.

"And relax," Reed added. "Everyone in the neighborhood goes there, not just gays. Like I said, cheap drinks. Besides, no one knows who you are."

"Not yet."

CHAPTER 2

REED

NINE YEARS AGO

Climbing the Hollywood hills was easy.

Climbing the Hollywood acting scene was nearly impossible.

I'd secured guest spots on popular TV shows over the past year and combined with modeling shoots, it paid the bills. But it was not the success that I'd anticipated a year ago, the one everyone back home in New York was rooting for.

A lead role. Movie offers. Film premiers.

I was still gearing up for my first big break.

And funny enough, my competition for many of the roles I wanted always came in the form of my roommate, Tate.

Not that he'd hit the big time, either. Not yet. Like me, he'd had steady work but nothing that catapulted him to stardom.

We made an odd couple—as roommates and friends.

He was intense, moody, and so focused on his future that he didn't see what was standing right in front of him. I admired his tenacity, his drive. Fuck, he had at least five to six auditions lined up every week, without fail. He was busting his ass to get ahead. To get noticed.

But I also recognized that he was running from something.

He'd only mentioned his hometown a few times, and only to say it was crap. I was sure that it was much more than that. Whenever we'd get into an argument, which could spark from something as simple as how loud the TV was, his anger exploded. And if you were nearby, look out, because the backdraft would knock you flat on your ass.

Not that he scared me or anything. His temper was vocal, not physical.

But I was the son of a therapist and I recognized trauma when I saw it.

My take? Acting was Tate's form of therapy, whether he knew it or not.

No one who met me, at first glance, assumed that I knew of such things. That was fine.

Sure, I was blond, and people often made quips about my matching sunny personality. Like being a positive person in this town was a bad thing. Or that my easy jokes and laid-back manner meant I wasn't as smart, or driven, or as adept at reading a room. Or a scene.

I didn't bother to correct anyone.

It was always better to be underestimated.

Not that Tate did that to me. Not since he moved into my place a month after we first met.

He learned right quick that I was not the himbo he'd assumed at first glance. And I had a temper at times too. Slower to burn.

Except with Tate. Then it was like striking a match.

But it was over as quick as it lit.

We joked, and fought, and the circle went on.

But while I was always a glass half-full kind of guy, that didn't mean I didn't see the empty space. I just chose to believe in the best in people.

And something about Tate, from the first day we met, called to me.

His brusque attitude and rigid demeanor were shields, ones that he fought hard to maintain. Except when I said something outrageous and coaxed a rare smile out of him. Fuck, if he smiled more in auditions, he'd probably be a superstar by now.

The only other time he mellowed was when he'd had a few drinks. The man was crying out for fun but rarely relaxed enough to do so.

In no time at all, he became my closest friend. I had a lot of them, but very few I trusted.

Most of my acting friends would stab you in the back for less than the price of admission.

But not Tate.

Despite our competition for the same roles, neither of us torpedoed the other. We traded the inside scoop on upcoming auditions. And we helped each other rehearse our lines and offered criticism. Some of it we took, other times it led to arguments, of course. Passionate ones, always. Ones that were becoming a bit too passionate. At least, for me.

Too bad Tate was straight.

Or so he said.

His constant reminders to me that he was *not gay* repeated like a bad case of reflux. I heard him the first time. And I never came on to him or flirted. Well, not intentionally. But there was a tension between us, and sometimes it made me wonder. Not to mention that I spotted him staring at me a few times. And I knew interest when I saw it.

But I didn't want to rock our friendship. Or push him in any way. Everyone came out in their own time. Or not at all.

And Tate was already a wounded animal—get too close or push too hard, and find out the hard way that yes, his bite *is* as bad as his bark.

But his constant refrain made me question things. Why

did he feel the need to keep telling me he wasn't gay? The behavior reminded me of the jocks in high school who were vocal about not associating with anyone queer, until after class, when they'd proposition me in the locker room.

And sure, I knew that openly queer actors had a harder time in this biz. Unfortunate, but true. But I had come out of the closet at sixteen and there was no fucking way I was ever going back in.

Not even for my career.

Which might finally be on the verge of spiking.

I'd finally secured an audition for a movie role. Not an extra, not a non-speaking role, but a good, solid supporting role.

Now all I had to do was break the news to Tate.

The door of our apartment slammed, and I heard my roommate's telltale footsteps down the hallway. He stepped into the living room where I was sitting on the sofa, reading my lines.

"Hey!" I greeted him, schooling my expression.

Tate had recently cut his hair, and the long brunet strands that once fell to his cheekbones were no more. The undercut suited him. Despite the scruff that covered most of his jawline, I noticed the rare pink flush that stained his cheekbones.

"Guess what?"

I could tell from his excited tone that something big had happened.

"You got the part in *Longford Medical*?"

Longford Medical was a long running hospital drama on TV. I'd auditioned too, but they wanted someone older.

He shook his head and whipped off his wayfarers, his amber eyes so bright I hardly recognized him.

Then he smiled, and shit, the effect it had on me was painfully intense.

"Even better. I got an audition for *Fallingbrook*!"

"The one directed by Lance Darling?"

"Yes! This is fucking it! I can feel it, Ree. This is the one!"

I launched off the sofa and reached over to hug him. For once, Tate didn't tense.

In fact, he squeezed me so tight I was sure my ribs were going to bust.

"I'm so happy for you!" I exclaimed when I finally leaned back.

"I'm still in shock. I just got off the phone with Henn. She was so excited."

Henny Pritchard was his agent and one hardworking bitch. I say that in all respect because being a bitch in this town is a necessity. She pushed for the clients she believed in. Tate was one of them.

My agent, a guy named Rik Grouse, was not the same. He'd been great in the beginning. But the number of new auditions he had in mind for movie roles was dwindling with each passing month, and I knew that something had to change.

"When do you get called in?" I asked, as I quickly stepped back.

Tate licked his lips, and I forced my eyes up to his. "Next Tuesday. You gonna help me rehearse?"

"Of course. But the same goes. When you're a big star on that movie set, you better invite me to visit," I teased.

Tate shook his head. "Better yet, as soon as I have the offer, I'll put a good word in with the producer."

"Confidence, I love it! Fuck, I'm so happy for you."

"Thanks. You feel like going out for a bite? My treat."

I grabbed my phone on the coffee table. "You're on."

"How about you? Any news?"

"Yeah, but I don't want to spoil yours. It can wait."

Tate glared at me, his eyes darkening. "Spit it out, Ree. Come on."

"I have an audition on Monday for a supporting role in *Just Like You*."

"The romcom?"

"Yeah. At first Rik wasn't sure about it. I had to push him. Hard. The movie auditions are getting fewer and fewer."

"Why wouldn't he jump on it?"

"I don't fucking know. TV, no problem, but he knows what my goal is. Now I'm starting to think he doesn't believe in me like he used to. Or maybe he sees a problem I don't. Christ, is it possible I'm just not meant for the bigger roles?"

The glass was half-empty for a change.

"Bullshit," Tate snapped and pointed a finger at me. "And don't ever repeat that. If you think that way, you're defeating yourself. You know you have what it takes. Maybe it's time to find an agent who feels the same way."

"You're right." I nodded, taking a deep breath. "But patience for shit like this is never my strong suit."

"That's 'cause you're the golden boy."

"Excuse me?"

"You've probably had people falling all over you since forever. Telling you you're beautiful and let's face it, when you look like you do, doors open. You don't need to bust them down like the rest of us."

I crossed my arms, my temper igniting. "Doors have not opened. And I work my ass off!"

"I didn't say you didn't. But I think you came to LA under the assumption that you were gonna make it fast. But the reality is, if you're not related to anyone famous, it ain't happening overnight. Even for someone as pretty and talented as you."

"Look who's talking, Mr. Dark and Dangerous," I scoffed. "Most of the people you meet are ready to drop to their knees for you."

"I told you how I feel about you saying shit like that," he bit out.

"Which part?"

Tate's face flushed a dark red. "All of it."

"Enjoy the rest of your night," I snapped, and started to walk around him.

Tate grabbed my arm. "Ree, I didn't intend to insult you. But you gotta admit, gorgeous people have an advantage. And sometimes it makes them lazy or complacent."

"This is LA, Tate, everyone is gorgeous! I'm not a stand-out. If I was, and if what you said was true, I'd be a star right now. And you call me lazy one more time and you can sleep on the goddamn balcony!"

"I said it makes *some* people lazy, not you. Don't twist my words."

I arched one eyebrow, but it had no effect on him.

He sighed. "I just meant that you had certain expectations when you got here and just because it's taking longer that you thought, doesn't mean it won't happen. You have a presence that draws people to you. Fuck, even grumpy asses like me. And your day is going to come. I know it. You know it too."

I took a deep breath and nodded. "I just want it so bad. And Rik keeps getting me auditions for bit parts on TV when I want the movie roles. And he won't tell me why. I mean, any job means money, but this is my dream. I'm a good actor."

"You're a great actor, but Rik needs to go. Want me to talk to Henn?"

"Why not? But quietly. I don't want to alert Rik just yet. Not until *after* this audition."

Tate nodded. "Are you still pissed at me, or do you want to go out?"

I cocked my head and planted my hands on my hips. "Mexican?"

"You know it."

The next week, I got the part. And then I switched agents. And Tate was right.

The stars were finally aligning.

Tate won his role too.

He jokingly called me his lucky charm. We celebrated our first movie roles by getting drunk and getting matching four-leaf clover tattoos on our hips, me on my right, him on his left.

We were riding high, and nothing could stop us.

But acting was a career with no clear direction. One week you were up, the next down, the next out entirely. There were no guarantees, no security.

You only had today.

Living in the present was easy for us.

But eventually, the past has a way of catching up.

CHAPTER 3

TATE

EIGHT YEARS AGO

"That's it. Just like that. Fuck, that's good."

My words were barely a whisper.

I was, after all, in my trailer, on the lot, on my break, and getting sucked off by one of the extras, a cute twink named Leo.

I couldn't afford to scream or shout and have a PA come barging in here.

Not that I was concerned they'd blab, because everyone here knew the drill. Fooling around with people on set was my usual preference. NDAs were already in place. It made it quick and convenient. And I liked to keep my private life, private.

Maybe next time, I'd have enough time to screw.

It had been a while since I'd fucked a man and the need was hitting hard. The women I dated publicly weren't doing it for me. They never would. But they looked good, or rather, we did. Out at parties and biz junkets. And cultivating my image was important.

This was my second movie role in a year, and for a

twenty-two-year-old from bumfuck nowhere, I was living the fucking dream.

Until a sudden knock at the door startled me—and the guy sucking my cock.

I started to push his head away when the door opened.

Reed stepped up into the trailer.

I was both relieved and panicked when I met my best friend's surprised gaze.

"Sorry," he quickly replied, turned, and slammed the door again.

"Oh shit," Leo whispered, his voice hoarse.

He looked up at me but all I saw was his dirty blond hair.

"No worries. Finish me off and do it fast," I commanded.

Leo groaned and took me back into his mouth. Fuck, he had no goddamn gag reflex and after a few bobs of his head, I came down his throat in a heated rush.

I almost cried out his name.

No, not Leo's.

Then I realized it was just a coincidence. Bad timing.

Leo pulled off and wiped his mouth with the back of his hand. I passed him a box of wet wipes and motioned to the door.

"Thanks."

I stood up and headed for the bathroom, giving myself a quick cleanup and a fresh spritz of cologne.

When I exited, Leo was gone. And Reed was sitting in my chair.

The chair where I just blew my load.

Christ.

My dick twitched but I ignored it and walked right up to my best friend.

"My apologies for interrupting," Reed smirked, his green eyes full of mischief.

"Fuck off, you're not sorry at all," I grumbled.

Reed laughed out loud, and the familiar sound made me shiver.

"You're so right," Reed replied with his sunny smile. "He's cute."

"I didn't notice," I said as I sat down on the chair opposite him. "It was only a blow job. Any warm, wet mouth will do. It doesn't mean anything."

I was still resisting the truth. Especially with Reed.

After almost two years of living in the same apartment, it wasn't the first time he'd caught me with my dick down some guy's throat. He knew I was gay. But I still couldn't say the words.

But I did have a theory as to why I was holding out.

Even though we were both making movies, I'd received the bigger roles and the higher pay. I sure as shit knew it wasn't because I was a better actor. I suspected that Reed's openness about his sexuality had something to do with it. He'd even brought men as dates to cast parties and events.

While LA in general and the movie business in particular was full of queer rep, it still wasn't the norm when you sat down in that movie theatre and stared up at the big screen.

Hetero relationships still ruled the box office.

Movie stars, too.

Unfair, but true.

And I wouldn't be happy until I was one of them.

"Speaking of sucking, I had a shit morning," Reed whispered as his luminous smile dimmed.

"What happened?"

"The assistant director, Donny Flood, wanted to hook up."

"Are you shitting me?"

Reed shook his head.

"He's like, sixty years old," I scoffed. "You're so far out of his league it's laughable."

Reed sighed. "Well, he didn't find it funny when I turned him down."

"I met him at a junket last month. With his wife. She's a horrible actress... Tina, Tara... I can't remember."

Fuck, I was terrible with names. Ironic, giving my ability to memorize lines and lines of dialogue.

"So what happened?" I asked.

"I politely turned him down. An hour later, I was informed that I was re-cast in a non-speaking role. When I confronted him about it, he said it was due to 'artistic refinement'. What a line of bullshit. Fucking prick. You know, sometimes, I really hate this town."

"He can't do that to you! Did you tell Henn?"

Reed scoffed. "Of course, I did. I called her right away. But there's nothing she can do. It's his word against mine. And decisions to re-cast are done all the time. It's not unusual."

I got up and began to pace. I was so angry at that asshole for punishing Reed.

It served as another reminder of the predatory nature of our industry.

So why then, did so many of us stay? The lure of money and fame is just too tempting to pass up. Not just that, but the whole culture of the business rewarded your ego. The chance at being immortalized on film fed into the basic human desire to cheat death.

"I have an idea."

Reed looked at me with a furrowed brow. "You're not going to slash his tires or anything like that are you?"

"What? No." I playfully smacked his shoulder. "There might be an opening here."

"What? How?"

"Keep this between you and me. Dylan Aylmer was found passed out in his trailer yesterday. Drunk. Again. He couldn't film at all. And we don't have the budget to delay any more, so I have a feeling he's going to be cut. I could put a word in for you."

Reed stood up in front of me and shook his head. "I can't let you do that. And doesn't Dylan have a major role?"

"No, he's a supporting actor in this one. A great guy, friendly and talented, but his drinking is getting out of hand and it's affecting his hiring. Too bad, he had top billing last year," I paused. "So, you want me to put a word in?"

"I couldn't ask you to do that," Reed whispered.

Reed was too nice for this cutthroat business.

"Why not? It'd be great. We could finally work together."

Reed turned away and glanced out the window. Not that there was anything to see outside but other trailers.

"I don't think so. I still have my commitment—"

"To a non-speaking role? And an asshole assistant director who'll probably make your life hell until you give in and fuck him?"

Reed flinched. "I don't want to get a reputation as an actor that can't hack it and quits on a whim. I'm not a diva and I take my work seriously."

Reed turned to me again, fire in his eyes.

"This is a better opportunity. You know it is!" I snapped. "Why are you being a stubborn ass?"

"I'm not! Just let it go, Tay. I'm sorry I brought it up."

"Are you?"

"Yes! I don't even know why I'm here. I should have stayed on the lot and had my break with the crew."

"Admit it, you missed me."

He shook his head but smiled. "You're so fucking arrogant, you know that?"

I preened at his remark. He was right.

"I better go," Reed murmured and headed for the door.

"Let me put a word in, please. You deserve better."

Reed reached for the door latch and paused. "I don't think it would be good for our friendship, or for your reputation. There might be talk. We spend enough time together as is."

"What do you mean?"

Reed turned and rolled his eyes. "Trying to get me this role might make people take notice. We still share an apartment. I'm just waiting for the press to get a hold of that. How much longer can you keep it a secret?"

"About that," I started, as I took a deep breath. "I've got enough saved now to get my own place. I was gonna tell you on the weekend, but since you brought it up… I'm moving out at the end of the month. That gives you three weeks to find someone else."

Reed said nothing at first, he just looked away and nodded.

"Sorry I interrupted you earlier," Reed sighed. "And as for your offer, thanks but no thanks. I'll stick with my current job. It's better for everyone. And I appreciate the heads up, I'll start looking for a new roommate right away."

As much as I was looking forward to my total independence and a place of my own, I didn't like the idea of Reed sharing his space with anyone but me. Strange but true.

But I didn't say anything. People moved up and moved on. It was time.

We'd still see each other. Our friendship wouldn't change.

Or so I thought.

Later that night, when I got back to our apartment, Reed wasn't alone.

When I got out of the elevator, just out of sight, I watched as the director Reed was complaining about was heading out of our apartment.

A sick feeling washed over me. I turned the corner and waited in the shadows until the older man quickly stalked towards the elevator. Once he was gone, I waited a few minutes and then walked over to let myself into our apartment.

"Ree?" I called out as I slammed and locked the door behind me.

He stepped into the hallway in his red silk robe, his hair disheveled.

"Hey, I thought you weren't back until after midnight?" Reed asked.

"We shut down at eleven. I guess a fourteen-hour day was long enough."

"Okay, well, I'm exhausted. I'm off to bed. Night."

He turned quickly.

"Ree?"

"Yeah?" He swiveled back to look at me.

Under the dim glow of the overhead light, I finally took notice of his face. The dark circles under his eyes. And the redness on his cheeks.

"Is everything okay?"

Reed let out a shaky breath and tightened the belt on his robe. "It will be."

Two days later, Reed had his speaking role back.

I never asked and he never said. It became the great unspoken secret. I had plenty of my own, but Reed? He was normally an open book.

There was a shift between us, a wall thrown up. One that neither of us was willing to climb.

And it turned out, we weren't that different, he and I.

Both of us were gonna make it, no matter the cost. Pride had no place in show business.

But I hated to think of my friend, who was a kind and sensitive man, being hardened like me. I didn't want that for his life.

Two weeks later, I moved out.

But every time I walked into my new place, I expected Reed to be there. Or his belongings, which were strewn in every room in our old apartment. He was fastidious about a clean kitchen, but a neat freak he was not.

What did I miss most? His boisterous laugh. And oddly

enough, the scent of those damn vanilla candles that he had everywhere.

I often heard the echo of his voice in my dreams. For the most part, that's where I saw him. I was busy, and so was he, and our friendship went from talking every day to texting once a week.

It took me four months to get used to living alone.

I hated every minute.

CHAPTER 4

REED

SEVEN YEARS AGO

"Reed, take the offer. It's a historical drama with a lot of potential. If it gets picked up, think of the royalties. We're talking lots and lots of money."

I was tempted to throw my phone across the room.

"I'm not saying no, Henn, it's just—"

"I know, sweetie, I know, but this is a good thing. It's a solid role, with writers that are known for their hit shows. No, it's not a movie deal, but it's still great money. And a regular schedule which will leave you time for other auditions. Plus, no creepy predators. That I know of. And who knows from there? Come on, most actors would kill for this kind of offer."

"You're right, I know you're right. I'll take it."

"Amazing! I'm emailing you the contract. Let's meet for lunch tomorrow to celebrate, your pick."

"Thanks, Henn."

I sighed, staring out my window. At the orange glow of the sunset in the distance.

My movie dreams fading as fast as the sunlight.

"Reed, you're a wonderful actor, and this is going to be good for you."

"I know," I replied and hung up.

I thought about my goals when I'd arrived in LA three years ago. And this was not where I thought I'd be by now.

Not like Tate.

My friend had launched—not all the way to the top, but close—and left me in his stardust.

I thought for sure he'd have pushed our friendship aside too, but he surprised me. Despite his success and hectic shooting schedule, he always made time for a text or a call. Sometimes a dinner at my place when he had a few hours to spare.

No, it wasn't like it was when we were roommates but then, nothing was.

And despite my busy work and social life, none of the men I met ever compared to him.

It was stupid and foolish. Tate didn't see me like that.

I was his friend, and only that.

And friendships were too rare to risk. Even for me.

Lovers I could pick up any day, but someone I could confide in?

Fuck, no.

I texted Tate to tell him about the contract.

He was always the first person I went to with any news. Even before my family back home. Sure, my mom, dad, and sister were proud of me. They were there when I needed a boost and vice versa. And my mom was a former drama teacher, so she knew all about actors.

But Tate was going through the exact same thing as me and he could relate in a way no one else in my family could. Working actors dealt with a seesaw of emotions, the ups and downs of our employment status playing havoc with our bank accounts and our confidence.

Not ten seconds after I sent the text, my phone rang.

"Hey."

"Hey? Is that the best you can do?" Tate yelled in response. I heard traffic noise in the background. Not surprising, since half of your life in California was spent on the road. "At least act enthused. You got a contract, Ree! This calls for celebration. I'm picking you up in half an hour."

"Sounds good. Where do you want to go?"

"How about a private party up in the hills hosted by none other than Kendrick Sloan, the producer? I snagged an invite from Erin."

"Are you… is she… coming with us?"

If so, it was a hard pass for me.

Erin was a model and socialite that Tate paraded around town for parties, and the like. Or maybe it was the other way around since she had more connections than he did. She was Tate's on-again, off-again girlfriend. Or fake girlfriend. I didn't know anymore. Leggy, blonde, and bubbly, she was nice enough on the surface, but I didn't like her. I didn't trust her, and I didn't like the way she held onto Tate.

Like he belonged to her.

I knew that Tate was using her, and it went both ways. That was the problem. I was worried she'd sell him out at some point. Still, I minded my business.

I was a nice guy, after all.

Most of the time. But mess with my friends, Tate especially, and look out. If she made Tate unhappy, I'd rip out her hair extensions without pause.

"She's in Miami," Tate replied. "And staying there."

"She's moving?"

"She's gone. Moved a few days ago. Met some guy in the hotel business there."

"Are you okay?"

I sure as fuck was. I was so relieved at this news.

"Why wouldn't I be? It was all for show. Besides, there's

now a roster of actresses and models looking to be seen with Tate Aduma."

"Jesus Christ, your ego is really getting out of hand."

Tate's responding laughter had all the hair on my body standing on end. It wasn't often that he let loose like that. I was extremely possessive of that laugh because I was one of the rare people that could pull it out of him.

Not even Erin could do that.

"I'll be there soon. Wait out back."

The line went dead. Typical Tate. Never say *hi* or *bye*.

I headed for my bathroom and took a quick shower.

Then I changed into a pair of navy-blue trousers and a short-sleeve button down. Twenty-minutes later, I was in the service elevator that led to the back of the building.

Surprisingly, when I exited the condo, Tate's red sports coupe was already parked nearby.

"You're early," I commented as I walked up to the car. "Mark this date down."

"Shut up and get in the car, Mr. TV big shot."

I gave him my favorite finger and then opened the passenger door.

"Nice fit," he murmured as he lowered his sunglasses and gave me a once over. "Looking for a hot man tonight?"

I was looking right at him.

"Always," I replied with a wink, then slid into the seat and slammed the door. "I could use a good dicking down."

Tate swallowed hard and pushed his sunglasses back up, then turned his attention to the road and shifted into drive.

He hit the accelerator, hard, and tore out of the alleyway.

"What about you?" I asked. "Now that Erin's gone, you'll be on the hunt for a new piece of arm candy."

"Don't be bitchy, Ree, it doesn't suit."

"Sure, it does. I'm not always nice."

"Yes, you are," Tate smiled. "As fluffy as marshmallow and just as sweet."

"Fuck off, Tay," I grumbled. "That's the most insulting thing anyone has ever said to me."

Despite Tate's easy laughter, and our usual banter, he seemed different.

Unsettled.

When we stopped at a red light, I noticed that he was fidgeting in his seat, tapping repeatedly on the steering wheel with one hand and using his free hand to rub his beard.

It wasn't like him. He wasn't a nervous person. Or, if he did have anxiety, he hid it well.

"What's wrong? You're jumpy."

"Just a long week. I also have to be on set early tomorrow morning."

"Why didn't you say? We can go out another night."

"No!" he yelled, and I startled. Then he shook his head. "Sorry, I mean, this is perfect. Erin assured me that this party is gonna be a good time."

Something was going on with him, but I didn't push.

If, when, he wanted to tell me, he would.

It took about an hour to get to our destination. We ventured the winding roads, climbing higher and higher, and finally arrived at a gated community at the top of a scenic cul de sac. Tate gave his name to the security guard, and we were waved through.

Every luxury car you could name was lined up along the street.

After we located a spot and parked, Tate motioned to the largest house on the street. We walked up the massive driveway, following the blast of music. But the closer we came to the front door, the more my anxiety spiked. And I had no idea why.

Maybe because Tate was still fidgeting.

I nudged his shoulder while he knocked on the door. "What's with you?"

"Nothing. Nothing this party won't fix," he replied.

This was not the Tate I first met, the one who couldn't stand the party scene.

He put on his professional smile when the door opened. A handsome man in his forties stood in the foyer.

"Tate! I wasn't sure if you'd show up. Without Erin, I mean."

"It is what it is. Life goes on," Tate shook his head and a lock of hair fell over his eyes. "She's happy in Miami, and I'm happy here."

"Who's your friend?"

"Oh, sorry," Tate replied. "Kendrick Sloan, this is Reed Larkin."

I offered my hand and Kendrick shook it. "Larkin... that sounds familiar. Are you one of Henn's clients?"

I smiled. "I am."

"Awesome, come on in. The party's just getting started. Here."

Kendrick handed over his phone to Tate first, then Tate passed it to me. I tapped on the eNDA and added my signature.

LA, gotta love it.

Once that was done, Kendrick ushered us inside. "Go mix and mingle. I'll catch up with you later."

This house was open concept living at it's most extravagant. The entire living, dining, and kitchen space all together was the entire size of my apartment, times four.

With floor to ceiling windows and minimalist décor, the house was all about the view: a panoramic slice of the city, lit up like a wash of glittering jewels. People were packed into every corner of the room, the music blasting out over the din.

Tate tapped my arm and I followed him through the crowd.

A dining table big enough for twenty was set up with bottles of champagne and liquor on one end and bags of coke down the other.

Plenty of people were lined up to score, one after the other, taking their turn. I stuck to alcohol and the occasional spliff. Coke made me jittery as fuck and that screwed with my ability to audition. But it was tempting, especially when the host was providing the goods to his guests for free. Only the biggest players in this town could afford to do that.

"Champagne or a margarita?" I asked Tate.

"Champagne. I'll be right back."

Tate let go of my arm, and I watched as he walked around the table, weaving in and out of the throngs of people. He was stopped several times by one person more famous than the next. But Tate didn't linger, he said a quick hello and kept rounding the table until he reached the other end.

"Would you care for a glass of champagne, sir?"

I startled at first because I didn't even notice the server standing nearby.

Nodding, I held up two fingers. "Thanks."

When he passed over the glasses, I took my first sip, glancing around the room.

I nearly choked on the bubbly.

It wasn't the champagne. It was Tate that caught me off guard.

I watched as he grabbed one of the gold cylinders littering the table and leaned down to snort a whole line of coke.

When he finally leaned back up, he shook his head and smiled, wiping his nose.

Tate made his way around the table again and I passed him a glass, my hands suddenly shaky.

"Never seen you do that before," I said casually as I looked at him.

He shrugged his shoulders. "Only the past few months. My schedule's been crazy and it's the only thing that keeps me energized. You know how it is. Plus, this current job has been difficult. Wait, that's not the right word. It's kicking my ass."

"Playing the bad guy is getting old already?"

"It's much worse than that," Tate hissed and downed his champagne in one long gulp. "Never done anything like it. My sleep has been fucked too. So, I need a boost now and then."

Now and then? Did he mean once a week or…

"I can see the wheels turning in your head, Ree. Relax. It's fun. Everyone does it. You have."

"That's right, so there's no judgement here. Just friendly concern," I replied and took another sip of champagne, hoping the alcohol would burn away the fear that was now swirling in my belly. "Tell me more about what's going on with this role."

"It's best that I don't. Except to say it's the most challenging job I've had. Ever. But it's a lot. It's haunting."

Tate was sweating now, his pupils dilated, his face flushed. He motioned for the waiter and grabbed another two glasses of champagne. I finished mine and took the offered second.

"See that guy over there? That's Neal Lockwin, my director."

Tate pointed across the room.

Sure enough, in the flesh, was Hollywood's most notable actor turned director. He'd been in the biz for forty years and was a studio heavyweight.

When he spotted Tate in the crowd, he waved him over. Holy shit.

"Are you serious?" I asked.

"Yeah," Tate nodded as we made our way through the crowd. "I met him at a party that Erin and I went to a while back. I thought I told you about him taking over my current project? The original director was canned two weeks ago."

"No, you didn't mention it at all. What's he like to work with?"

"Demanding."

"Erin was helpful to your career, I'll give her that. What are you going to do now that she's gone?" I asked as we proceeded to work our way through the party to the other side of the room.

"I'll be fine. I've learned enough and I know what I need to do. Whatever it takes, right?"

The coldness of his tone made me shiver. Tate was always single minded in his ambition.

Then again, I was the same. I'd even slept with someone I didn't want to, in order get ahead. Or rather, to keep my job. Not my proudest moment and I didn't plan on doing it again, but there it was.

And Tate's rise from just another face in the crowd to where he was now, was impressive. But sometimes I wondered if it was the job or the accolades he was seeking. All actors needed to feed their egos, but some couldn't handle it if they weren't always in the spotlight.

"Tate, my leading man," Neal boomed and drew him in for a bro-hug and a slap on the back.

A shorter, stockier man standing next to Neal was sipping his drink and staring at us like we were something he picked off the bottom of his shoe. I got the ick factor right away.

"Tate, I want you to meet my agent, Victor Sills."

"Nice to meet you, Victor." Tate shook the man's hand and turned to me. "This is Reed Larkin."

Neal looked at me and his face iced over. "I'm familiar with Mr. Larkin. If you'll excuse us, I need to talk shop with Tate and Vic. Privately."

The director's sharp dismissal was unsettling.

"Uh, sure."

What the hell just happened? I looked over at Tate, but he shrugged.

"I'll go find Kendrick," I stated. "See you later."

I turned and headed back for more booze. When I glanced

over my shoulder, I watched Tate deep in discussion with Neal and Victor.

A sudden tap on my shoulder startled me. I turned to find Kendrick giving me a knowing smirk.

"Don't mind Neal. He's old school. And by old, I mean he's a homophobic prick. He hates to work with queers. Even though he doesn't mind taking our money, whether it's from producers like me or moviegoers in general."

"I still can't believe people think that way. It's 2017 for Christ's sake."

"It's a shit world, sweetheart. And I don't like it any more than you do, but in this town, you get used to shaking hands with the devil."

"Neal's still got a lot of power?"

"He does indeed," Kendrick remarked. "And it looks like Tate is Neal's next leading man. You know what that means."

I did. Tate was going to be looking for a new girlfriend.

And our friendship?

I had a bad feeling I was going to be written right out of the script.

CHAPTER 5

REED

SEVEN YEARS AGO, THE SEQUEL - A MONTH
LATER

Tate was ignoring my texts. And phone calls.

Hell, any attempt to get in touch with him.

A month had passed since that party, and he'd all but disappeared from my life.

And I knew why.

And me? I wasn't coping well at all. My best friend was slipping away, or rather, he'd already gone.

For reasons I knew but didn't understand. For reasons that made me angry, but most of all, for reasons that hurt.

So, I called the one person that I turned to when everything else in my life went to shit.

"Hey, Mom."

"What's wrong?"

"How do you—"

"Hold on," she replied.

I waited silently and heard her yell *'Roman, get down here!'*, calling for my dad. There was a muffled *'What is it, Rose?'* reply in return.

A few seconds later, she and my dad got on the line.

"Okay, Reed, spill it."

That was my mom. Get right to the heart of the matter.

As a former teacher and acting coach, Mom was used to dealing with melodrama—on and off the stage. She was my inspiration, not just when it came to acting, but for life in general. My mom lived in the present, laughed often, and loved fiercely.

And of course, being married to my dad, who was a psychotherapist, meant that no issue was above discussion. Everything and anything that needed to be said in our family, was said.

"It's Tate. He's not talking to me," I confided. "And I don't know what to do."

"Did you have a fight?" she asked.

"No, nothing like that," I replied and stood up, staring out my front window. "We went to this party about a month ago, and ever since, he's pulled away."

"Something must have happened," Dad interjected. "You know what it is, you just don't want to say it out loud."

As usual, nothing got past him.

"I think it's because I'm open about being gay," I confessed.

"What? But you've been friends for three years," Mom replied. "Why is your sexuality suddenly an issue?"

"I've told you how ambitious Tate is. And he's convinced that only hetero-presenting actors can get to the top. Plus, his new mentor is none other than director Neal Lockwin."

My comment was met with unexpected silence.

"Hello?"

"Sorry, it's been a while since I've heard that name. I've never met him, mind you, but I know people who've worked with him," Mom added. "Neal's reputation as a misogynistic asshole is well known in acting circles."

"I don't doubt that at all. But it gets worse," I sighed.

"Neal recognized me at the party and refused to talk to me. I didn't understand why until the producer who was hosting the event told me that Nate's a homophobe."

"In Neal's case, I'm not surprised to hear that," she sighed. "And now Tate's working with him?"

"Yup. Neal's his mentor or something. Tate thinks Neal is his ticket to the top. And Tate will do just about anything to prove himself worthy. I get being driven, but this? This, I don't understand. How can he push me away because of this prick? Wait. What am I saying? This is Hollywood. I should be used to this shit by now. No one cares about anything except their fucking career," I snapped. "But I thought... I thought Tate was different. That our friendship was different."

"Sounds like you need to let him go," Dad announced.

"What?" I shouted into the phone.

"If Tate is willing to do as you say, to throw away your friendship in order to get ahead, then it might be best if you let him."

"But I don't—"

"Your father's right. You love him, Reed."

A lump formed in my throat and refused to budge.

"I never said anything about that," I whispered.

"You don't have to. I'm your mother. And I can hear it in your voice every time you talk about Tate. You have a soft spot for wounded things, and from what you've told me about him, I'd say Tate is all that and more. But you don't want to get trampled while he makes his way to the top. If he wants to let you go, you need to let him. If he really is your friend, if he cares about you at all, you'll find a way back to each other in time."

"Mom—"

"There's a time to let go and a time to fight, and son, it's not time to fight," Dad added. "You can't figure this shit out for him. He has to find out for himself."

"But I can't just… I mean, the thought of—"

Fuck, the thought of letting Tate go was unthinkable.

I couldn't breathe.

"I can't tell you what to do, of course—" Dad started.

"Even though you just did," I snarked. "Both of you."

"Don't be fresh with your parents," Mom teased.

"Sorry."

"You know in your gut what's right. Even if your heart is saying something else, your gut is the one you need to pay attention to," Mom reminded me. "You love hard, Reed, just like me, just like your dad. But the first person you need to give that love to, is yourself."

My parents, of course, were right.

But that didn't make facing the truth any easier.

Tate

"I said *cut* goddamn it! Jesus Christ, how many takes do we need? I've seen more emotion from a freaking mannequin. What a fucking waste of reel!"

Neal's booming voice had everyone on set, me included, silenced. I shook my head, sweat slipping down my face, hell, all over my body. And it wasn't from the heat of the set lights.

Neal got up off his chair and up in my face.

"What the fuck was that, Tate? I need to see your rage! All I'm getting from you right now is petulant angst. What kind of a male lead are you? Can you actually perform in this role or are you just wasting my fucking time?"

I could take raised voices without flinching, but the minute someone (anyone except Reed) stepped into my personal space, especially in anger, I was done. My heart was pounding so fast I thought for sure I was gonna drop dead any moment.

"You hear the tone of my voice?! This is the kind of anger I'm talking about!" Neal screamed, so close I could smell the stale coffee on his breath. "Ten-minute break. Everyone, get the hell off my set!"

Shaking, I hauled ass to my trailer, my hands trembling, my stomach roiling.

The scars on my back itched like crazy.

"Hold up your shirt, boy."

Whack.

"You're disgusting, acting like a fucking sissy ass."

Whack.

"Stop sniveling, you little shit. Take it like a man."

Whack.

The memory of my stepfather's voice was suddenly as loud as Neal's.

A ghost that I needed desperately to shake off.

I tried to.

After I stumbled into the bathroom and emptied my stomach contents into the toilet.

This movie was turning out to be a disaster. My role was cutting way too close to home for comfort.

It would look great on my portfolio. But it was hell on my sanity.

Acting like the kind of man I despised was fucking with my head. And every day that passed, the tension on set grew higher. I couldn't retain dialogue and I had a hard time concentrating. Restless sleep followed, along with little appetite. The longer I was in character, the worse I felt. Until I was heaving my guts out by the end of the day. Every day.

It wasn't only the job that had me in a bad way. It was my relationship with Neal. My mentor.

Getting ahead, especially with the showbiz heavyweights in this town, came at a price.

At Neal's insistence, I'd dropped all contact with Reed, and guilt gnawed away at my gut like a painful ulcer.

You're an asshole. And a hypocrite.

I was all that and more.

Reed was too good for the likes of me. He deserved better.

Maybe leaving him alone was for the best. Letting him go was the kindest thing I could do, my last act of friendship.

That reasoning didn't make me feel any better.

I wiped my mouth and leaned back to take a much-needed breath.

Once my stomach settled, and while I was still on my knees, I frantically searched under the sink for a familiar plastic container. It was hidden, taped behind the pipe.

I ripped off the tape and grabbed the container, then stood up on wobbly legs. Opening the box, I reached for the baggie and the metal straw, dumped the entire amount of coke into the counter, and sniffed until every single white speck of it was gone.

Fuck, that was good. So good.

I should've done a line before I headed on set this morning, but I only had one baggie left, and I'd wanted to save it for the end of the day to relax. The cast would often party at night, and I needed social lubrication. That was my usual routine.

But now, I needed a boost in the morning to prepare myself for the day ahead. And at times like this, a midday reliever.

Pulling my phone out of my pocket, I texted my dealer, demanding more.

I had another month of filming and there was no way I was going to get through it sober. Not today, and not for the rest of it. No fucking way.

Leaning up, I glanced at my face in the mirror.

The ghost stared back at me, and I shook my head to dispel the image.

I looked like shit. Pasty, despite the layer of makeup, and my brown hair was almost black with sweat.

Splashing water on my face and over my head, I told myself it would all work out.

I could do this. Everything was under control.

By the time I'd dried off and downed a glass of water to get rid of the taste of bile, the vicious voice in my head was gone.

Bad memories? Bad decisions?

Vanished.

That the was the power of this drug. Even though I looked like crap on the outside, inside, I was burning bright again.

Nothing could stop me.

When I finally made my way back to the set, my shakiness was gone, and I was ready to go.

I didn't care about other people or their judgements. Not even an angry director.

"I want to wrap this scene up today, so hurry the fuck up!" Neal yelled when he saw me walking back to set. Then he turned to the crew. "Makeup, fix Tate's face, now!"

But I didn't hear the yelling or notice the furious glare.

I was pumped and primed. I was Tate fucking Aduma. Ready to unleash the beast that Neal wanted.

When filming resumed, I was in the zone. I became the character I despised.

Neal got the scene he wanted, and by the end of the month, the movie he envisioned. And me? I proved my mettle as an up-and-coming A-lister.

But highs never last forever. Reality can never be fully eclipsed.

Pain eventually, always, breaks through.

CHAPTER 6

TATE

SIX YEARS AGO

> Reed: I heard you collapsed on set today. Are you in hospital? What the fuck is going on? What happened?

> Reed: Your agent won't answer my calls. Are you all right?

> Reed: If you don't text me back, I'm coming over to your house and camping outside. I'm not joking. I'll buy a fucking tent and live on your front lawn until you talk to me!

I laughed out loud at the last text and started to cry at the same time.

I paced my living room, my heart racing, and my mind along with it.

Christ, I needed a hit. And I needed it bad. But I had to wait one more hour for my dealer. Then it would be okay. Just one more score to give me that much needed courage to reply to my best friend.

Not that we were 'best' anymore. Or friends, even. Not after a year of silence.

And whose fault is that?

Not that a year of no contact could erase him from my mind. Reed often popped up in my dreams, those unforgettable eyes haunting me.

I thought about him incessantly.

Especially when I was fucking a guy. And I fucked. A lot.

But even that was hitting a low point lately.

I'd picked up a sexy twink late last night, over on Sunset Boulevard. Ten minutes later I was parked in an alleyway, pounding his ass in the back seat of my SUV. Or I started to. Until my cock stopped cooperating.

I'd heard about whiskey dick, but too much coke can apparently do the same.

So, of course, I lost my temper along with my hard on, and kicked the guy out of my car. Texted my dealer and got high again.

And I felt great. For a while.

But I was too wired to sleep, and I made the mistake off popping a few sleeping pills. I woke up when my alarm blared four hours later. When I arrived on set, everything went to shit. The room began to spin and then, nothing.

I woke up in a private hospital three hours later. They gave me a lecture on addiction and seeking treatment, which I ignored.

I signed myself out and headed home.

I still had the shakes and it made it difficult to even hold my phone, never mind type on it.

And what could I say to Reed?

After all this time. After all the missed calls and texts.

After I'd pushed him away. For the sake of my career.

Reed didn't deserve the silent treatment.

And he deserved a hell of a lot better than me.

I was consumed with working my way up the Hollywood

food chain, but I wasn't the only one having professional success. Reed's TV show became a hit. He wasn't as widely known as me, but he was getting there.

Living the dream.

And my life? It was a goddamn nightmare.

Funny, because over the past four years, I thought that I was the one who was making it to the top and Reed was following in my footsteps.

Not anymore. And I hoped he never did.

Victor, the agent Neal had introduced me to the night of that party, convinced me that he was my ticket to the top. So, ten months ago, encouraged by Neal, I switched agents.

It turned out to be the biggest mistake.

Vic kept harping that 'gay by association' was just as bad for my career as if I'd come out myself. He told me to cut Reed loose for good and carefully managed my image on a level that was intrusive to an extreme. Yeah, he knew what condoms I preferred, what kind of lube I ordered, and arranged for discreet men to show up when I needed to fuck. He introduced me to a top-notch dealer. And he had women showing up at my door every day.

I was never without a female escort in public, ever. It was annoying as fuck, but I was too busy filming and snorting half my earnings up my nose to give a shit. Or, to do anything about it.

After all, Vic kept telling me that our plan was working.

I was in demand.

Directors wanted me, fellow actors envied me, and producers loved me. No matter how tired, sick, high, hungover, I always delivered.

Always.

Today was the perfect example. Okay, maybe not the best example. But even though I felt like death, I'd show up tomorrow. Showing up meant success.

I should be thrilled.

I had arrived. I made it.

I had everything I ever wanted.

Multiple movie offers and a big-ass mansion in Pacific Palisades. Fast cars. A cook and a housekeeper. A massage therapist and a stylist on call. The adulation of fans and fellow actors.

An empty fucking life that only saw company in the form of my dealer or some escort that I had to pretend to like.

But I couldn't step off the hamster wheel. I just kept running and running. No matter what role I got offered, it wasn't enough.

When would it ever be enough?

I was twenty-four going on twenty-five, and so fucking young when I looked in the mirror. And yet, inside, I was beat down. Weary. I felt like seventy, never mind fifty.

I thought I'd left my shitty life back in Alabama years ago. But I was still running.

The only person that had ever managed to still me, was Reed.

My phone rang and I didn't have the heart—which some would argue I didn't have to begin with—to ignore him.

"Ree, everything's all right," I answered straight away.

"About fucking time you took my call! Are you okay? Where are you?"

Oh God, the sound of his voice made my eyes well up again.

A fierce ache bloomed in my chest.

In the rare moments when I was at home, alone, I'd turn on his TV show just to see his face and hear his voice. Pathetic.

And TV was no match for the real thing.

"I'm at home. Resting."

Pacing the floors. Climbing the walls.

"I'm coming over."

"Don't!" I yelled. "Vic will throw a fit."

"And he rules your life now?"

"Pretty much, yeah."

"He's a first-rate asshole!" Reed continued. "And a homophobic prick! You deserve better than him."

I didn't deserve fuck all.

"You haven't taken my calls or returned my texts for nearly a year, and I know it's because of your stupid agent," Reed bit out. "And then I find out through the Hollywood grapevine that you collapsed on set? What's going on? Talk to me. Please."

I let out a breath that was near painful.

Despite feeling like absolute shit, I was relieved that I could finally unburden myself to someone.

To him.

"I overdid it on the coke last night. When I got home, I took some sleeping pills, and I guess the combination fucked me up. When I arrived on set this morning, I was dizzy, and I passed out. They sent me to a private clinic, pumped my stomach, then pumped me full of saline. I signed myself out an hour ago."

"You're using regularly?" Reed asked quietly.

"Every fucking day. I need it to keep up, Ree. I'm always exhausted."

Tired from working non-stop. From hiding. From lying.

From everything.

I waited for the lecture, the derision. But of course, this was Reed. I should have known better.

"You're not the first—or last—person I know who's dealing with addiction. But Tay, you need to talk to someone. Today was a warning. Your body is going to quit on you if you don't cut that shit out."

"I know, I know. It's just that Vic has me lined up for back-to-back movies this year and I need the energy. He found me a dealer who gets me the good stuff, none of that low-grade shit. Vic said—"

"Fuck what Vic said! He just wants to keep you coked up so he can shove you back out there to make more money to line his pockets."

"He's an agent, that's the way they are."

"Not all of them. Besides what he's doing to you, working you to death and encouraging your addiction, there's the other shit that's going on. Are you even aware of the talk about him? He sexually harasses his female clients. It's the worst kept secret in town."

My head was pounding now, throbbing like a motherfucker.

"I... I didn't know."

Well, I'd heard the rumors. But I ignored them. As always, my career took precedence.

"I'm such a selfish bastard," I sighed. "Why the fuck are you still my friend?"

"You're not selfish, Tay, you're ambitious. To a scary degree. But you don't need to push so hard anymore. You've made it."

"It's never enough," I confessed.

"That's why you need to talk to someone. I can refer you to my therapist. She's great. But it sounds like you need detox for the coke. Take a few months away from work and get your body healed," Reed encouraged. "But the first thing you should do is cut Vic loose. A day of reckoning is coming and he's going to be held accountable for his actions. And you don't want to be associated with a man like him. It'll ruin everything you've worked for."

Despite my headache and body chills, I knew Reed was right.

Somewhere in my foggy brain, the warning he issued clicked.

"Text me the contact info for your therapist," I replied. "I think I'll call Henn, too. If she'll ever talk to me again."

"It's done. And I'm sure Henn will happily take you back as a client."

"I hope so."

"Can I come over now? I need to see you," Reed insisted.

"I don't want you to see me like this."

The line went dead, and I was left staring at my phone.

It was the first time that Reed had ever hung up on me.

Five seconds later, my phone buzzed. It was Reed forwarding the contact details for his therapist.

I'd texted Vic that I didn't want to be disturbed the rest of the day.

So, while I didn't have my agent in my back pocket, I called Reed's therapist and set up an appointment. Then I talked to Henn and told her everything. Well, the shortened version.

A knock at the door a half hour later filled me with both dread and relief.

It was my dealer.

Except, when I glanced at my security camera, it wasn't.

It was Reed.

Even disguised in a baseball cap, sunglasses, and a fake mustache, I could tell it was him. I'd know that long, lithe body anywhere.

Despite feeling like death, I practically ran to the door.

When I opened it, Reed said nothing. He pushed past me and stalked into my home.

I slammed and locked the door and leaned back against it, completely out of breath.

"Jesus, Tate," he exclaimed as he threw off his hat and sunglasses. "Jesus, you look—"

For the first time ever, he walked right up to me and cupped my face in his hands. All I could do was stare into those electric eyes of his. I'd never seen anyone look at me with such concern. And for once, I didn't flinch or pull away.

"What's with the attempt at a disguise?" I asked. "Not that I didn't know it was you right away."

"In case of the paps. Or your fucking agent."

"Thanks, but you didn't need to do that."

I shook my head.

Reed suddenly let go of me and I nearly slid down the door. My knees and every other part of me was shaking.

"I've been such an asshole to you," I admitted.

Reed nodded. "You have."

"So, why are you here?"

Reed sighed and yanked off his fake mustache. "You're not the only one who can't say no."

"What does that mean?"

Reed ran a hand through his blond hair. "It means I'm your friend. For better or worse."

I snorted. "I thought that was marriage."

"That's any relationship worth holding on to. And I know that despite your douchebag behavior, you're still the man I met four years ago. You may act like an ass, but it's your defense shield. We both know that there's much more to you than meets the eye."

"I'm so fucked up, Ree."

The words were barely a whisper.

"Hey." He stepped back up to me and gripped my shoulders. "Everyone is fucked up."

"Not like me."

"You've endured a lot."

I stiffened. "What are you talking about?"

"We lived together for two years," he said softly. "Did you think I didn't notice the scars on your back?"

My body locked up tight, but the tears came fast and hot.

"I can't... I can't talk about that."

"I know. I've always respected your privacy. But someday soon, you'll have to tell someone."

"Are you an actor or a shrink?" I snapped, wiping the tears off my face, not wanting him to see them at all.

"I'm the son of a therapist, remember? Between that and acting, I've been taught to observe."

I swallowed hard and stared at him. "And what do you see?"

"A man who's pushed himself to the brink trying to prove his worth. Trying to hide his pain. And someone who's afraid to let others see the real person behind the persona."

I shivered. Why was he always spot on?

"Anything else?"

Reed shook his head.

"You, Tate. The only thing I see is you."

CHAPTER 7

REED

FIVE YEARS AGO

I stood in the entryway of the rehab center in Ojai, waiting for Tate.

Just like I had on the third Sunday of every month for the past three. The months when Tate was finally ready to have visitors. That included me, our agent Henn, and Charlene, our favorite casting director.

When your life implodes, people scatter. And while it can be painful to realize that many of the friends and colleagues you spent so much time with couldn't care less about you (and sometimes, you about them), it simplified life. Housecleaning, if you will.

Time to let go of people and things that don't support you and start fresh.

Tate's timing, despite the difficult year he'd had, was still spot on.

A month after his on-set blackout, Tate cut ties with his agent, Vic. Two months after that, Vic was brought up on charges of harassment and assault. One accusation turned into a major lawsuit as more women were coming forward.

Once an agent who managed the biggest players in Hollywood, now Vic had nothing to say. Only his lawyer spoke for him.

There was a major shift happening in Hollywood and for once, it had nothing to do with earthquakes.

But speaking of forces of nature, I watched my favorite one walk down the hallway towards me.

Tate looked healthy and vibrant again. And intense as always.

Just like five years ago, standing in the hallway of that drafty warehouse, my breath caught at the sight of him.

And my heart?

That poor sucker still wanted what he couldn't have.

My gut clenched with a warning, but my heart overruled it.

It didn't matter. Any bit of Tate that was mine, I relished.

My mother was right about this need I had to rescue wounded things. And yeah, I knew Tate was hurting inside. Not that he'd ever admit it. He'd come close, and I hoped to hell he'd unburdened himself to his therapist. If Tate endured what I suspected he did, the longer he avoided it, the harder it would be to heal. And trauma always has a way of rising to the surface.

It wouldn't be easy. Not for someone who made their living taking on other people's lives instead of examining their own.

I put my worries aside for the moment and soaked him in.

His hair was longer now, and he'd let his beard grow out. It suited.

"You didn't have to come and drive me home."

That was my Tate. Never a 'hi, how are you'. Get right into the meat of the script.

"Yes, I did."

I met him halfway and reached up to pull him in for a hug.

Despite his initial stiffness, he notched his face into my neck, his rough beard rubbing against my skin. I did my best not to react, but it wasn't easy.

God, he even smelled the same. Leather and amber. That damn cologne of his was *my* addiction.

Why did no man ever smell as good as Tate?

"You ready to go?" I asked, my voice hoarse as I finally pulled away.

"As I'll ever be. I just wonder what's waiting out there for me. No one will probably remember my name."

Tate had entered a local rehab the day after he fired Vic. But only for two months.

When he got out, he relapsed.

Six months ago, I'd finally convinced him to try this place, about two hours north of LA. A few actor friends had gone through their program and said it changed their life.

But typical Tate, his main concern was his career.

That hadn't changed.

I rolled my eyes. "Sure, that's why Henn has been fielding calls about your return."

"Really? Who from?"

"She's not going to tell me, that's your business."

Tate nodded. "And the house is okay?"

I'd been keeping an eye on his place. And I'd added a few touches to make it more welcoming for his return. The modern space was crying out for warmth. I had it re-painted (in Tate approved colors), added plants, and artwork. I was going to get him a cat for company but that was stepping over the friend line, even for me.

"The house looks amazing if I do say so myself. It finally feels—"

I stopped myself.

It felt like home. Because it was Tate's.

"Feels like what?" he elbowed me as we made our way through the front doors.

"Feels less clinical."

Tate barked out a laugh. "Yeah, well, nesting was never my thing. I always had one foot out the door. In fact, I hated being there alone."

"Too much house?"

Tate shook his head. "Too much time spent with myself."

We stepped into the bright sunshine, another cloudless day in California. Passing a garden full of succulents, we wandered along the gravel path to the parking lot.

"Well, you're going to love it now. You won't want to leave."

"You're confident."

I shrugged my shoulders. "Well, I am a TV star. That's only natural."

"And how's the third season taping going?"

"Good. We're starting contract negotiations for season four. Henn's playing hardball. If I don't get offered more, I'm walking."

"You're serious?"

"Yup. I've got enough offers coming in for other stuff. Maybe it's time to try for a film role again," I replied. "You want to stop and grab lunch first?"

"Thanks, but I just wanna head home. I don't want to risk getting photographed just yet."

Just because or because he was with me?

"And no, it has nothing to do with you, Ree. I'm just not ready for the paps yet. And I promise, I'm going to do better. You know, be an ally. I'm sorry I've been a shit person."

"You're not a shit person. You've just made some shitty decisions. And things are changing," I stated as we got to my car. I unlocked the door and slid into the driver's seat. "Queer actors are demanding rep. More films and movies are going to reflect that."

I left it at that. Tate was free to tell me. If he ever wanted to tell me.

"That's good. I'm happy for you."

For me.

He was still holding on to some of his secrets.

My good mood began to waver.

"What's the plan when you get home?" I asked, changing the subject.

I started the car and pulled out of the lot. The gates opened and I sped onto the main road that led to the highway. So far, I didn't notice any cars following us, but you could never be too careful.

"I need to get myself into a regular routine. I've got the name of a sober living specialist who'll help me get adjusted. And I have a meeting with Henn. I want to get my feet wet again. Nothing major, but something. You know I'm no good with time on my hands."

I chatted about the latest Hollywood gossip as we drove, ending up at the winding hills of his gated community.

The security guard at the entrance recognized us and waved us through with a smile.

"It feels like I've been gone for years, never mind months."

"Do you want me to stay with you for a while?" I offered.

"No, I couldn't let you do that. You've done enough. I don't even know how to begin to thank you."

I waved him off as I pulled into his driveway. "No thanks needed. I'm just glad to see you looking healthy again."

We unloaded his bags and brought everything inside.

"Wow, it's so different," Tate murmured as he dropped his jacket and looked around.

Gone was the builder beige paint, and in its place there were warm terra cotta walls that set off the southwestern style of his furniture. I'd added lots of chunky knit throws and pillows, leafy plants, and wood accents. And with some new paintings on the walls, it was warm and inviting. At least, I thought so.

"It's amazing," Tate continued as he stepped into the living room. "I love it."

I lit up inside with immense pleasure. And relief. I wanted Tate to have a space that he wanted to be in. A refuge from the chaos of Hollywood life.

"I'm glad. I was going to buy you a cat but then I thought, that has to be something you pick out yourself."

"A cat, eh?"

"They're good company."

"And that's why you have so many?" Tate chuckled.

"Smart ass." I gave him a choice finger. "I can't choose, you know that. If I could, I'd adopt all of them."

"Why don't we go together, next week, and each pick out a cat? Then we can split pet parent duties when one of us is out of town."

I was stunned by his suggestion. "That's a big commitment."

"I know. I'd only do this with you."

I stopped short and stared at him. Did he even realize what he'd just said?

"Unless, of course, you don't want to," Tate backtracked. "It was just an idea. I mean, with your work schedule and your dating life, you probably don't have time for a pet."

I wandered over to his kitchen and opened the fridge, pulling out a bottle of sparkling water. I selected two glasses from the cupboard and placed them on the counter.

"I have time. And my personal life has been quiet."

"No special man in your life?" Tate asked. "I mean, besides me."

I knew Tate was joking but it still made my chest ache.

"Nope. I'm all about a fun, casual time."

"You want more, you're just afraid."

"Me?"

"Yes, you. You want it all. But in this town, it's hard to find someone real."

I poured two glasses and passed one to Tate. "Truth? I've only been in love once. He didn't return my feelings and so, it kind of put me off romance for good."

"You never told me that. Who is this mysterious guy? Have I met him? Worked with him?"

Oh, you've met him, Tate.

"Yes, but I'm not telling you. It serves no purpose."

"Well, whoever he is, he's a fool," Tate declared.

"No, he's not. And I don't regret my feelings. Falling in love is never a mistake."

Tate scoffed. "Like I would know."

"Never?"

Tate hesitated for a split second.

"Never."

"Now that you're sober, maybe things will change."

Tate took a sip of his water and shrugged his shoulders. "Doubtful. I wouldn't be a good partner for anyone. We'll see if I can take care of myself first."

"In that case—" I paused as I walked around the kitchen island to open the patio doors. "We'll be single together."

"It feels like five years ago."

"It does."

Between us, nothing had changed.

CHAPTER 8

TATE

FOUR YEARS AGO – PART 1

" hate these fucking things," I muttered to myself as I stood in front of the mirror adjusting my bowtie.

I was struggling with the stupid tie and struggling to stay calm.

It was my first red carpet appearance in two years, and I was mentally bracing myself for the onslaught of press and peers.

My only relief was knowing that Reed was also going to be in attendance.

With his date.

A fellow actor named Julian Brennan. Jules, as he was known. A guy with a smile even a dentist would envy. A man Reed had seen more than once. And he rarely double dipped. Was this one serious?

The idea of Reed and Jules as a permanent couple made me nauseous and irrationally annoyed.

Then I berated myself. I wanted my friend to find love, to find a partner. He acted like he didn't care about finding a special man, but I knew that's what he wanted. There was a longing in his eyes when he talked about his parents' happy marriage and growing up with his sister, Rissa. I knew Reed wanted it all—the marriage, the house, the kids.

I should be happy for him. Maybe Jules could give him that.

Then I remembered the first time I'd met Jules, at a party two weeks ago. He'd eyed up every hot man within range and he wasn't subtle about it. I was tempted to warn Reed, but it wasn't my place. Reed hadn't called the guy his boyfriend or mentioned they were exclusive. Maybe they had an open relationship? Lots of people did.

Not that I understood it, but then again, I hardly understood any relationship that wasn't transactional.

Well, except my friendship with Reed.

But I had no business thinking any more about him or his date.

I had my own to worry about.

The limo was arriving in five, and then we were off to pick up my date for the evening, an actress named Celia Cantrell. She was another beautiful blonde, and no doubt I would be the envy of every hetero man in attendance. Whatever. To me, the date was just another trip on the endless merry-go-round that was my life.

The life made for viewing.

Not the one behind closed doors.

And rushed blowjobs with faceless men in the back seat of my car weren't cutting it anymore. I was afraid of being outed, but also terrified that my fake life was making me restless again.

But I was used to putting on the usual act. Hell, it was as easy as slipping on this tuxedo jacket.

I didn't stop when the director yelled cut. Not me.

I kept right on playing my part.

And Christ, now *wasn't* the time for a quarter life crisis.

Once I was satisfied that my tie was on straight, my breath

was minty fresh, and my hair was stylishly disheveled, I grabbed my phone and keys and headed for the front door.

"Be good, and don't sleep on my pillow," I warned my cat, Cary, who was sitting on the arm of my sectional, staring at me.

Ha. I was silly, thinking that this headstrong creature would listen to anyone, let alone me.

I'd made good on my promise to Reed. We went to that animal shelter not long after I came out of rehab and adopted cats. We named them Cary and Grant, our Hollywood icon in feline form. Of course, Reed's cat, Grant, a tabby-Maine coon mix, was friendly and adored scritches and belly rubs, whereas mine, a ginger-haired devil, hissed and clawed at me if I dared to reach out and pet him.

The only time Cary cuddled up to me was in bed, at night, on the pillow next to mine. Otherwise, his royal grumpiness sauntered around my house, clawing at the furniture, and staring at me with those big green eyes of his like I was the enemy.

The enemy who fed him specially formulated cat food and bought him a three-level scratching palace.

But despite Cary's obvious displeasure at being my roommate, I liked the company, and the knowledge that someone was waiting at home for me. It made it less lonely. And I had to admit that while Cary didn't like physical touch—mine at least, Reed was another matter—he was a good listener. Not that I would tell anyone that, but it was true. I'd lie in bed at night and confess my innermost thoughts and secrets to my cat.

My Hollywood life was so glamorous.

I shook my head at my ridiculous musings and checked myself one last time in the foyer mirror. I was good to go.

I activated the alarm and shut the door behind me.

The limo was already parked in my driveway. The back window rolled down and I spotted Henn, waving at me.

"Wow, I haven't seen you this dressed up in ages. Looking good, Tate."

The driver got out and opened the back door for me.

I thanked him and slid in beside Henn, who looked glamorous as always. Henn was somewhere around fifty, a former actor herself, and she was still model gorgeous. She'd had work done, like everyone in town, but at least when she smiled her face moved. With long auburn hair and dark blue eyes, she appeared ethereal, delicate.

"Thanks. I don't mind the suit, but the tie is already annoying."

"Much like your complaining. Suck it up and stop fidgeting," she replied and gave me a glare that meant business.

Delicate, she was not.

"Sorry, *mom*."

Henn rolled her eyes. "Why are you nervous? Besides the obvious fact that this is your first red carpet appearance in two years."

"My date. I wish I'd gone without. I hate making small talk with new people. It's so goddamn painful. Not just that, I'm tired. Tired of pretending I adore these women. When I don't."

Henn glanced at me with knowing eyes.

"You could've gone solo. No one thinks twice. And you don't need to keep up appearances anymore with fake dates."

The limo began to move as we headed out of my neighborhood. I rolled down the window to get some fresh air.

"I can't seem to stop doing just that. It's stupid, but why can't I just... fuck, I can't even say it."

I still couldn't tell people I was gay. Even though Reed and Henn knew. They'd caught me on occasion with one man or another, so of course they knew. And my therapist, and my sponsor. But despite all the progress I'd made, I still wasn't there.

It had been drilled into me for years that being gay in my

stepfather's house was a fate worse than death. Fuck, Kenny had a hair trigger temper about everything, but queers, liberals, feminists, and kids topped the list. I learned to keep my mouth shut no matter what.

Even then, it wasn't enough.

"If you can't say it, you're still not ready," Henn whispered.

"Will I ever be?"

Henn sighed and patted my hand. "Only you can make that call, Tate. I'm not in your shoes. It's a big step. One that you have to be prepared for. Especially in the public eye."

I nodded instead of saying anything else on the matter.

"So, we're picking up Celia first and then Reed and Jules," Henn announced while she pulled out her phone and began to type.

"I didn't know that Reed was riding with us."

"There's the possibility that both of you will be cast in Jared Elwood's upcoming production. He's the youngest director in town and everyone has nothing but great things to say about him. Jared thought it might be a good idea to start the PR machine early. Get the bromance going. The press will love that you're already friends and soon to be co-stars."

Bromance?

My earlier nerves kicked up good and hard.

And my urge for cocaine slithered to the forefront of my brain.

The drug made me feel invincible, like I could take on the world, and talk to anyone, do anything. I wasn't self-conscious like I tended to be when I was out in public.

"So," I started as I pulled on my tie, trying to loosen the chokehold. "What's the expectation? Reed and I pose side by side for a couple of photos?"

"Exactly," Henn replied. "Make a few comments about Reed's work, what you think of him as an actor, and that you look forward to working with him someday."

I could do this. He was my friend after all.

The press knew that. Our friendship was now the worst kept secret in Hollywood.

I glanced at the bottle of champagne in the mini bar. "I need some liquid courage."

Henn passed me the bottle, then grabbed two glasses. I popped the bottle open and gave each a generous pour.

Before either of us could make a toast, I took a huge gulp.

The sweet bubbles hit my tongue. It wasn't nearly as satisfying as that first hit of coke, but it would have to do.

We arrived at Celia's place twenty minutes later. She slid into the limo and sat on my other side.

She looked elegant in a black sequin dress, but she could have been naked for all I cared. I could put up with the fake smiles and the overpowering perfume but when she grabbed my thigh and squeezed, that was it. I pushed her hand away.

"Let me make something clear," I whispered in her ear so Henn couldn't hear. "This is for show. You get the photo ops you need, I get mine, we smile, maybe have a dance and then go our separate ways, understood? Don't touch me when we're not in view of the press."

Celia's eyes rolled. "No problem. Not that I'm surprised."

"What do you mean?"

"Come on, Tate. I know you by reputation. This really is a very small town when it comes to gossip. People talk."

I stilled. "And what do they say?"

Celia leaned in closer. "That you're a—"

My heart was pounding so hard, I could barely hear her voice.

"—complete bastard."

Well, I couldn't argue with that.

CHAPTER 9

TATE

FOUR YEARS AGO – THE SAME NIGHT, PART 2

I asked Henn for another glass of champagne and my nerves calmed a bit by the time we got to Reed's house.

But as soon as he slipped into the limo, my night took an unexpected turn.

I'd seen Reed dressed up before, nothing unusual about that.

Like me, he'd chosen a classic black tux. Except, he wore a crisp white shirt with a dark green tie, and a matching pocket square. The slim fit suited him to perfection. His blond waves were tamed with product, and he was sporting a bit of scruff on his face that brought all the attention to those plump lips of his.

In short, he was sexy as fuck.

I never allowed myself to stare at Reed for too long, but right here and now, I couldn't look anywhere else. He was so beautiful that I nearly swallowed my tongue along with the champagne.

And when Reed sat down across from me and caught my stare, something flashed in his gaze.

My heart jumpstarted.

It's just pre-event nerves. It's nothing.

His date slipped into the seat next to him. I nodded at Jules, but I didn't offer my hand. I didn't like Jules and I wasn't about to pretend otherwise.

I wasn't *that* good an actor.

Introductions were made all around and everyone began to chatter away.

Except me, of course. I was the odd one out, silent and brooding, all up in my head.

Thankfully, my musings were interrupted by Reed's phone ringing.

"Hey, can I call you back?" Reed answered. "I'm just on my way to the event."

He paused, then burst out laughing, and the familiar sound filled me with an intense kind of ache.

I rubbed my chest and reasoned it was heartburn.

"Hold on on a sec." Reed held his phone up with one hand and motioned to me with his other. "Tate, Henn, lean in together."

For once, I didn't need to fake a smile. Looking at Reed, and him looking at me, it was one hundred percent genuine.

"My sister insists on a picture," Reed explained, tapped his phone, and brought it back to his ear again. "I just sent it. Now do you believe me?... What?... Okay."

Reed offered me his phone. "Rissa wants to say hi."

I took it, clearing my throat, suddenly unsure what, if anything, I should say. I'd never met any of Reed's family, even though he talked about them a lot. The times when they had visited him in LA, I was either off shooting, or in rehab. And I wasn't sure that given the latter, they'd ever want to meet me.

"Hey, this is Tate Aduma."

"Nice to talk to you, Tate. Reed's told me all about you, but every time I've asked him to send a picture of the two of you, he says no. I started to think he was lying about being your friend."

I barked out a laugh and everyone in the limo turned to stare.

Shit.

"That's 'cause he knows that I hate taking pictures. I mean, it's part of our job, but other than that, I'm not one for photos."

"Well, you take a great one. That smile is something else."

Your brother is something else.

And goddamn it, what the fuck was with my head tonight?

I glanced over at Reed, and he was sitting back, watching me intently. Reaching up with my free hand, I tugged on my tie.

"You caught me at a rare moment," I added. "But it's nice to speak to you too. Reed has told me good things."

"Did he tell you about our psychic connection?"

"Oh, yeah. But I'm not much of a believer in all that."

Reed suddenly leaned forward and mouthed *what are you talking about* and motioned for me to give him back the phone.

Rissa began to laugh. "I bet he's making a face right now, wanting in on the conversation and asking you to give him back the phone."

"Hell, maybe you are psychic," I blurted out.

"Not really, it's just that I'd do the same thing. We're both terribly nosy."

I let out another laugh. "Well, nosy or not, it was nice talking to you."

"You as well, Tate. Have fun tonight."

I passed the phone back to Reed and when he reached for it, our hands brushed. Another spark ran through me and fuck, I didn't know if my heart could take any more shocks tonight.

When we arrived at the event, Reed leaned forward and tapped my knee. "Did Henn tell you about the promo?"

"I'm good."

I was sweating like I was in detox.

Celia and Henn stepped out first, then me, Jules, and Reed. I turned and started to offer my hand to Reed and realized my mistake.

But not before I caught his surprised stare.

Instead of berating myself, I quickly pivoted and waved to the press and the crowds of people gathered on the sidewalk. Flashes went off like snaps of lightning, and I walked beside Celia until we reached the press gallery.

Reed stepped up beside me and my hands began to tremble.

One journalist yelled out Reed's name. "Can we get a shot of you and Tate together?"

"I don't know about that," Reed teased the journalist. "This guy may be my friend but he's a photo hog."

The joke eased some of my tension and I fired back. "Don't listen to him. He's the former model. He never saw a camera he didn't love."

We stood, smiling, side by side, as the flashes continued to pop.

"Is it true that you two are signed up to star in a movie together? A project with Jared Elwood?" another reporter yelled out.

"Maybe. If Tate can pass the audition," Reed quipped.

I turned to him and shook my head. "You mean, if you can work for more than three hours a day."

"Ouch," Reed placed a hand on his chest and then smiled at the cameras. "You see what I put up with?"

There were fake laughs at our cheesy jokes and more photos. Without thinking, I placed my hand on his lower back.

And then, surprisingly, he did the same to me.

I fought the urge to step closer to him. More reporters yelled out our names as we smiled and did our bit.

It was the most natural I'd ever felt on the public stage and yet, the most nerve-wracking.

Celia and Jules stepped on either side of us and the four of us posed altogether. Then it was me and Celia, and Reed with Jules. There were the usual questions about our dates for the night. I forced back an eye roll but just barely.

Once our bit was done, Henn ushered us inside.

"Great job, you two. You had the press begging for more," Henn gushed. "Let's ensure we also take some photo ops when we leave tonight. Keep the buzz going."

"I need to speak with Tate for a moment. Business," Reed interrupted. "Will you all excuse us?"

Before I could say anything, Reed was pushing me through the venue, down the hallway towards the bathrooms.

"What's wrong? Did I say something to the press I shouldn't have?" I asked.

He pulled me around the corner into a dark alcove.

"What was all that?" Reed hissed.

"All what? I smiled and did what I was told to do," I snapped. "It's called promo and it's part of our job."

Reed ran an agitated hand through his hair. "What's with the... you know... touching me when we're on the carpet?"

"You mean, the back thing?"

"Yes. And when I was about to step out of the limo."

"I was just being supportive. What's with you tonight?"

Reed scoffed. "I could ask you the same thing."

I stepped closer to him. "What did I do wrong?"

"Nothing. You did nothing wrong," Reed sighed and stepped back. "I'm just nervous. Sorry."

"About what? What's going on?"

"Jules, he—" Reed bit his lip. "Jules asked me to move in with him."

I swore my heart stopped beating. All the air was sucked out of my lungs.

"Is that—" I coughed, clearing my throat. "Is that what you want?"

"I thought so," Reed shrugged. "Maybe? I don't know."

"Why are you hesitating?"

"I don't love him. Not like—"

Reed paused and stared up at me.

He couldn't mean…

I watched his throat move as he swallowed.

I locked on his perfect pink lips and all kinds of dirty thoughts about my best friend flooded my mind.

Suddenly, his mouth was the only thing I wanted.

Cupping his face, I leaned in, our noses touching, our lips sharing the same breath.

"Don't," Reed warned. "I'm not one of your secret fuckboys. You can't do this to me."

Fuck.

He was right. I was screwing up. Again.

I dropped my hand and stepped back, cursing myself. Then I did what all actors do when they've run out of script— I left the scene.

I avoided Reed as much as I could for the rest of the night and focused on my 'date'.

That night was another turning point for our careers and our friendship.

The movie collaboration we teased to the press, the one directed by Jared Elwood? It made Reed and I the biggest stars in Hollywood.

But like everything in this business, when one thing rises, something else falls.

I just never thought that it would be us.

CHAPTER 10

REED

THREE YEARS AGO

"I'm worried Tate's using again."

Henn's statement wasn't surprising but it was alarming all the same.

"I went round to his house to check on him and there was a man there that I didn't recognize," she continued. "I don't know if it was one of his hookups or his dealer, but Tate and, whoever it was, looked strung out in a bad way. I booted the stranger's ass out of the house. Then Tate ordered me to follow."

I stared silently at Henn as we sat in my backyard.

My stomach flipped over in the worst possible way, but at the same time, what could I do?

Tate wasn't taking my calls again and I was so pissed off, I couldn't form words.

"What happened?" she asked me. "He was doing so well, and then for the past year, you two just stopped talking."

I sighed and took a sip of my gin and tonic. It was only noon, but whatever. A meeting with my agent, even one I loved as much as Henn, called for liquor.

Especially if we were talking about Tate.

"What happened was, he—" I paused and stared at her. "You cannot repeat this, Henn. Swear to me on your botox."

"I swear."

"At the gala last year, when we were doing the photo op, I thought he was acting strange. He never touches me in public. So, I pulled him aside and asked him what was going on. Then he… he tried to kiss me. But I wouldn't let him. Because I knew, I just knew, that once he had, he'd deny it ever happened and then I would be devastated. We didn't even kiss and I was fucked up afterwards! My relationship with Jules tanked and then Tate stopped contacting me. The only time I saw him was on the set of our fucking movie and even then, he refused to talk to me unless we were filming. And the whole thing is his fault! He was willing to throw almost six years of friendship down the shitter that night because he was horny! What the fuck was he thinking?"

Henn swore up a storm and shoved her sunglasses to the top of her head.

"Jesus Christ, you are two of a kind! And I don't know what he was thinking, Reed, but my best guess is, he finally realized that he has feelings for you. Feelings beyond friendship."

I scoffed at that.

"Tate doesn't do romantic feelings. And even if he did, he's not out, and probably never will be. I can't do that to myself. I won't."

Henn stared at me with knowing eyes. "You're still in love with him."

I took another long sip of my drink and shook my head.

"I was. Past tense. Not anymore."

Tate wasn't the only one who was good at lying. I'd told myself that I wasn't in love with him so many times over the years that I was finally starting to believe it.

"I'm going to drop by his place today to see how he's doing," Henn whispered. "Come with me, please."

I let out a dramatic sigh and slammed my glass on the table. "Fine. One time only. But that's it."

Since Henn wasn't drinking, she drove.

By the time we go to Tate's, I was all but jumping out of my skin.

What if he was using again? Just the thought of Tate being sick or worse made me shiver.

We got out of the car and headed up the walkway to the front door.

And then I heard the shouting.

"Stay here," I instructed Henn.

I knocked on the door.

When the yelling continued, I disabled the alarm (typical Tate, he hadn't changed the code in over a year) and I entered the front door.

I took several steps, past the foyer and into the living area, and stopped short.

Tate was standing in his bathrobe, yelling his head off at a naked man who was giving it right back to him.

"You've got five seconds to get out of my fucking house!" Tate bellowed.

"Or what? You're gonna call the cops? I don't think so, asshole. Now, you owe me for last night, so pay up!" naked guy yelled back.

"I don't pay to screw. I don't have to. Now get your shit and get gone!" Tate shouted and picked up a pile of clothes from the couch, throwing them at the guy.

"I made it very clear last night that I expected payment. And I ain't leaving until I get it!"

"You got coke, that's payment enough!"

"That's not how it works, honey."

"What the fuck is going on here?" I interrupted.

There was a second of silence as Tate finally noticed me.

He looked like day-old shit, his face ashen, purple circles under his bloodshot eyes.

He'd also lost weight. A lot of it. Jesus, when he moved, his bathrobe fell open. I could see his ribs.

"Who the fuck are you?" The stranger snapped, then did a double take. "Holy shit, you're Reed Larkin!"

"Jesus Christ, you're fan girling over him?" Tate swore. "Get out!"

Naked guy shook his head and crossed his arms.

Fed up with the yelling, I pulled out my wallet and offered the stranger three hundred dollars, in cash.

"Will that cover it?" I asked.

"Not enough for putting up with his sorry ass," he replied and gave Tate the finger. Then the guy bent to pick up a pair of shorts and a tank top. "But I won't say no. A boy's gotta survive."

I pulled out another hundred while Tate's man of the night got dressed. The guy took the money with a nod and stuffed it in his pocket.

"You were never here," I warned him.

"I wish. Closeted queens are the worst."

Tate's trick for the night stalked past me and I let out a sigh of relief when I heard the front door slam.

"You're using again?" I bit out as I walked up to Tate. "Are you out of your fucking mind?"

"It's under control! We were partying last night, just having fun. Then I needed another hit to wake up this morning. And why the fuck am I explaining myself to you in my own home? I didn't ask you to come here!"

"But it's a good thing I did, right? When are you going to stop doing this to yourself?" I shouted back.

"Doing what?"

"Living a lie. Denying your past. Denying who you are. And then using coke to deal with it."

"I'm not lying or denying anything! You and Henn know

the truth! I'm gay, and I fuck men. There! Is that what you want me to say? Are you happy now?"

I shook my head. "I have never, not once, pressured you about your sexuality. Don't you dare try and act like your unhappiness is my fault!"

"Why not? If I was out when I attempted to kiss you last year, would you have been okay with it? Or would *I* have ended up just another one of *your* fuckboys?"

"What?"

"I'm not the only who likes to live in denial."

I flinched at his words, and he caught it, his eyes narrowing.

No matter how long we'd been apart, I could never erase the image of those amber eyes of his. Even tired, even high, he was still the most intense man I'd ever met.

Why, why couldn't I ever stay away?

"I'm not in denial about anything!" I snapped back.

"Not even your feelings for me?"

He knew he'd hit his mark, with that telltale smirk on his face.

"Fuck you, Tate! And fuck our friendship!" I screamed. "I can't do this anymore. I can't watch you slowly kill yourself. You want to ruin your life, go ahead. You want to live with your trauma forever, you want to hide who you really are, fine. But I'm out! Not that it will change much. You don't want to talk to me anymore anyway."

Tate's face fell and he stepped forward, reaching for me.

It was too late. I pushed his hands away.

"You can never say goodbye, Tay. But I can."

I turned and headed for the door.

"No, Ree! Wait!"

My heart was telling me to stop, but my feet kept moving.

I slammed the door behind me and waited.

Five seconds, ten, twenty.

A minute passed, then another. Henn walked up to me,

but I couldn't talk. I just stood there, shaking, tears sliding down my face, feeling like a fool.

Tate was lying again. He made no move to stop my leaving.

He just… let me go.

And I wasn't wrong.

Tate needed to sort his life out on his own. And once again, I needed to let him.

I finally had enough sense to keep walking towards the car. I got as far as his front yard and I puked, my gut heaving, my throat burning. I clutched my stomach, and more tears fell.

The rest was a blur. Henn tried to comfort me, steering me into the car and offering me a bottle of water. Over and over, she asked me about what had happened. I gave her thanks for the water but said nothing else.

I just wanted to go home and be alone.

She dropped me off at my house and I proceeded to finish that bottle of gin.

And another.

I stayed in bed for three days straight.

Good thing I was on break between filming.

The whole time my phone was blowing up. Tate had managed to text and call more times in those seventy-two hours than he had all year long.

I wanted to reply to him, but I didn't. I held firm.

It was too late.

Unfortunately, a month after our run-in, I got word that I was going to be working with Tate again. Or rather, Jared Elwood was planning a sequel to the hit that had brought us our fame. I loved working with Jared because he was progressive and pushed the status quo. He was the antithesis of Neal Lockwin.

But I wasn't sure I could do this again. Jared wanted both me and Tate in the production or it was a no go.

At first, I said forget it. Henn told me I was nuts.

The payout was incredible, and the shoot wouldn't start for another year. Plenty of time for me to deal with the death of my friendship with Tate.

And a few months later, I was finally convinced to take the offer.

Or rather, it took one quote from an entertainment article to change my mind. An interview with Tate where, when asked about our relationship, he described me as a 'former friend, if you could call him that, and a mediocre actor at best'.

I signed that fucking contract the same day and issued my own statement in return, calling him 'narcissistic and overrated'.

When the time came, Jared would be in for one hell of a movie production.

It wasn't just Tate's comment about me that changed my mind, but also a phone call from another Hollywood A-lister, a friend and fellow actor Dylan Aylmer. Dylan, like Tate, had battled addiction.

And his phone call, on a gray March morning, broke my resolve.

"Reed, it's been a long time. How you been?"

"I'm okay Dylan, how about yourself?" I asked.

"Living in Palm Springs, so pretty damn good. Quiet, but good."

"You sound great."

"I've been sober four months and I know that doesn't sound like much, but every day I'm getting better."

"I'm so glad," I paused. "I'm sorry I haven't called lately. Trust me, it's not you."

"I know, I just talked to Henn. She's really worried about you."

"She shouldn't be. She has other clients to worry about."

"Speaking of that, how's Tate doing?"

A sudden lump formed in my throat.

"I have no idea. Our friendship is done, Dylan. Finished. We had a big blowout and that was it. He even spoke about it to the press. Henn didn't tell you?"

"She just said you were going through a hard time, but gave no details. And I haven't been reading the usual gossip. My therapist wanted me to detox off that too."

"Smart idea. But maybe you could give Tate a call? I'm sure he'd be happy to hear from you," I suggested.

I knew that Henn kept tabs on Tate. She'd only mentioned in passing that he was in rehab again and left it at that. I didn't push and she didn't offer. But that didn't stop me from worrying, and wondering, and second guessing my decision to cut off contact.

"I'll do that. And I'm sorry to hear about you and Tate. You guys were close, and for a while there, I thought that—"

Dylan paused.

"We were just friends, Dyl. Only that."

"Yeah, Tate fed me the same line. But I know chemistry when I see it. And since I'm a country boy at heart, I also know bullshit when I smell it."

"Still as charming as ever."

"You can take the man out of Texas—"

I laughed. For the first time in ages.

"I've got a break between acting gigs. Would you be open to a visitor? I mean, is that okay?"

"That would be great! I can tell you one thing for sure. When you hit rock bottom, you find out right quick who your real friends are."

The pang of guilt about Tate hit me full force again. But then I remembered that I had my own heart and my own well-being to look after.

"How about Sunday?" I asked. "Does that work? I'll probably stay a few days."

"Text me the details. I look forward to it."

"Will do. I'll see you soon."

Dylan's call left me strangely homesick. When my cat, Grant, hopped up on my lap and began to pester me for scritches, I gave in to his charms. Like always.

Even the damn cat reminded me of Tate.

Grant pawed at my hip and I looked down. I'd almost had that fucking tattoo on my hip lasered off, but I couldn't do it.

I left it as a reminder, a warning.

Even the luckiest of charms are just that.

Luck isn't love.

Instead of wondering about the demise of my relationship with my former best friend, I picked up my phone and called my oldest one.

When my Dad answered, everything came flooding out.

And his advice? It was simple.

Go back to Tate. Don't leave anything left unsaid.

This time, it was time to fight.

Unfortunately, Tate refused to talk to me.

It turned out to be too little, too late.

CHAPTER 11

TATE

TWO YEARS AGO

"Will you tell Mr. Larkin that I don't need or appreciate his advice when it comes to this scene? I know what I'm fucking doing!" I yelled.

Of all the actors I had to work with, it had to be my best friend.

Former, I reminded myself. Not friends and not best.

Not anymore.

Yes, I had fumbled again last year and succumbed to my addiction.

But this time, Reed walked out of my life. For good. Just wrote me off.

Like I wasn't worth anything.

Confusion and hurt turned to anger. Mostly at myself, but Reed was an easier target.

And that's where I stayed.

I was an asshole on the best of days, so my temper was nothing new to the crew.

And my anger grew as I stared at Reed and the smug look on his handsome face.

"And will you tell *Tater* here that he's not fooling anyone," Reed sneered. "This scene requires real emotion, something he knows very little about. Maybe his stunt double would be better off in his place?"

"Why you fucking ass—"

I lunged for Reed but the production assistant, Hugh, and our director, Jared, got in between us.

"Don't touch me Tate, or my lawyer will have you replaced faster than you can snort your next line of coke," Reed snapped.

"I'm clean now! Screw you!" I shouted back.

"Stop it," Jared interrupted. "Both of you."

Jared didn't yell back, but the warning in his voice silenced both me and Reed.

I managed to calm myself and stepped back.

"Listen to me and listen good, we are a week behind schedule," Jared continued. "And I want to get this sequel finished as much as you do, probably more so I don't have to listen to your incessant bickering. Save your critiques of each other for after hours. Do your job and do it well. You know the acting world. Word travels fast and if you're difficult, work will be difficult to find."

Thinking about that, I kept my mouth shut.

I was already dealing with naysayers thanks to my last stint in rehab. I didn't need this on top of everything else. After all, my work was the only thing that kept me going.

"It's fine. I'm good," Reed announced and ran a hand through his hair. "I'm a professional."

Jared looked at me with a question in his eyes. "Tate?"

I nodded. "I'm here to work. Let's get on with it."

Jared sighed and held up his hands. "Okay, everyone, places! Let's get this scene wrapped up!"

Thankfully, Reed and I were playing enemies. Two

lawyers who were once again on opposing sides. It made for interesting banter and tension. And given our status, it hardly felt like acting at all, at least, for most of the scenes. This was one was more emotional, though, with my character finally opening up to Reed's.

And Reed wasn't totally off the mark. The heavy scenes in acting were often cathartic, but painfully real. Sometimes, hitting too close to home.

Then I realized that if I didn't bring my A-game to this role, despite my feelings for Reed, I'd only be screwing myself over.

I'd finally started to understand, through therapy, that it was better to lance that poison than to let it fester. And if emotion was needed, emotion was what they were going to get.

I got into place and Reed stepped forward, until we were almost nose to nose.

I was used to the intensity of the set lights and the fact that there were dozens of pairs of eyes on me.

But I was not prepared for the intensity of Reed and this new dynamic between us.

Once, his eyes were the only peace I knew.

And now, there was so much turbulence there, it made me want to look away.

"I didn't call you down here to my office to rehash old cases, Nik. I called you down here because I have a problem on the current one."

At least I remembered my lines…

"I shouldn't even be talking to you!" Reed shook his head.

No shit. Then I remembered, this was Nik, the character, not Reed.

"Then I'll make this as quick as possible. Someone is trying to blackmail me. And I think it's someone on the jury."

"What?"

I looked over at the desk to my right and pointed at the envelope. "I received that today. Open it."

"*You* trust *me* with your secrets?" he scoffed.

Holy fucking hell, talk about art imitating life.

"Just open it."

He walked over to the desk and opened the envelope. Out fell a picture along with a note.

"That's you and me standing outside my condo building," he replied and shrugged. "Big deal. I live near the courthouse. We were just having a discussion about the case. We've only spoken at designated meetings in preparation for the trial or at trial."

"I know that! But nothing in that picture can confirm that. It doesn't look good. And read the note."

"*If you paid more attention to your client, and not the opposing counsel, you'd have won the case by now. Is that why you went easy on the prosecutor's witness? Your cross-examination needs work. Take a plea deal or this picture, and more, will be released.*"

"More? What the fuck is this person talking about?"

"I have no fucking idea, but I don't want to find out. This is serious, Nik. I won't let my client take the fall for something he didn't do."

"So you say."

"Jesus Christ, this picture is not just about me. Your life will be fucked too if there's any hint of impropriety!"

"Alert the judge. You'll need to step aside."

"Me? You should recuse yourself as well. It's both of us in that picture, my friend."

"I'm not your fucking friend, Tate!"

Shit.

"Cut!" Jared yelled out. "Reed, come on!"

Reed raised his hand. "Sorry, sorry. Let's do it again."

An hour and five takes later, we finally got the scene wrapped up.

Despite the constant tension between me and Reed, I was

glad that I'd gotten through that scene. We could do this. I'd worked with plenty of people I didn't like, so why should this be any different?

It was getting late, though, and we still had two more scenes to finish tonight.

This was when my urge for coke hit hardest.

Also, when I was alone.

Cocaine was a siren's call for the lonely.

Instead of giving in to the need, I asked one of the supporting actors to practice lines with me. Then I called my sponsor.

Next thing I knew, it was time to report on set again.

As I sat in the chair getting my makeup touched up, I realized that I wasn't the only one looking worse for wear.

Reed came into the dressing room and sat down beside me. Despite his easy smile and upbeat demeanor with the rest of the crew, I noticed the dark shadows under his eyes and the fact that he'd lost some weight. He was always slimmer than me but looking at him now, it sparked a worry.

And the longer I stared, other, more dangerous feelings rose to the surface.

An ache, a longing I never felt for anyone. Only for him.

You're ridiculous.

He's fine. You're fine.

And you don't need him, right?

"Too many late nights?" I quipped as I looked at him in the mirror.

"Fuck off."

"Ooh, touchy. Can't get laid?"

"You're such a pain in the ass," he snapped. "I'm having problems sleeping, all right? Not that it's any of your fucking business."

"That's not like you."

"Well, a lot has changed in a year."

"No shit."

Then there was an awkward silence as our makeup artists worked quickly to finish up.

"So, have you—" I started.

"Don't," Reed interrupted. "I don't want to make small talk. Just leave me alone."

But of course, I couldn't. That wasn't me.

"Can't we just—"

Reed ripped off his protective gown and stormed out of the dressing room before I could finish my sentence.

"Don't mind us," I murmured to the make up artists. They just rolled their eyes.

No doubt they'd be repeating everything they heard the second I was done.

Once my makeup was finished, I wandered back out to find Reed in deep discussion with Jared. My former friend better not be trying to convince the director to kick me off this movie or so help me…

Instead of patiently waiting my turn, I walked right up to them.

"—I can't do this, Jared. There's too much—"

"What's going on?" I interrupted.

Jared glanced at me with weary hazel eyes, then back at Reed.

"Look, I don't know what happened between you two and I don't need to know," Jared replied calmly. "But I was an actor once too, and I know about working closely with people you don't get along with. It's not easy, but I'm sure you've faced it before. Haven't you?"

Reed nodded. "Yeah."

"Yes," I muttered.

Yes and no.

I'd never had to work with someone I once considered my closest friend. The man that I compared against all other men. Reed could barely look at me now and when he did, there was nothing there but disgust. It made me feel even lower than I already did.

It made me want to crawl back into my trailer and never come out.

"Let's get on with it, then. The sooner we're done, the sooner you guys can go your separate ways. Although, you really should consider talking this thing out. I've never seen either of you so angry before and it's not healthy," Jared sighed. "There. That's my intervention for the day."

Jared walked off and left Reed and I alone again.

"I don't know if I can do this," Reed whispered.

"The role?"

"No, for Christ's sake, this!"

He pointed between the two of us.

"I'm clean now, Ree. And in therapy. I swear this time is different."

Reed bit his lower lip and shook his head. "That may be true and if it is, I'm glad for you. But it doesn't change things between us. I just… I can't go back."

"Is this," I paused and looked around to make sure no one was overhearing us. "Is this because I'm not out?"

Reed eyes flashed. "I've said it time and again, I would never pressure anyone to do that. Ever. And are you really that clueless?"

"What? What else is there?"

"Don't you remember our last conversation? What you said to me?"

"I was high on cocaine, so no, I don't!"

Reed angry expression turned to resignation. "Then it doesn't matter. It's not relevant anymore anyway."

"I have no idea what you're talking about!" I roared.

"Exactly!" Reed yelled back. "Leave me alone!"

He stormed off and left me standing there, more confused than ever.

What had I said to him that day? I wracked my brain but

all I could remember was shouting, and the look of devastation on Reed's face. And then he was gone.

And he never came back.

Then I thought back to the night of that red carpet event a year prior. My fumbled attempt to kiss him. Was it possible that Reed wanted… no, he'd turned me down. And he was right. If we had kissed, it would have changed everything. And not in a good way.

I wasn't ready to deal with that. Still wasn't.

Shit, I was so fucked up.

But at least I had plenty of stuff to talk about with my therapist on my next visit.

CHAPTER 12

REED

ONE YEAR AGO

Why did I sign on for another movie with Tate?

Make that two in one year.

Was I a masochist? Was I stupid?

Yes. And yes.

It was also the drug of success. Tate wasn't the only one with addictive tendencies.

Last year's sequel was a smash and made us even more popular. And brought us accolades, nominations, and more opportunities.

Personally, the two of us together were a disaster, but professionally, Tate and I were box office gold.

First came *Field of Blood*, a film we shot in France. Also directed by Jared.

Tate and I started the production by going out with the crew to celebrate our first week of filming. We ended up getting drunk, getting into a near fistfight, and arrested for public mischief.

Thankfully, our lawyers got the charges dropped.

My nice guy image took a hit, but for Tate? The incident only fueled his bad boy image.

Contrary to Jared's warning, the feud between me and Tate turned out to be profitable for both of us, and for the movie PR. We got so much press and attention that Henn was constantly fielding offers.

And when I heard about *Jagged Edge*, a script that Jared was planning to film in Thailand, I approached him and convinced the director to take another chance on me. It wasn't easy, but I secured my role. Then I found out about Tate doing the same.

I guess the buzz around this script was too tempting for either of us to pass up.

As usual, I ignored all the warnings signs flashing in front of me.

It was the opportunity to work with Jared again. And a few months away from the smog and grind of LA.

Even if that meant working with the one man I couldn't exorcise.

I felt like a shell of myself, like he'd taken a piece of me and I'd never be whole again. I couldn't bear to look at him, but I couldn't stop thinking about him.

Okay, that was probably the third reason why I accepted this latest role.

It was pathetic.

Our friendship had imploded, but I was still in love with Tate.

And I hated that I was in love with him.

It didn't stop me from seeking out pleasure with other men. But it did leave me with a restlessness that was never satisfied.

I met, I fucked, and I was done.

I had a small circle of friends that I hung out with, most of whom were starting to pair up. Which made me happy for them, but sad for myself.

Since I was running on empty.

Maybe it was time to put this ridiculous warfare of ours to bed. *Don't even think about bed and Tate in the same sentence.* To rest, to be accurate.

That was the plan.

Until I arrived in Bangkok, along with Dylan, who had also landed a role in the film. I was looking forward to having at least one friendly face to talk to.

But now, only three days into filming, it was turning into a disaster.

It started with a rewrite to the script.

Suddenly Tate and I had to kiss, and when he found out— or when I asked him if we could rehearse it before taping—all hell broke loose.

Tate freaked out and locked himself in his dressing room until Jared talked him down.

And he wasn't the only one who was panicking. I just did a better job of hiding it.

It probably had to do with the fact that I'd had a drink beforehand to help my nerves. A mistake on my part.

Me, alcohol, and Tate was a dangerous mix.

It was one scene, mind you, but still, nothing in nine years of professional acting had prepared me for this. And I'd kissed a lot of men, mostly for pleasure but occasionally for work.

It was a short clip, probably only ten seconds of reel. But I was never so nervous in my life.

For the first time ever, I thought I might puke on set.

What a way to set up a kiss.

"Places everyone, quiet!"

I could do this.

It's just a kiss. Nothing to it.

I walked up to Tate, determined to get this shot in one take. I didn't want to be in his personal space any longer than was necessary. And once I was done, I was heading straight for that bottle of gin again.

"In three, two, one… action."

Tate froze for a split second and I, as usual, took the first step.

The lips that I'd longed to taste more than any other were right there in front of me.

Without pause, I reached up and shoved my hands into his hair, cupping the back of his head.

Fuck, it was amazing to touch him. I hadn't been this close to him since that red carpet event.

We shared one heated breath and my body locked up tight. A barrage of emotions hit me full force and my hands began to shake.

Or was that him? Was he trembling too?

His amber eyes bored into mine, so intense that I was all but drowning.

I forgot about everyone watching us and the fact that I was supposed to be acting.

And then, we moved at the same time. Like we'd been doing this forever.

I leaned up and he reached down, and when our mouths collided, a shockwave snapped through my body, from the tips of my hair to the soles of my feet.

I'd dreamed of kissing Tate, but the reality was different, so much better, than my imagination.

It was painfully sweet and sinfully hot.

And I figured, if I only got one chance in my life to kiss Tate, I was going to *kiss* Tate.

My tongue playfully teased his soft lips and he groaned loudly in response, parting his lips.

So, I went for it.

But as usual, Tate turned the tables on me.

Next thing I knew, it was him, not me, taking control of

the kiss. His rough beard teased my lips while his tongue greedily sucked on mine.

And I was only too happy to return the favor.

Even in this, our kiss turned aggressive, mauling, as we fought for dominance.

Hey, it was us, so that wasn't surprising. Neither of us wanted to give in to the other.

But neither of us could stop.

I'm pretty sure I heard Jared yell 'cut' but Tate and I kept on kissing.

It wasn't enough.

I needed more.

His hands cupped my ass and pulled me in tight, and when our hard cocks brushed against each other, I moaned into his mouth. He gently bit my lip and then soothed the sting with that wicked tongue of his.

The man was a complete and utter ass, but fuck, he knew how to kiss.

"Hello? I said cut!"

Jared's voice boomed in my ear, and I finally paused.

Tate must've heard it too and before I knew it, he pulled away. Leaving me a trembling wreck.

"Okay folks, let's take a break."

I was too stunned to move, let alone acknowledge our director.

Crew members walked around us, but I barely paid any attention.

All my focus was on watching Tate as he ran a nervous hand over his beard and his swollen lips.

He hadn't run off like I'd expected.

And then his eyes met mine.

He was staring at me like he'd never seen me before.

Tate

Kissing Reed imploded nine years of self-denial.

Granted, we were supposed to be playing our parts. But there was no acting involved, not for me.

Not for him either.

Hard dicks don't lie.

I finally kissed my best friend. Former. Or maybe not former? I didn't know anymore.

Whatever the case, I wasn't playing a character when I touched him.

And our kiss? Fuck me, that kiss.

My skin was torched, my lips tingling from shock and awe.

We kissed like everything else between us—with passion that bordered on aggression. Lust and hate were so closely tied together, I didn't know which was which anymore.

But I knew that there was no going back from that kiss.

At least, not for me.

For Reed, on the other hand…

After filming wrapped that day, both of us headed back with Jared to the yacht he was staying on. He was hosting a dinner with his friends, his lead bodyguard Alex, his lawyer, Aiden, and our castmate, Dylan. There was privacy here and security on every level of the ship, one bodyguard more scary looking than the next.

Normally I was the troublemaker at social gatherings, but Reed was the one throwing back the alcohol faster than anyone.

And when he started flirting with Alex, things got heated.

Especially when Reed asked Alex if he'd like to go back to his hotel with him. I lost it, Aiden snapped at him, and everything went downhill from there.

Did Reed really want to fuck Alex? Granted, the man was hot, and ripped, and he had that strong, silent thing going on.

But how could Reed act like that kiss we shared meant

nothing? Or maybe on his end, it did. Maybe he was a better actor than I gave him credit for?

If so, I felt like a fool.

And it made my anger darken at the slightest provocation.

"Slow down on the booze, Reed, or you're gonna have a hell of a hangover tomorrow. You don't want to delay production. Again," I snapped.

Guests began to get up and leave the table.

"Relax, *Tater*, I can h-handle my d-drinking," Reed scoffed, slurring his words.

I shook my head. "You're making an ass of yourself. Go sober up."

"Don't tell me w-what to d-do! And you're one to talk about s-sobriety."

"I've been clean for a year. Stop throwing that in my face."

"But it's better than getting up in your face? Right?" Reed reached for his wine glass, taking another long gulp.

"Shut it," I hissed.

"Oh yes," Reed leaned forward and placed a finger to his lips. "Be q-quiet. But only about who you fuck, right Tate? Secrets, that's what you're good at."

"You're so obnoxious when you're drunk."

"At l-least I'm honest," Reed waved his glass around, spilling the contents all over his hand.

"Really?" I asked and tossed him a napkin to clean up. "And what about that kiss today?"

Reed stared at me with glassy green eyes. "It was so fucking hot."

I couldn't help the bark of laughter at his blunt admission.

"Yes, it was."

I said it. Why not?

Chance are, Reed would forget this convo by morning.

"Wait! I need to m-mark this day down," Reed announced. "Tate admitted that he l-likes kissing men."

Only the seagulls nearby heard him.

"I admitted that kissing *you* was hot," I corrected him.

Reed was suddenly silent and set his glass down. Then he put his arms on the table and dropped his head down.

"Reed?" I asked.

When he didn't answer, I got up and walked around the end of the table. "Reed, are you—"

A loud snore interrupted my question. He was passed out cold.

"I guess he's done for the night."

Dylan's sudden voice startled me. I turned around to find him, Charlie, one of the deck crew, and Kiernan, one of the bodyguards, staring at me.

Had they all heard our conversation?

"We'll get him to a room so he can sleep it off," Charlie assured me.

Charlie walked over and gently shook Reed's shoulder. I watched as he and Kiernan helped him get up. Dragged him, more like.

Shaking my head, I walked over to the other end of the deck and leaned on the railing.

"Reed's fighting something. Hard," Dylan remarked as stood beside me. "I just hope he faces it soon. Drinking ain't gonna solve nothin'."

"It was a stressful day. I'm sure by tomorrow, he'll be okay."

"And what about you?"

"Me? I'm fine," I answered automatically. "Nothing happened."

"Sure." Dylan shook his head. "That's why you were fucking his mouth on set today."

I choked on nothing but my own spit and air. "We had to kiss, so we kissed."

"It's me, Tate. I've been on enough sets to know the difference between acting and real passion. I know what I saw."

"But—"

Dylan held up his hand. "Don't worry. I won't say anything."

Maybe it was time I finally told the truth to my friend.

"I'm gay."

Holy fuck, I'd actually said it. And sober too.

"Besides Reed, my therapist, and Henn, you're the only other person I've told. But for some reason, I still haven't been able to come out," I paused and shook my head. "Where I come from, there's no such thing as gay. You're either straight or you're dead. And that fear is so instilled in me, I don't know if I'll ever shake it loose."

Dylan studied me for a long moment.

"You're not alone in that fear. It took me a long time to come to terms with my sexuality. Hiding was part of the reason for my drinking. Always worrying that I might be found out. Pushing my desires into dark corners that never saw the light of day. I didn't know how being bi might affect my career. But things are different now. It ain't ten years ago. And I can tell you this, Tate. The moment I started living my truth, that was the moment I started living."

Dylan patted me on the shoulder and left me standing alone on the deck.

Coming out was one thing.

Facing my feelings for Reed was another.

I looked out to sea, and while the water appeared calm, dark clouds rolled in, and the wind picked up.

A perfect storm was brewing.

And I had no idea if I was going to survive the wreckage.

CHAPTER 13

REED

PRESENT DAY

I f acting taught me anything over the past decade, it's to expect the unexpected.

Tate and I reached a stalemate of sorts thanks to that trip to Thailand.

I don't know if it was *the kiss* or me making a drunk fool of myself, but the anger that had fueled us for months and months had slowed to a simmer.

We managed to complete filming without delay, or getting arrested, or pissing off the crew.

A win in my book, even though things were still tense because we were both too stubborn to make the first move and talk about what happened. Despite seeing each other at various industry events, Tate and I pretty much ignored each other.

I guess silence was better than fighting.

Thank fuck I was busy.

I had two movies in production this year, both for streaming services.

It left me with little time to worry about the ghost of Tate Aduma.

Was I finally letting him go?

Or perhaps I had just accepted the fact that my relationship with him was like a puzzle I could never quite figure out.

One that was missing one important piece.

While getting my makeup prepped for the shoot today, my phone buzzed. I smiled when I saw my sister's name appear.

Rissa and I had always had a strong bond, only being a year and a half apart. And despite my life on the west coast and hers on the east, we always made time to talk. We joked about our psychic connection, often calling each other at the same time.

"Hey, sis, can I call you back at five when I'm on break? I'm just getting my makeup finished."

"This can't wait, Reed. Are you alone? Are you sitting down?"

Her voice was so low, barely a whisper. I knew immediately something was horribly wrong.

"Hold on."

I placed my phone to my chest and politely asked the makeup staff to leave my trailer. Once they were gone, I put the phone to my ear again.

"Okay, what's going on?"

"It's Mom. She—" I heard a sniffle and then a gut-wrenching sob. "She's dead."

Thank fuck I was sitting down because I was about to pass out.

"No. No, that's not right. I just talked to her three days ago, what—"

"Mom was driving to the gym early this morning," Rissa choked out. "Another c-car hit her head on, they were driving in the wrong lane. They think it might… it might have been a drunk driver."

No. This couldn't be happening. Not to my family.

Not my mother. *No.*

"Rissa," I gasped, refusing to believe what she'd told me.

But her sobbing grew louder, and there was no denying the truth.

I looked up, catching a glimpse of myself in the mirror. I didn't even realize that I'd started to cry until I saw the tracks of tears on my face.

"I'm going to book the first flight out," I finally managed to reply. "I'll be there as soon as I can."

"Dad's still in shock, they've given him a sedative. We're at the hospital. Norwich General."

"I'll text you as soon as I land."

I texted Henn first and then went in search of the production coordinator.

A half hour later, I was in a rideshare heading for LAX. And I didn't care if the paps spotted me. If they dared to approach, I would scream bloody murder.

Nothing felt real.

I was numb. My brain, my heart, every part of my body.

I'm sure I talked to people at the airport, at security, but I don't remember any of it.

All I knew was that the person who'd supported and loved me all my life was gone.

My vibrant, fifty-nine-year-old mom was taken from us. What would our family be without her?

When I landed in New York, there was a driver waiting for me. Henn, my rock, had arranged for it. Good thing too, because I was not fit for the almost two-hour drive north to Norwich.

I had sunglasses on to hide my swollen eyes and I was still shaking.

My phone buzzed and I sighed, not in the mood to deal with anyone.

> Tate: Henn told me. I'm so sorry about your mom. Are you…

There was a pause while three dots appeared, then disappeared.

> Tate: I mean, fuck, nothing I can say will be of any comfort to you. Except that I'm here if you ever need to talk.

More tears erupted as the irony of Tate's words hit my heart like a sledgehammer, shattering what was left of it.

How long had I been waiting for him to say that exact thing? On top of losing my mom, it was too much. I was hysterical, sobbing and choking on air at the same time. I'm sure the driver thought I was completely off the rails.

When I finally managed to get a hold of myself, I typed out a response with trembling hands.

> Reed: I'm still in shock. But thanks for reaching out.

> Tate: Call me. Anytime.

I wanted so badly to make that call. Even if it was only to hear him say something sarcastic about me. It was weird, because he should've been the *last* person I wanted comfort from.

But there it was.

Suddenly, I felt incredibly alone.

Rissa had her husband, Darren, and the kids. Dad… God, I couldn't imagine what he was going through. He was dedicated to my mom for the past thirty-five years. I looked at their marriage as the gold standard.

When I arrived at the hospital, I called Henn to thank her for the car service.

She'd warned me that the news of my mom's death was already making the rounds and there might be reporters sniffing around the hospital.

Christ, that made me angry. It made me want to say *fuck it* to my Hollywood career. I couldn't take a shit lately without it making headline news and now the press was going to circle over my mom's passing like a pack of hungry vultures.

I texted Rissa and she instructed me to head on up to the third floor.

When I got off the elevator, I spotted her blonde ponytail and rushed over to greet her.

"Reed," Rissa called out when she saw me.

I pulled her in for a hug, both of us shaking and crying.

"Where is she?" I managed to whisper.

Rissa leaned back and wiped her face. "They just transferred her to the morgue. They have to do an autopsy."

"Jesus Christ."

My voice broke and both of us held on to each other, sobbing.

Darren was suddenly beside us and put his arm around Rissa.

"Dad is awake and wants to talk to you," he murmured.

Rissa nodded, too overcome to speak.

"Thanks Darren," I replied and gave my brother-in-law a hug.

Rissa led me to the last room at the end of the hallway. My dad was lying in a hospital bed, his normally ruddy complexion ghostly white.

Then when he spotted us, fat tears rolled down his cheeks. "Is it true? Is she really gone?"

We reached his bed, Rissa on one side and me on the other, taking his ice-cold hands in ours.

"I'm so sorry, Dad."

There was nothing else we could say to comfort him.

· · ·

Tate - Five days later

Death has a strange way of bringing people together.

Henn and I took a private plane to New York for Rosalin Larkin's funeral.

But as we grew closer to our destination, my earlier confidence that I was doing the right thing began to waver.

A week ago, Reed was the last person I would talk to. Now I was flying across the country to see him.

Every instinct, ever since I heard the news, told me *yes, go to him.*

I'd been fighting the urge to hop on a plane from the moment Henn called to tell me Reed's mom had died. I knew how close he was with his family. I'd never met his mom in person but from Reed's stories, I felt like I knew her. Reed always described her as the fulsome heart of their family.

Her son certainly took after her.

I remembered how caring he'd been with me when I was in rehab in Ojai, and how he'd made my house a home I wanted to return to.

A lump the size of California lodged in my throat and stayed there for the entire five-hour flight.

Would he want me there? Or would I just upset him?

Given our volatile relationship, anything could happen.

And the last thing he needed was more stress.

What would I say? What could I say?

It didn't help that Reed would have to grieve in the spotlight. News of his mom's death, and the drunk driver who killed her, was still making the rounds. Every time I saw a new picture of the crash scene, I wanted to scream on Reed's behalf.

Henn informed me that his family was holding a private service, and that security would be on hand, just in case. Hopefully, Henn and I would make our entry and exit without any media fuss.

I didn't know how long I'd be able to stay anyway.

Funerals were something I avoided.

Rosalin's death made me think about my own family.

Something I never wanted to do.

There was no one left. Just painful memories that I couldn't get rid of.

Shortly before I turned nineteen, my mom died from a massive brain hemorrhage, the result of a final beating from my stepfather.

He, in turn, died in jail after being arrested. Much as I wanted that bastard to rot in prison for the rest of his life, his death gave me a relief that I didn't dare express.

"Tate."

Henn's voice startled me.

"Yes?"

"We're ready to leave."

Fuck, I was so caught up in my head that I hadn't even realized that we'd landed.

We exited the plane to a cloudy and wet New York afternoon. I shivered and pulled my suit jacket tighter. Thankfully, our SUV was waiting nearby.

"They're not having a wake. The viewing will take place at the funeral home, just prior to the service."

"Shit, I forgot about sending flowers."

"Already taken care of."

"Are you sure me being here is a good idea? I mean, Reed's going to be upset enough as it is. I don't want to make it worse."

Henn pinned me with her blue eyes. "Good or bad, you've been a part of his life for a decade, Tate. Put your ego aside for one day and think about him. If you were in his position, would you want him here?"

Of course, I would.

There was no question.

Two hours later, we pulled up to a massive estate that turned out to be the funeral home.

My eyes couldn't get used to the lush greenery. LA was always so dry and dusty.

We stepped out of the car to be greeted warmly by the manager.

He guided us quickly inside. The place was already packed with people and the heady fragrance of roses. Everywhere I looked, there were displays of pink flowers.

Immediately, my eyes locked on Reed standing at the other end of the room, next to his mother's casket.

I jolted at the paleness of his face, the look of utter devastation.

Then I noticed his sister, who could've been his twin. She was standing beside a man I assumed was her husband. Reed had mentioned them a lot, always lovingly. I thought back to that one time I'd spoken with her. Not many people made me laugh but, much like her brother, Rissa had managed the impossible.

Instead of waiting, I worked my way through the crowd of people.

The moment Reed turned his head and locked eyes with mine, I knew I'd done the right thing.

"Tay," Reed whispered as fresh tears welled up and spilled down his cheeks.

I didn't say anything.

Instead, I reached for him. We hugged tightly, so tight I was sure I was going to have bruises the next day.

Not caring who was watching or what was going on around us, I finally pulled back and cupped his lean face in my hands. His normally sparkling green eyes were bloodshot and swollen from crying.

"I am so, so sorry, Reed."

Reed bit his bottom lip and nodded, and I wiped his tears away with my thumbs. I had no idea what prompted me to do that, since I wasn't one for showing affection. Or affectionate gestures in general.

Reed took a deep, shaky breath and stepped back, and I dropped my hands to my sides.

"This is my sister, Rissa, and her husband Darren," Reed started. "This is—"

"Of course, I know who this is. I wish we'd met under other circumstances, Tate, but thank you for coming."

Rissa offered her hand to me. When I shook it, she gripped mine in both of hers.

"I can't remember if you and Reed are friends again or still fighting, but our family appreciates you being here."

Given our surroundings, I bit back a grin at her bold statement.

"Reed and I are at odds, but rest assured, it's entirely my fault," I admitted as I looked at Reed. "Maybe one of these days, I'll get it right."

CHAPTER 14

REED

TWO MONTHS LATER

I t was seven AM on a Monday morning, and I was drunk.

Okay, not drunk, but severely hungover.

I should've been on set, returning to work. I'd been back in LA for a month now.

But I couldn't give a fuck. I didn't care anymore.

Not about my work, not about my friends, not about anything.

My mom was taken from us, leaving my dad a shattered mess. Leaving my family a mess.

And the man who killed her? He was out on bail.

On bail.

Out living his life like nothing had fucking happened. Like he hadn't destroyed our family in one morning.

And I was so goddamn angry about it that no one could talk to me. And I sure as fuck didn't want to talk to anyone.

Especially *him*.

Tate had left numerous voicemails and texts. While I responded to the first few, I ignored the rest of them these past few weeks. I was too busy emptying out my liquor cabinet.

It was ironic and sad, like I was suddenly living out one of my Hollywood dramas.

I felt guilty coming home to LA, but Rissa insisted that I needed to get back to my home and my routine for my own health.

Not that I gave a fuck about that either.

I couldn't sleep, but I didn't want to get out of bed.

I couldn't stop crying, but I hated being emotional.

I didn't want to feel, but pain was the only thing I knew.

So, I locked myself in my house and drank and drank and drank. Getting drunk and passing out was the only thing I wanted. Oblivion. I could forget about all the bad shit.

Pot barely relaxed me. Coke woke me up, and I sure as fuck didn't want to be awake.

But gin and tequila? They burned all the way down and I welcomed that fucking fire.

Pain wanted pain.

I'd been tempted, just once, to cut myself. But given that I passed out at the sight of fake blood on set, and my stomach roiled just thinking about touching a knife to my skin, I brushed that idea aside.

I stuck to the pretty tasting poison instead.

My house was littered with empty bottles and garbage everywhere. It looked like I'd ransacked a bar. It smelled like one too, plus add in the stench of my unwashed body. I couldn't be bothered to care about any of it.

Including the state of my bedroom. And that's just where Tate found me.

Fucking Tate.

I glanced up from my drool-crusted pillow to find him standing at the foot of my bed. Or was I still drunk and imagining him?

"Yes, it's me! What the fuck, Reed? This place reeks, and so do you."

I glanced at him—from his shaggy hair to those amber eyes, to the full lips that were locked in a perpetual pout—and gave him my preferred finger.

"How the hell did you even get in here?" I yelled back and immediately regretted it.

My head felt like I'd taken a few hits and my ears were ringing.

"Jesus, how much have you had to drink? We exchanged keys back when we were actual friends, remember? I never gave you back yours, and apparently, you never changed the security code, genius. Now get your ass in the shower. We're going to clean up this mess and change Grant's litterbox since you obviously haven't done either in weeks."

"Not that it's any of your business, but I fired my house-keeper. And I can take care of myself! I don't need you cleaning anything. Get the fuck out of my house!"

I finally pushed myself upright and everything began to spin. But I didn't let that stop me. Shoving the sheet aside, I stood up quickly, and nearly lost my balance.

Tate grabbed my shoulders, but I pushed him off. "Don't touch me!"

"Reed!"

But it wasn't Tate calling my name.

I blinked and I realized that it wasn't just Tate standing there, but Henn and Charlene too.

Henn was picking up empty bottles off the floor, and Charlene had what looked like a stack of my clothes in her hands.

"What the... what the fuck is going on here?" I demanded. "Why are you all here?"

"Your sister called me," Tate snapped and rubbed a hand over his beard. "You haven't responded to her messages for three days. The last time she spoke to you, you weren't making any sense, slurring your words. She's worried out of her goddamn mind!"

"How did she get your number?"

"We exchanged them at the funeral, remember? Jesus, it was only a month ago, Reed!"

I held my face in my hands as the throbbing headache grew sharper.

"Stop yelling!" I shouted, which didn't help matters at all.

Instead of saying anything else, Tate gripped my left arm and pulled me towards the bathroom.

"Let go of me," I hissed, trying to pull my arm back.

But I was so dizzy that I couldn't get my proper footing, and nearly tripped.

"We can do this the easy way or the hard way. But one way or another, Ree, you're getting in that fucking shower."

I gave up trying to pull away from his iron grip and let him guide me. I was too weak from lack of sleep and not eating.

Next thing I knew I was shoved into my shower and hot water sprayed my body.

"I guess I should be grateful it's not freezing cold!" I snapped.

"Don't tempt me," Tate replied.

I blinked the water from my eyes and realized he was standing in the shower with me. In his jeans and t-shirt which were now soaking wet. I glanced down at my naked body, leaner now, and in bad need of manscaping.

Like I gave a shit about how I looked. What did it matter anyway?

Years ago, I'd have dreamt of this moment. Well, not me being hungover, but being in the shower with Tate. Then I mentally berated myself for even going there.

"This isn't how I imagined our first shower together," I muttered sarcastically and turned my back.

Turning away from Tate.

"Me neither. Now shut up and wash up. You reek worse than a high school locker room," Tate snarked. "I mean it, Ree, or I'll scrub you down myself."

I turned back to him at that comment and snatched the offered bottle of vanilla bodywash out of his hand.

"I'm going to ask one more time, Tate. What the fuck are you doing here in my home?"

Tate shook his head and stepped closer to me, his wet clothes rubbing against my bare skin. I full on shivered despite the hot water.

"I'm trying to be your friend."

"We're not—"

"The fuck we aren't! We might like and hate each other in equal measure at times, but nothing will change this." He pointed between us. "No matter what, we end up here."

He said it with such conviction that I, despite my hazy mind, believed him.

Tate was right.

Somehow, despite everything, we always found our way back to each other.

Was it healthy? Probably not.

But I didn't give a shit about healthy. I just wanted the pain to stop.

I forgot about the bottle until he gently took it from me and squeezed a small amount in his hands. He lathered it up and began to wash me. And I leaned back against the tiles and let him.

With each passing minute, my mind began to clear a bit more.

Then I remembered Mom was gone, and I wanted to crawl back down another bottle.

"I need a drink," I murmured when he finally turned me around and washed my back. "I can't sleep, Tate. I can't eat. I just… think about her final moments in that car and I imagine her screaming for help and there's nothing I can do—"

Fat tears rolled down my face and mixed with the spray of the shower. I was shaking so hard, my teeth rattled.

"I know, baby. I know."

Tate slid his arms around my waist and pulled me into his bigger body, my back to his chest. I don't know if I was shocked by his words, his gesture, or if it was my gin-soaked brain, but I grabbed hold of him and I didn't let go.

He was the only real thing.

My center of gravity while I spun out of control.

And that was a total mindfuck. Tate was the steady one? How the fuck had that happened?

How long did he hold me?

It might have been five minutes or thirty. I don't know.

But he didn't let go while I sobbed and sobbed until I ran out of tears. And water.

Then I was ushered out of the glass enclosure and bundled up in a bath towel. I turned to find Tate doing the same, his wet clothes now a pile on the floor.

"Come on, we'll get some clean clothes, and have coffee."

I didn't say anything but I let him lead me out of the bathroom.

All the empty bottles had been cleared away and there were clean sheets on my bed.

"Sit."

I sat on the bed with my eyes closed while I listened to him rummaging through my closet. When I opened them again, he'd thrown on a pair of my sweatpants and a t-shirt. They were tight on him, and I cursed myself for even noticing.

He kneeled before me and put socks on my feet. Then he rose again and gently slipped a t-shirt over my head.

"Stand."

"Sit. Stand," I repeated. "What am I? A dog?"

"Most dogs are a hell of a lot more agreeable than you right now. And you forgot roll over. And fetch." Tate smirked and passed me my grey sweatpants. "Can you get these on, or do you need help?"

Instead of answering, I took the pants and slid one leg in, then the other, and yanked them up. I wasn't shy about my body, but for some weird reason, I didn't want Tate to see me vulnerable like this.

And I hated to give him any credit, but I felt marginally better.

"Let's go have something to eat."

"You're being nice to me and it's freaking me out," I admitted.

He looked at me with a cocky grin. "You're such a liar. You're not freaking out at all."

"Asshole," I grumbled.

He snorted and steered me out of my bedroom and into the living area, where Henn and Charlene were busy hauling bags of bottles out of the house.

I sat down on the sofa and watched them cart out those big ass recycling bags.

Holy fuck, had I really drunk all that?

"Jesus, you guys don't have to do this. I can get rid of that later."

"It's no worry," Henn said as she sauntered back into the living room and sat down across from me. "But you are."

"Everyone want espresso?" Tate asked as he walked over to the kitchen island.

"Make mine Irish," I added and looked around. All three of them were glaring at me. "What? Too soon?"

Charlene sat down beside me and patted my knee. "You're not known for your comedic timing, Reed, so keep the jokes to yourself and listen up. After we get caffeine and food into you, we're taking you to the doctor. Maybe a detox center if you agree."

"What? I'm not sick! And I'm not an alcoholic!" I scoffed.

"Five bags full of empty liquor bottles disagree with that statement," Henn added.

"Aren't I entitled to grieve?"

"Of course, you are," Henn continued. "But refusing to leave the house, refusing to talk to anyone, including friends like us and family who are concerned about you, is troubling. And so is binge drinking. It's not going to make the pain go away. You need to talk to someone."

"I'm not Tate," I growled. "I don't have an addiction. I'm in control."

Tate snorted and I turned to watch him make himself at home in my kitchen.

"You have a comment you'd like to share with us?" I snapped.

"Yeah, I do. Looking at you now is like looking in a fucking mirror, Ree. Except, you have a family that cares about you. Haven't they been through enough? Do they need to watch you self-destruct on top of losing your mom?"

"Fuck you!" I yelled and stomped off back to my bedroom, slamming the door.

Everyone could just go straight to hell. They had no fucking idea what I was going through.

I heard the door open, and I barely held back a scream.

"Don't, Tate. I don't want to hear it. I'll drink as much as I fucking want. I'm awake, I'm talking, so you can see I'm fine. All right? I don't have a problem. It's under control."

"Bullshit," he snapped. "Are you going to get in your car in the near future?"

"What?" I whirled and stared at him. "Where did that come from?"

"Answer the goddamn question. Do you still drive?"

"Of course, I drive! I live in California. How the fuck am I going to get around? And what does that have to do with anything?"

"You won't stop drinking, and that's your choice. But one

of these days you're going to leave the house, right? And because your brain will be so fucked up from downing alcohol day and night, you're gonna think you're fine and you'll get in your car and then guess what Ree? Are you freaking kidding me? You're going to become just like that asshole who took your mom's life!"

Tate likening me to the monster who killed my mother hit me like a punch to the solar plexus.

"No! You take that back! I am nothing like that piece of shit!"

My chest locked up so tight, I couldn't breathe.

I was not that person.

Tate shook his head and stalked up to me. "If you keep going like this, you'll turn into him. Is that what you want? Do you really want to do that to your father and sister? Your niece and nephews? I know how much you love your family, Ree, so I'm going to give you back some of your own advice. Please, please listen to me."

"I just... I can't deal with it. I can't do anything. All I feel is pain," I choked on another sob.

"I know. It's not fair that she was taken like that. But you can't drink or snort your pain away, Ree. Trust me, I've been there, I've tried. It only makes things worse. Don't repeat my mistakes."

I let his words sink in as Tate headed for the door. "I'm calling your sister and telling her what's going on. I think she should fly out here to help you."

"No!" I walked towards him and grabbed his arm. "No. Please. I won't do that to her. I... I'll go to the doctor. I'll go. But on one condition."

"Anything."

"You come with me."

CHAPTER 15

TATE

A MONTH LATER

I'd been true to my word and went with Reed to his doctor.

For the first time in my life, I was thinking about someone other than myself.

And it felt damn good.

I hadn't been able to save my mom when I was young, but maybe fate was giving me another chance to do right by Reed.

Reed's grief over the loss of his mom though, even three months in, was fresh, and he was still struggling.

His doctor monitored his detox off the alcohol and suggested an anti-depressant medication, which Reed agreed to. And therapy.

He was having a hard time staying asleep at night and consequently, he struggled to get out of bed in the morning. But at least he wasn't isolating anymore. He talked regularly to his family back in New York and to Henn and Charlene, as well as his therapist and a sober living specialist.

And of course, yours truly.

Because he couldn't avoid me.

I'd landed on his doorstep a month ago and I hadn't left. I'd even taken a break from movie projects for the first time in my career so I could keep a close eye in case he relapsed.

Camping out in his guest bedroom, which was as nice as any five-star hotel room, wasn't exactly a hardship.

I stayed up with him in the middle of the night when he woke up from nightmares and I coaxed him outside even when he didn't feel like socializing. I made sure he ate regular meals, that he swam in his pool every day and loaded up on sunshine, and that he got plenty of exercise in the form of hiking in the nearby hills.

I'd also brought my cat, Cary, with me, and he and Grant were happy to be reunited again.

Cary was happy to be near Reed, with both cats sleeping in his bedroom.

Sometimes I'd look in on him and find them curled up, one cat on either side of him. They knew, instinctively, that he needed them more than I did.

But I reminded myself that this, us being roommates again, was only temporary. Until Reed was himself again.

Not that I imagined he'd ever be quite the same.

Death changed you. I knew that all too well.

I just hoped that the sunny spirit of my friend was only temporarily sitting in the shadows.

I'd hate for him to turn into a brooding pain in the ass like me. There was only room for one of those in our relationship.

"Why are you scowling at my blender?"

I looked up to find Reed standing on the other side of the kitchen island, in his favorite grey sweatpants and a pink t-shirt, a cat in each arm. Like the freaking pied piper. Both cats clung to him and gave me a dirty look, like, *what are you still doing here, asshole*?

Shaking my head, I grabbed the container of protein

powder and the frozen berries and continued making our morning smoothies.

"I'm thinking about you."

"Ouch. That bad, huh?" he murmured as he walked over and sat on one of the stools.

The cats jumped on the island and made themselves right at home.

"No. Just that there's only room for one moody ass in this relationship and that's me."

Reed let out a laugh and I was so relieved to see him smile again.

"I can promise you that despite my ups and downs, I will never, ever, be as grumpy as you."

"Good. Do you want an espresso?" I asked.

"No, thanks. I'm cutting out the caffeine. It disrupts my sleep."

I finished adding everything to the blender and pressed start.

"I got a new script today. Do you feel like reading it with me?" I asked.

Reed hadn't shown any interest in work. I didn't want to push him hard but at the same time, he needed a bit of a shove.

"Sure. Who's the writer?"

"Max Lowell. Dylan's fiancé."

"Really? I didn't know Max was a screenwriter. I thought he taught English."

"He does, at a university near San Diego. This is his first attempt at screenwriting. He was a ghostwriter in his spare time, that's how he met Dylan, working on his autobiography. Max wanted to try his hand at a project with Dylan, which led to this script. Apparently, they've already had producers fighting over buying the rights."

Reed's interest was piqued. I could tell by the curious glint in his eye.

"Now I have to read it. What's it about?"

"I have no fucking idea."

Reed laughed out loud again. "Well, that's helpful. Thanks."

"Dylan wanted to tell me, but I said no. I prefer to read a script with fresh eyes. No pre-conceived bias."

"It's too early in the morning for all those big words of yours, Tate."

I poured his smoothie in a tall glass, added a glass straw, and slid it over. "Shut up and drink your breakfast, smart ass."

Reed pretended to scratch his face with his middle finger.

I was so goddamn happy that our relationship was finally back on track.

"Did he email it to you or send it via courier?"

"Email," I replied and then took a long sip of my own drink.

"Where's your laptop?" Reed asked, getting up.

I shook my head and put down my glass. "Have your smoothie. I'll get the laptop. It's in my bedroom, somewhere. Under a pile of my crap."

Reed snorted. "Your bedroom?"

"Fuck, yeah. Squatter's rights," I quipped as I made my way to the back of the house.

I wasn't joking. Reed's Spanish style house felt more like home to me than mine.

And sure enough, I found my laptop on my bed, under a pile of (hopefully) clean laundry. I also found the charger and headed back out to the living room.

Reed was leaning against the island, sucking down his smoothie with gusto. Watching his cheeks hollow and his throat move made my dirty mind kick into high gear.

Not that my mind needed to go there.

We'd finally circled back to being friends again. I didn't want to let my stupid hormones fuck everything up.

Instead of being a perv, I sat my ass down on the sectional, opened my laptop and typed in my password.

"Your password is our old apartment address?"

I glanced over my shoulder to find Reed leaning over the edge of the couch.

"Do you mind?" I sneered at him.

Of course, it had absolutely no effect.

"No, I don't," Reed replied with a smirk and stood up.

He walked around the sofa to take a seat beside me.

The cats decided I was fair game and began to crawl over my lap as I tried to type. Grant's fluffy gray tail hit me in the face, and I heard Reed's snort-chuckle.

"What's with the butt in my face?" I complained while Reed pulled Grant back into his arms.

"Too hairy?" Reed teased.

I was glad to see his sense of humor returning, even if it was at my expense.

"Exactly. Now, where's that email that Dylan sent me," I whispered to myself as I searched my inbox. Once I found it, I forwarded it to Reed's email. "Done. Do you have your tablet to read on?"

Reed held up his tablet in his other hand.

"How come Dylan sent this to you now?" Reed asked. "Normally, a producer buys the script first and then goes looking for actors."

"He and Max already had us in mind for the major roles. Dylan's searching for a producing partner. Which is why he also sent it to Jared, who's one of the interested buyers."

Reed placed Grant on the cushion next to him and swiped his tablet. "I think it's cool that Jared's making independent films now. No more out of touch studio bosses crawling up his ass."

"Yeah. But only a project or a two a year going forward. He's cutting back."

Reed glanced at me. "Quality over quantity. He might be on to something."

I didn't know if it was everything I'd witnessed Reed going through over the past three months or just the nature of entering my thirties, but the idea of taking time to breathe in between movies was beginning to appeal to me.

There was more to life and surprisingly, more to me, than acting. Exactly what that was, I'd yet to figure out.

"I love that he gives his actors leeway when it comes to working a scene. I guess that's why I kept going back for more of his films," I admitted.

"Even if it meant working with me?" Reed commented.

I glanced at him. I was so relieved to see his eyes clear and calm. There was still a sadness that lingered, but it wasn't sharp like before.

I smiled at him. "We had our squabbles, but you can't argue with on-screen chemistry. Can you?"

Not just on-screen, but twenty-four seven.

Reed licked his lips and nodded, then looked back at his tablet. His face was flushed, and it looked gorgeous on him, highlighting those sharp cheekbones and the pale dust of freckles. I could stare at his face day and night and never lose interest in studying him. Even after ten years, every time I glanced at him felt like the first.

"Do I have cat boogers on my face?" he asked as he continued to stare at his screen.

"What?" I laughed out loud. "No."

"Oh. Cause you were staring, and I thought maybe, you know, I had something on my face."

I felt my own heat in response.

"Just looking at that thing you call a beard."

"Hey." He turned back to me and stuck out his tongue. "Not all of us can grow a full mountain man beard in two hours. And I've been told that my scruff is very sexy."

I reached out and cupped his chin, rubbing the soft blond

hair against my thumb. "I wouldn't call it scruff either. More like peach fuzz. And you couldn't grow this out in two weeks, never mind two hours."

No way in hell was I going to admit that Reed was right. It was sexy as hell.

He was sexy as hell.

I prepared for him to push me away, but Cary beat him to it, his paw batting my hand.

"Hey, what do you think you're doing?" I glared at my ill-mannered cat.

"He's coming to my defense."

Cary jumped over Reed and curled up on his other side, next to Grant. "See?"

"Traitor," I muttered.

"Quiet," Reed hushed me. "I'm trying to read."

I made a zipping motion over my lips and opened the attachment in my email.

Duology was the name of the script. Sounded heavy.

The setting was London in the late nineties.

I read the logline, the hook. This was a love story between a closeted bisexual man and a widower struggling with grief.

Despite my initial surprise, I kept reading. And reading.

Twenty-year old Tate would've refused to even glance at this script.

Thirty-year old me said it was about fucking time.

CHAPTER 16
REED

TWO WEEKS LATER

"Are you sure you want to do this?" I asked Tate as we waited for Dylan and Max's arrival at my house.

The couple were driving up from San Diego for a celebratory dinner. Jared was backing *Duology* with Dylan, and Tate and I were taking the lead roles.

"If I wasn't, I wouldn't have signed the contract," Tate replied as he stood in the kitchen, preparing a salad.

"Remember how freaked out you were in *Jagged Edge*? That was only one kiss."

"That was last year. Things have changed. I've changed."

What did he mean by that?

I watched Tate move between the sink and the fridge, so at home in my house. He'd moved in here six weeks ago and hadn't left my side since. I was, hopefully, starting to come out of the worst of my grief, but some days were better than others. And now that I was feeling better, I didn't think I was in any danger of relapsing. I knew it, Tate knew it.

So, I wondered why he hadn't left.

And why he was so fucking calm about this movie. What had changed?

I paced my living room, a nervous wreck, while our cats watched on with bored interest.

Tate and I had readily agreed that the script for *Duology* was the most intense, heartfelt work we'd read in ages. It offered two lead roles that were filled with detailed backstories and incredible dialogue. Characters that any actor would fight to play.

But this was a love story that we had to play out.

And pretending to *fall* in love with the man I pretended *not* to love, was a mindfuck.

Okay, so I'd be pretending to fall in love with the character he played but still, this was Tate. When I acted with him, it was never just about playing a part. The reality of who we were always seeped in.

"The entire movie is about the intimate relationship that develops between these two men. Do you get what that means?"

Tate rolled his eyes.

"Duh, I read the script, just like you. Fuck me, some of those sex scenes were hot as hell. All I can say is, bravo Max," Tate snorted. "And lucky Dylan."

"This isn't a joke! We have to act out those very scenes. And why are you so calm? Do you realize this is probably only the fifth major movie production in the past two years that centers on queer relationship rep? Do you know how big of a deal this is going to be when it comes out? How much attention we're going to get?"

"Yes, to all that. And I'm calm because the writing is fucking gorgeous. These characters, their story, it's painful and beautiful at the same time. Shit, Ree, you felt it too. It's the most incredible role I've ever been offered in my entire career. I'm honored that Dylan and Jared chose me. Chose us."

He wasn't getting it.

"Agh!" I let out a growl of frustration and walked over to the island.

"What's with you?" Tate asked. "Is this because I'm not out yet?"

I stopped moving.

"Yet?"

"You might want to sit down for this bit of news, but it's gonna happen, Ree. I've done a lot of thinking the past few months. Well, to be honest, for years. But I think that I might be finally ready."

"You can't just think, Tate, you need to be sure. Someone like you, like me, in the public eye, there's no taking it back."

"I realize that."

"No," I snapped. "I don't think you do. You don't get the hateful emails, or the nasty comments on social media or—"

Tate held his hand up. "I grew up in a household that was ten times worse. I'm sure I'll be able to handle whatever shit comes my way."

All my annoyance vanished at his blunt admission. I walked around the island to stand beside him.

"That's the first time you've ever mentioned… I mean, I had an idea, but you never talk about your childhood," I paused, "I'm so sorry."

He didn't look at me. Tate nodded and set the food prep aside.

"You've seen the scars on my back, and I'm sure you've speculated about how I got them. Even after plastic surgery, they're still there. I'll never get rid of them. Courtesy of my stepfather, Kenny, and his regular efforts to beat 'the gay out of me'. And I use that term only because that's exactly what he said to me. Usually accompanied by his leather belt or whatever weapon he could find during one of his rages."

My stomach flipped over in the worst possible way, and the sudden, bitter taste of bile filled my mouth. Suspecting what had happened to him and hearing it were two different things.

Tate shook his head and then turned to me.

"My mom grew up in foster care and had me on her own when she was a teenager. She struggled all her life. Barely made ends meet. Until Kenny came along when I was fourteen. She'd been laid off the year before from her job at a local plastics factory, so she was desperate for a lifeline," Tate paused and rubbed his beard. "And then our life of poverty became a living hell. See, I wasn't into the usual shit he thought a boy should be into. And I wasn't always this big. Until I hit my late teens, I was small and rail thin. I was an easy target for that bastard's anger. He hated having a kid around. He hated kids in general. And gays, women, fuck, anyone who wasn't a nasty, violent piece of shit like him."

I reached for his arm. "Jesus Christ, Tay. How long did—"

Tate inhaled sharply and shook his head.

"Years. Until I hit a growth spurt around seventeen and he backed off. Well, until I fought back. When I turned eighteen, I was done. I had some money saved up so I moved out. Worked two jobs to support myself in a one-room apartment in town. Told my mom to leave him, to come live with me but she refused. Just like she refused to go to the police all those years. In hindsight, I couldn't blame her. Kenny was friends with the local sheriff, so what were the chances they would take her seriously? Then, about a year later, he... he beat my mom so bad—" Tate took a deep breath and paused, "So bad, she died as a result. He was arrested and died in jail shortly after."

Tate finally looked over at me, his amber eyes welling up. He blinked the tears away before they could fall.

"My God, Tate. I... I don't know what to say."

"I don't expect you to say anything. But I need you to understand, Ree. I've known, since I was thirteen, that I was gay. I knew then just as much as I know now. But there was no coming out for me in my situation. Not then, not when I first moved here, and not until recently. That vile, hateful shit he spewed at me for years is still lodged somewhere in the back of my brain. It created a fear within me that is the hardest fucking thing, outside of his beatings, that I've ever had to deal with."

My vision blurred and tears spilled down my face.

Tate reached out to touch me, gently wiping the tears away. I wanted to hold his hand to my cheek, but I resisted the temptation.

"You're ruining your makeup," he teased.

I shook my head. "How can you joke right now?"

He shrugged. "Deflection is my survival mechanism."

"Tate."

"I was born Joshua Tate Hanratty, but he's gone. I'm not that scared boy anymore."

I jolted at the mention of his birth name.

"But I'll always have scars. The internalized ones are the worst," he continued, "The biggest turning point was when I finally told my therapist everything, after my last stint in rehab. I can't let what happened to me in the past continue to haunt my present. I can't use coke or anything else to deal with my trauma, and my fear. To pretend to be someone I'm not. I'm not gonna say that coming out will be easy for me. I'll probably freak out at some point."

"That's normal."

Tate nodded. "It just sucks, you know. Hetero actors never have to prepare a statement about who they are. They don't have to justify their sexuality."

"No, they don't."

"But coming out means I don't have to hide anymore, and the fear doesn't win. And I'm so fucking sick of hearing that man's voice in my head. He's been in there for half my life but no more. I need him gone for good."

Tate's passionate voice, his fierce expression, it was pure determination.

I looked at him like it was the first time I was seeing him.

He'd opened up in a way that he'd never done before. With a pain that he'd been carrying around for so many years. One that I couldn't even imagine.

His confiding in me meant everything.

CHAPTER 17

REED

"Thank you for telling me," I whispered. "For trusting me. I know that wasn't easy. But I'm really glad you did."

"Me too." He nodded and wiped his eyes. "I wanted to tell you years ago, but I just couldn't do it. I came close a few times but... I wasn't ready. I was always better at running from my problems than facing them."

"You were young, Tate."

"On the surface."

He bit his lower lip and blinked away more tears.

I took another step closer and gave him a hug, needing to comfort him in whatever way I could.

His body tensed for a moment and then relaxed against mine.

Holding him felt so fucking right.

Tate gripped my waist in return. "So, back to my original question. Are you still concerned about filming together?"

I was, but for reasons that I wasn't ready to reveal.

"Well, actually—" I started as I reluctantly stepped away from him.

"Because I don't want to get into a massive argument before our guests arrive."

"There will be no argument, massive or otherwise," I countered. "But are you sure you're still up for having visitors?"

Tate nodded.

"Now more than ever. But can you finish the rest of the dinner prep? I need to go for a swim."

"Of course."

Tate walked around me and opened the patio doors, heading straight outside.

I watched as he stripped off his clothes and dove, naked, into my infinity pool.

He swam several laps, then rested for a moment with his hands on the edge of the pool.

I stared at him, the reflection of the sun highlighting the sharp angles of his profile.

The pain that consumed him was etched all over his face.

I swallowed back the urge to cry again as shockwaves coursed through my body.

For a moment, I considered joining him, but I knew when he wanted to be alone. And his break was short-lived. Soon, he was diving back under the surface of the pool like a seal.

Respecting his need for distance, I turned back to the kitchen.

But my mind was still processing everything he'd told me. I swiped at the dampness on my face and took a deep breath. The truth was worse than I'd imagined. And I was so upset and angry on his behalf, at how he'd been abused and left to fend for himself. He'd had no one to turn to. Not even his mom, who was also a victim.

I heard another splash and looked over to find him swimming laps.

Just like I knew that exercise was one form of therapy, I knew Tate. What he needed now was a return to normal.

Gathering my emotions, I got to work.

I finished the salad and placed it on the table, then went about oiling the indoor grill for chicken kebabs.

Once I got those cooked and set aside, I wiped off the counter. I turned to find a wet Tate standing at the edge of the kitchen, watching me, one of my bright orange beach towels wrapped around his hips.

"Smells good. Everything set?" he asked.

"It's all done."

I watched his face for any remaining signs of distress.

"You sure you're up for this?"

"I'm fine," he replied with a nod. "And I hope they get here soon. I'm fucking starving."

The doorbell rang.

"I'll get it," Tate announced.

"No, I'll get it. Go put some clothes on."

"You mean, I can't answer the door like this?" Tate quipped as he wandered down the hallway to his bedroom.

The towel around his hips slipped lower and lower, until I got a glimpse of one tan ass cheek.

"I guess it depends on who you're expecting."

Jesus, what was wrong with me?

Months of celibacy, that's what.

Tate's responding chuckle made me warm all over. And fuck, just hearing him laugh untied the knot that was my stomach. I could breathe again.

Placing the kitchen towel aside, I headed for the foyer, glanced at the security screen, and then opened the door.

"The Hollywood hit makers have arrived," I greeted Dylan and Max.

"That's Max," Dylan smiled at his fiancé, who in turn, blushed and shook his head.

"Don't give me all the credit. You helped me write the script."

"Oh yeah. Those steamy sex scenes. It required a lot of research and practice to get them just right."

Dylan winked at me.

Max's brown eyes rolled, and he adjusted his glasses.

"Come on in, dinner's ready. Tate's just getting changed."

I ushered them inside and guided them to the living room.

"He's still living here with you?" Max asked.

"For now. I'm sure in a week or two he'll be back at his house."

I didn't even want to think about that. How quiet and lonely my house would be without Tate's presence.

It was eight years ago all over again.

"How're you doing, Reed?" Dylan asked. "You look healthy but are you coping all right?"

"I'm much better, thanks. Sometimes the grief hits me hard and the urge to drink follows. But every day, I feel a bit better. I'm proud to say that I'm still sober. I've had amazing support."

Speaking of which…

"Dylan, Max, so great to see you again!" Tate walked up to the couple and gave them hugs in turn.

Which was another new thing I'd noticed. Tate wasn't a hugger by nature.

Except with me.

But lately, with our inner circle, he'd been different, affectionate.

This sweet side to him only made my feelings that much more intense.

And troublesome.

"What would you guys like to drink?" I asked. "We've got iced tea, sparkling water, and all kinds of fruit juices. Sorry Max, we're a dry household."

"Tea would be great." Max nodded. "And no worries, I've cut out alcohol for good."

"I told him he didn't have to because of me—" Dylan started.

"And I told you, I don't miss it. I sleep better and I feel better. End of discussion."

Max leaned over and kissed Dylan. The smile they shared with each other said everything.

"Where's Cary and Grant?" Dylan asked.

"Probably hiding in my bedroom."

As soon as the words were out of my mouth, guess who sauntered into the room. Both cats hopped up on the couch and made themselves at home with our guests.

I walked over to the fridge and grabbed the pitcher of iced tea, and a bottle of chilled water, and Tate brought over the tray of glasses.

"Reed and I were just talking about how excited we are to film this movie," Tate commented as he poured several glasses of tea. "But I did have a question for you, Dylan."

"Shoot."

"How come you didn't want to play a lead role? Or any role, for that matter? Especially given that you had a direct hand in writing the script."

Dylan smiled at him. "Timing. I've got other priorities right now so I'm leaving the acting in your capable hands."

"You're not coming to the UK with us at all?" I asked. "Not even as co-producer?"

Dylan shook his head. "No. Max and I are already working on another project together. One that's personal, not professional."

Dylan looked at Max, who turned to us.

"In addition to planning our wedding, Dylan and I are expanding our family. We're going the adoption route, like I did with my daughter Blake."

"Holy shit! Congratulations!" Tate exclaimed and stepped over to give them each a hug.

I got up and did the same. "I'm so happy for you guys!"

When we finished offering our congrats and sat down again, Dylan and Max both had tears in their eyes. And huge smiles on their faces.

"See? This is exactly why I wouldn't be able to work on set," Dylan admitted as he wiped his eyes. "My emotions are all over the damn place. It would take me forever to film one scene."

"That's understandable," I replied.

I was incredibly happy for my friends, but also envious.

I'd always dreamt of having a family of my own. I knew that someday, whether I had a partner or not, I was going to be a dad. There was still time, after all. I was only thirty-one.

But I also longed for a man I could share my life with, and after so many years of dating and hookups, I wondered if I was ever going to find him.

If I'd ever get over Tate...

I glanced over to find him watching me. Of course, the look in his eyes was knowing. He knew exactly where my mind had gone. The family part, at least.

I wanted to be annoyed that he could read me so easily, but what was the point?

No one knew me better.

And right then and there, I faced the truth.

Like it or not, my heart would always belong to Tate.

CHAPTER 18

TATE

TWO MONTHS LATER, THE UK

I was confident about making this movie.

Up until the moment our plane landed in London.

Then, the realization that I was about to film an epic love story with my best friend had me panicking.

I could refuse to leave the plane. Or pull some other stunt to get me thrown off the film. But I wasn't a dramatic diva. Okay, sometimes.

But I wanted this role. I'd read the script so many times that the lines were permanently burned into my memory. And I'd prepped with a dialect coach until my accent was on point.

I was prepared. I was ready.

I was freaking the fuck out.

And all because my personal feelings were... problematic.

I'd always accepted my attraction to Reed. Even when we hated each other, he still fucking turned me on. That had never changed.

But our friendship meant more to me than screwing and I

was never ready for a relationship. And I wasn't sure he was ready for me either.

Or at least, that's the excuse I always used.

I wasn't out, and I hadn't fully accepted myself.

Now, though, things were different.

I'd talked to Henn, and we'd made a plan. When I was back from filming, but before the movie was released, it was gonna happen. I was going to come out.

My personal life was going to take center stage.

And fuck, all the reasons why I'd held back from Reed were disappearing, one by one.

And as those roadblocks crumbled down around me, the only thing I could see was him.

I had no desire to fuck anyone else. Even after I'd moved back to my house. And Reed never talked about anyone either. Not lately. I didn't see him go out with other guys and he didn't mention hooking up with anyone.

I'd often pop over to his place for breakfast, unannounced. There were no visitors coming or going.

So, we were friends again. Maybe more than before? But less than I wanted.

And my want for him was getting so intense it was all I could think about.

But what if we crossed that line and sex fucked everything up? I don't think I could survive another breakup.

"You're freaking out, aren't you? Am I going to have to haul your ass off the plane?"

I looked up at the sound of Reed's voice to find him standing in the aisle with his carry-on bag in hand, sunglasses already in place.

"I'm not panicking. I was just thinking," I replied. "Stop with the doomsday shit, already."

I slid my wayfarers down off my head to hide my eyes. I'm pretty sure if I looked at Reed now, he'd know right quick that I was not panicking about the movie, but about him.

Fuck, if only he knew how much I wanted to do dirty, dirty things with him.

Like joining the mile high club.

Reed scoffed. "Don't bullshit me. I can read you better than anyone."

I grabbed my backpack and turned to face him, leaning in close, until my cheek touched his. "Really? And what am I thinking now?"

I heard his sharp inhale as my lips brushed his ear.

When I leaned back, I gave him my trademark smirk.

I couldn't see Reed's eyes, but I'd bet anything they were rolling.

"Move your ass, movie star," he replied, shaking his head.

"You're always fixated on my butt," I quipped as we made our way down the aisle to the exit. "Any particular reason?"

To be fair, he wasn't the only one who had ass on the brain. Christ, the way his tight, round cheeks filled out those jeans? Fuck me.

"I could say the same for you." He turned and lowered his sunglasses. "Gotcha."

I shoved his shoulder playfully. "You got nothin'. Keep walking. I need my hotel room and a full English."

"You better be talking about breakfast."

I responded to his joke with nothing but a filthy chuckle.

Once we disembarked and went through the boring-ass process that was customs, our assistant got our luggage sorted.

The plan was to head straight to the hotel, have a snack, sleep for a few hours, then meet up with Jared and his fiancés, Alex and Aiden, in the evening for dinner.

That's right. I said fiancés, as in two of them. I couldn't imagine dealing with one boyfriend, let alone two.

Then again, Jared was an expert at managing a cast of characters. I guess his personal life wasn't any different.

As we headed for our car, I didn't notice any paps following us, but I was prepared.

The project was still under wraps as far as the press was concerned, but any day now, someone would leak something. Intentional or not, it was the Hollywood way. Money so easily talks.

It took us just over an hour to get to our hotel, and then me and Reed headed our separate ways. Or rather, to separate rooms on the same penthouse floor.

I was out to the world as soon as my body hit the mattress and woke up five hours later to a growling stomach and a dry mouth.

It was nearing seven and we were meeting up with Jared at eight.

After a quick shower, a shave, and a much-needed sandwich courtesy of room service, I headed down the hallway to knock on Reed's door.

Instead of being dressed, he was still in his bathrobe.

"Cute but too casual for dinner," I teased as I leaned against the doorframe.

"Haha. I woke up five minutes ago. I slept through my freaking alarm," he grumbled and waved me in. "And I don't know what to wear."

I followed him down the hallway to his bedroom.

"Seriously? We're gonna be late because of that? Just pick something. You're beautiful no matter what you wear."

Reed tripped and nearly did a header down the hallway. I caught his arm before he had a chance to faceplant.

"You okay?" I asked. He didn't say anything, just nodded and pulled his arm away. "Wear something like you had on the plane. Jeans and a sweater. It's dinner with Jared and his partners, not His Majesty the King."

I sat down on Reed's bed and watched him saunter over to the closet. The white robe began to slip off one shoulder. Then I imagined him taking the whole thing off. Slowly.

And just like that, my cock began to throb like a motherfucker.

I quickly glanced behind me and grabbed one of his pillows, placing it over my lap.

Leaning forward, I tried to feign boredom, but when Reed turned around, he raised one eyebrow.

"Stealing one of my pillows? Aren't there enough in your room?"

"Yours are softer," I lifted the pillow to my face. "And they smell like vanilla. Like you."

Reed's eyes flashed with something I could have sworn was heat, but maybe that was wishful thinking on my part?

"Don't fall asleep," he commanded. "I'll be ready in five."

Reed grabbed several items from his closet and walked into the bathroom.

I fell back on his bed with a groan.

"What the fuck are you doing, Tate?" I asked myself out loud.

A sudden vision of Reed lying naked on top of me was so fucking hot, and that didn't help my poor dick at all.

I was lost in my lusty daydream when the bathroom door opened a few minutes later. Startled, I bolted upright.

"Ready?" Reed asked.

Dressed in tight black pants and a blue patterned button down with the sleeves rolled up, he walked over to stand between my legs. I fought the urge to shove him down on this mattress and show him how ready I really was.

"Tate?" he asked, concern on his face.

"Yes. Of course. After you."

I followed him out of the bedroom, quickly adjusting myself.

Thankfully, it was a quick elevator ride to the lobby and our rideshare was already waiting in front of the hotel. Twenty minutes later, we pulled up to Jared's condo.

One of his fiancés, Alex, greeted us. I remembered him

from that trip to Thailand and I could see why the director had fallen hard for his bodyguard. The man was seriously intense. And handsome in a rugged way, with pale blue eyes and a grip that was just shy of painful.

"Come on in, gents. Jared and Aiden are just finishing the preparations for dinner. Did you have a good flight?"

We stepped inside their home, and something smelled amazing.

"It was great, except for Tate's turbulent snoring, which kept everyone on the plane from sleeping."

"I don't snore! You're just a light sleeper."

"Please. Jet engines are quieter," Reed scoffed.

"Are you two arguing already?" Jared yelled out.

He walked down the hallway with his arm wrapped around Aiden, the other fiancé.

Funnily enough, Aiden reminded me of my cat with his auburn hair and prickly demeanor. He had a face that was all sharp angles, not to mention a fierce expression. I recalled how possessive he was about Alex and Jared on that trip. How angry he'd been that Reed was flirting with Alex.

No surprise how that ended up.

"Bickering, Jared, bickering. There's a big difference," I insisted as I offered my hand to him and then Aiden.

"That's what I tell him all the time, but he never listens," Aiden commented. "Nice to see you again, Tate, Reed. Jared has been telling us more stories about your recent movies."

"Oh, shit," Reed blurted out.

Aiden chuckled. "Exactly."

"And yet, Jared keeps hiring us," I replied with a smirk.

Jared rolled his eyes. "That's because when you finally do get your heads out of your asses, magic happens."

"I always thought the magic happens when the head is in my ass," I quipped.

Aiden's bark of laughter echoed loudly.

"Tay! What the hell?" Reed shook his head, his cheeks flaming red.

"Tate, you and I are going to become very good friends," Aiden announced.

"Oh, shit," Jared and Alex said at the same time.

———

Two hours, and a three course Italian feast later, we settled in Jared's living room with green tea for Reed and Jared and espresso for the rest of us.

"How goes the plan with Henn?" Jared asked.

I'd been telling people in my inner circle about my sexuality, including Jared. I found it easier to do it this way, one at a time. So far, so good. And this way, when things rolled out, I'd have a support system in place.

"It's well in hand. I'll do a press conference when we return to LA. She still has a few concerns, though, when it comes to my brand deals. But that's for her and a lawyer to review."

"I'd be happy to provide an impartial consultation if you need it, no charge," Aiden offered.

"I might take you up on that," I replied with a smile. "I don't have any morality clauses in my contracts but Henn's worried that some brands might drop me or refuse to renew when I come out. But I told her, and she agreed, that if they drop me, they drop me. If a company has an issue with my sexuality, I don't want to work with them anyway."

"You might lose some, but gain new ones," Reed added.

"Jared can put me in touch with Henn," Aiden suggested. "I'll have a look of your contracts and let you know if there's anything you need to be concerned about."

"Thanks, I appreciate that."

"What about security?" Alex asked.

"What do you mean?" I glanced at him.

"You're a high-profile celebrity, and often, coming out can bring out the haters. And I'm not just talking about online. You might want to hire a protection detail for the foreseeable future as a precaution."

"That's a good idea," Reed added.

"I don't know if I need that," I mused. "Henn was more concerned about online trolls."

"Think about it and let me know," Alex replied. "I've sold the business, but I still have contacts. In fact, I know of one bodyguard here in the UK that's looking for work."

I glanced at Reed. "Do you really think I need protection?"

"I'd look into it. Can't hurt," he replied. "I dealt with a stalker a few years ago and I had a bodyguard for four months. It was well worth it for my peace of mind."

"What?! You never told me that!"

Just the thought of anything bad happening to Reed made my stomach seize and a cold sweat break out all over my body.

"We weren't talking at that point and the only time we communicated was when we worked together. Even then, it was name calling and yelling. So how could I tell you? And seriously, you didn't notice the guy following me around on set?"

"I just thought it was added security for the movie. Jesus, Ree. What happened?" I asked. "Who was this asshole harassing you?"

"I don't know. The emails stopped after a few months and that was that. Unfortunately, whoever it was probably found someone else to fixate on. It was nothing."

I reached for his hand before I realized what I was doing. "Promise me you won't ever keep something like that from me again."

He placed his other hand on top of mine and gripped it tightly. "I didn't keep it from you. We were—"

"I know. I know."

God, we'd been such idiots.

Then I realized that the rest of the room was silent, and I looked over to find Jared, Aiden, and Alex staring at us.

"Sorry," I blurted out as my cheeks heated.

"Nothing to be sorry about," Jared replied as he gave me a knowing smile.

I glanced at Reed again, and the idea that someone had frightened him, frightened me.

I couldn't lose him. That possibility was unthinkable.

And Jared was wrong.

There were a shitload of apologies due.

CHAPTER 19

REED

Tate was acting weird.

Or maybe it was me.

It seemed like no matter what we were doing or where we were, he was in my personal space. Had he always been like that? Was I too caught up in my own feelings for him in the past to realize?

Or was this new? Or my imagination?

Whatever the case, everything felt like us, but different. More intense.

He was possessive of my time and person more than usual. Not to mention, I caught him eye-fucking me the other night. But I dismissed it. Or, I didn't let on that I noticed.

The realization was heady, but it also scared the crap out of me.

This was my best friend, not a guy I could walk away from.

Not again.

And there was something about Tate *now*, how comfortable he was in his skin, how open he was with me and with our friends, that made my heart squeeze so tight it was about to burst wide open.

I thought for sure he'd be the one panicking when it came to working our first scene together, but it turned out to be me.

Would everyone else on set know how I felt about him by the way I spoke my lines? Bringing emotional depth to my character was not going to be a problem. As soon as Tate and I were in the same room together, our natural ebb and flow took over.

"Okay, people," Jared yelled out. "Here we go. Places!"

I was already seated, in my spot. Tate was just off set, waiting for his cue to walk into the room.

In the opening scene, Oliver the grieving widower, AKA me, is waiting in the funeral home as a handful of mourners offer their condolences on the loss of my partner, Kingsley. The story takes place in the late 90s, when gay marriage wasn't legal. Oliver and Kingsley aren't recognized as husbands in the eyes of the law, or the community at large, even though they've been living together for fifteen years. Fellow queer friends and my character's brother are the only ones who show up to the funeral. And, of course, Tate's character, Ambrose, one of my husband's coworkers.

Looking around at everyone's solemn expressions, the scene was eerily reminiscent of my mom's funeral.

It wasn't difficult for me to slip into my role and back into the hell that was grief.

"Camera ready?" Jared continued.

"Ready!"

"Lock it up. Quiet on the set," Jared paused. "Roll sound!"

"Rolling."

"And… action!"

I took a deep breath and stood up to greet the mourners. One by one, in their turn, they made their way into the room to speak to me.

But I was all too aware of Tate waiting at the end of the line, in his herringbone suit, his face solemn.

When it was his turn to come forward, I started to tremble.

I looked up in his eyes and I saw warmth and a wariness reflected.

He offered his hand, and I gave mine.

When our palms touched, a rush of heat pulsed through my body.

He was shaking my hand, but my hand was still shaking.

"I'm sorry for your loss, Oliver."

Tate's British accent was so crisp and foreign to me, that I blinked, hardly recognizing him.

That's the whole point, idiot. Now, get into character.

"Thank you, Ambrose. You're the only one of Kingsley's colleagues that showed up."

Tate let go of my hand and reached up to nervously adjust his tie. "Yes, well, barristers are known to be complete sods, aren't we?"

I fought back the urge to laugh, despite my sadness. A tear slipped out and I wiped it away.

"True, but I would hardly characterize my husband that way."

"Kingsley was a very rare man, kind and ethical to a fault," Tate nodded. "And how are you doing?"

That question brought more tears. "I've just lost the love of my life, how do you think?"

Tate grimaced. "Yes, well, I'm sorry. That was a stupid question. As Kingsley probably told you, I'm useless outside of a courtroom. Please do accept my condolences, such as they are, and take care."

Before I had a chance to say anything else, Tate stalked away.

I glanced at the figure of my husband in the coffin and then back at Tate, holding my stare.

"Cut!" Jared shouted. "And that's how you do it, folks!"

I startled when one of the makeup artists stepped in front of me to fix my face. The crew went about moving items for the following scene.

The next one was going to be a challenge.

Giving a eulogy, even a fake one, was not an easy task.

Horrible memories flooded my mind, making me feel like I was back in my hometown months ago, about to step up to the mic to talk about my mom.

Almost as if I called out to him, Tate was suddenly beside me. "You all right?"

"I'll be fine," I whispered as the makeup artist finished with my face and made her leave. "It's hitting a little close to home, but that's to be expected, right?"

Tate leaned over and pulled me in for a hug. I couldn't help but soak up his strength, my face against his shoulder.

Being held in his arms was so fucking good.

So real. And right.

"Um, guys, are we ready to go?" Jared asked.

I didn't realize we'd drawn an audience. Sure enough, when I backed away from Tate, I looked around to find the crew in their spots, ready to go on to the next scene.

I nodded. "I am, but you'll need to get wardrobe out here. I got makeup on his suit."

"You did indeed," Jared glanced at Tate with a smirk. "Can someone help *Tater*, please."

Several crew members began to laugh.

"What have I told you about that nickname?" Tate sighed and pointed at me. "This is your fault, Ree. You started it."

"So sensitive." I shook my head, glad for the comic reprieve. Suddenly I was a whole lot lighter. "*Tater tot.*"

More chuckles erupted around us, and Tate threw up his hands. "Okay, everyone's in on the joke now."

Film crews were notorious when it came to shit like that. The last time I called him that nickname on set someone sent a tater tot casserole to his trailer. He was not amused, but everyone else thought it was funny.

"Okay, people, back to work," Jared announced.

Six hours later, we wrapped up taping for the day.

Tate and I took a rideshare back to the hotel. Despite my exhaustion, I was wired, unsettled.

When we arrived at our floor, Tate insisted on walking me to my door.

"I said I was fine, stop fussing over me," I grumbled.

I opened the door and Tate followed me inside.

"Um, your room is down the hall," I reminded him.

"I'm keeping you company for a bit."

I didn't want to admit it, but I was grateful for his kindness. Today had been a productive day, but emotionally, I was fucking drained. And I didn't want to be alone.

We wandered into the room and Tate kicked off his shoes and made himself at home on my bed. Before I did something stupid, like crawl on top of him, I headed for the bathroom.

After enjoying a relaxing shower, I slipped on my bathrobe and headed back out to the bedroom.

Tate was out cold, snoring softly.

I walked over to the closet and pulled out a blanket, then placed it over him.

Walking around the end of the bed to my side, I toed off my slippers, turned off the light and slid under the duvet.

Unlike Tate, my sleep just wouldn't come. And no, it wasn't because my roommate was snoring.

I was trying to work out my emotions.

I'd always managed to keep my feelings about Tate to myself, but lately, it was getting harder and harder to hide how I felt about him. After everything we'd been through, there were no protective walls left around my heart.

It turns out, he'd snuck in there ten years ago and never left.

I watched the rise and fall of his chest, then my gaze moved higher, to the dark lashes that kissed his cheekbones. His hair was a tumbled mess around his face.

He was so goddamn beautiful that everything in my body ached just looking at him.

With a loud sigh, I snuggled under the covers and scooted over so I was almost touching him. I always envied his body heat since I ran cold.

Gradually, I began to relax.

His face was the last thing I saw before I closed my eyes.

———

When I woke up the next morning, I was lying on my other side and Tate was wrapped around me like I was his personal body pillow. Trying to extricate myself without waking him, I slowly moved his arm away from my waist and started to slide away from the bed.

"Where do you think you're going?"

Tate's sleep-roughened drawl had me frozen in place.

His arm latched onto me again, and I couldn't move.

"We need to get up and get dressed. We're due on set in an hour," I reminded him.

"No."

"Tate, seriously, let go. I need to get up."

"No," he growled, and I nearly squealed when his hot breath hit my neck.

"What is with you?" I whispered.

"You always smell so fucking incredible. Do you know that?"

My dick certainly understood. I began to squirm in Tate's grasp

"What are you talking about?"

"You. Smell. Amazing," he sighed and kissed my neck.

Just like that, my semi turned to a raging hard on.

"Sorry I fell asleep on you. How are you feeling?"

"Fine," I squeaked, then cleared my throat. "I'm good. I was too tired to talk last night anyway. But I appreciated the company, even in silence."

"We could've just shared a room, you know. Better for the film budget and the environment."

I turned my head to stare at Tate. He chuckled, his eyes watching me with amusement.

"What is with you on this trip, Tay? Are *you* feeling okay?"

"I'm fucking fantastic. Best I've ever been."

He pulled me in even tighter and his hard cock sat snug against my ass cheeks.

Oh fuck. Oh no.

This was not happening. Not now. We had to report to work shortly, and if he so much as tried to kiss me right now… just, no.

When, if, I ended up kissing my best friend (and not on set) I'd need time afterwards for the nervous breakdown that would inevitably follow.

And I sure as fuck didn't have that luxury this morning.

He gave me a wicked grin. "Sooner or later, Ree, it's going to happen, so be prepared. I'm giving you fair warning."

How did he always read my mind?

"All's fair?" I asked.

In love and war. That was always us.

"You better fucking believe it."

CHAPTER 20

TATE

Reed had all but avoided me this week. When we weren't on set.

But no more.

We'd left London and headed for Oxford to film the next portion of the movie.

This time, however, I was sharing a house rental with him for the next three weeks. A stately mansion, right in the heart of the city. It gave us privacy but also easy access to roam and play tourist when we had time off.

I don't know if it was being away from the grind of LA or the fact that I was finally getting comfortable in my sexuality, but every passing day gave me greater confidence.

Not just in myself but in my feelings for Reed.

We'd been circling each other for ten years and it was time to stop.

But I also knew him. He was frightened.

I was too.

Reed and I had the potential for a spectacular crash and burn. No special effects required.

Not that I was going to let that stop me.

While he was on set filming a solo clip, I did a run through of the house we were calling home for the next while. It had three levels—a living and kitchen area on the first, two bedrooms and two baths on the second, and a main suite with a huge bath and library on the third.

I'd given Reed the top floor, since I knew he couldn't live without his soaker tub. And he would love the library, complete with a reading nook under a big window that looked out onto the busy street below.

I liked being in the frenetic heart of the city. There were always people around. Unlike the gated community where I lived in California, where I'd be lucky to see a neighbor once a month. I mean, I liked the privacy, but at the same time, it was lonely when you lived alone.

Reed and I were recognized a few times in London but not as much as we were back at home. And I now understood why Jared had readily moved here. It was nice to be able to walk out the door without paps in your face. I'm sure things would be different if we were local celebrities.

But it was the people here, not just the paps, that I'd noticed. They were calmer, unobtrusive. Don't get me wrong, fans were always welcome, but sometimes I just wanted to go the store and do my shopping. Be normal and do normal things.

After checking the house over, I got my luggage sorted and headed out for a long walk.

Since I had no filming and I didn't need to report on set until tomorrow, I decided to grab a few items to make dinner. I got a couple of double takes when I entered a local bakery on High Street, but everyone was kind and helpful, no fuss.

There was something about the history of this area that appealed to me. It wasn't all shiny glass towers and neon signs like LA. Instead, weathered stone facades and gothic arches greeted me at every turn.

I walked under cloudy skies and intermittent rain, and I wasn't missing the sunshine at all.

Though I did miss *him*.

A few hours later, I headed back to the house and began to prep dinner. A Sunday roast with smashed potatoes and gravy. Dessert was store-bought. I was a decent cook but baking, not so much.

Once the roast and veg was in the oven, I got the fireplace going and selected a playlist that suited a relaxed evening for two.

I expected Reed back by six, but seven rolled around and there was no sign of him. My good mood plummeted.

> Tate: You heading back to the house? I made dinner.

When I didn't get a reply within ten minutes, I texted again.

> Tate: If you're not coming back until late, just let me know. Thanks

A minute later, I got my reply. But not the one I was hoping for.

> Reed: Sorry, a bunch of us went to a pub after filming wrapped.

Shit, I hope to fuck Reed hadn't been drinking. Between his late response and now this, my stomach did a painful somersault.

> Reed: Don't worry, I didn't drink. No urge lately. I'll be back in a bit.

Then he sent me a few snaps from the pub. I smiled when I spotted the usual crew members.

But one picture caught my eye.

It was Reed sitting close to a man who was familiar to me, but not a member of the crew.

Dark blond hair, a beard, copious tattoos…

Then I remembered the yacht in Thailand. It was Kiernan. Kiernan Doyle. The bodyguard who worked for Alex. Except the last time I'd met Kiernan, he had long hair, and now it was short.

The guy was ripped, with a killer smile. And he was aiming that smile at Reed.

Everything in my body tensed the longer I stared at the photo. I tried to think of a subtle way to find out just why Kiernan was there.

> Tate: Is that Kiernan Doyle sitting next to you?

But I was much better at being direct.

> Reed: It's his twin, Korry. He had a security job in London that just ended so he's in between gigs. Alex told him we were filming here and suggested he come meet us. He's coming back to the house with me tonight.

> Tate: Why?

I'd lost my southern manners years ago. Apparently, they were never coming back.

> Reed: To talk to you about a possible protective detail. Remember, the conversation with Alex? The timing is perfect.

The timing sucked.

> Tate: Okay. I've made enough food. Bring him over.

> Reed: On our way

Reluctantly, I set the table for three instead of two. But the longer I waited, the grumpier I became.

When Reed and Korry finally arrived, the food was over-cooked, and my temper was about to burn whoever spoke first.

The fact that the two of them were laughing when they walked in together didn't help my temperament either.

"Am I interrupting?" I asked as I stood in the hallway, arms crossed over my chest.

Reed ran a hand through his wet hair, and shook his head, giving me a glare that sent lesser men running.

Then he mouthed 'be nice'.

I stepped forward and helped Reed get his soaked denim jacket off, drops of rain flying everywhere. Korry slipped off his hooded rain coat and reached his hand out.

"Korry Doyle, a pleasure. Reed's told me all about you."

I offered my hand in turn and nearly squeaked when his grip crushed mine. And I had a strong fucking grip.

"Funny, Reed's told me next to nothing about you," I snapped back. "Except that you're Kiernan's twin. If it weren't for the hair, I'm not sure how I'd tell you apart."

"The tats. I've got none on me hands."

I looked down and sure enough, there were no Celtic tattoos on his hands.

"Come on in, dinner's ready," I announced. "I hope you don't mind roast beef that's overcooked."

"If there's gravy, I'll eat anything." Korry smiled at me and then turned to Reed. "You should go up and change, that designer jacket of yours was hardly protection against the downpour. You should've taken my coat."

Reed shook his head. "I'm fine. But I will go upstairs and change real quick."

I noticed that his pale blue button down was wet too, clinging to his chest and shoulders.

"I've put all your stuff on the third floor," I added.

Reed nodded and walked up the stairs. My eyes followed his ass until I remembered we had company.

I turned back to Korry. "I'm afraid we don't have any alcohol on hand."

"No worries, I had a pint at the pub. I could use a coffee though."

"Espresso?"

"Feck, yes," he replied and rubbed his hands together.

I didn't want to be charmed by this man. Bad enough Reed already was.

We headed for the kitchen and made the usual introductory chit chat. After I made two espressos, we sat at the dining table, waiting for Reed to join us.

We talked about Kiernan mostly. He was dating Charlie, and training to work alongside his boyfriend on the yacht. Then we talked about my plans, and Korry's availability to come to the US when and if, I felt I needed protection.

When Reed finally re-appeared, in clean jeans, a tight white t-shirt, and bare feet, I wanted to tell Korry to take his plate and take off back to the hotel.

Instead, I sat there staring longingly at my best friend while he took the seat across from me.

"Why didn't you guys start eating?" Reed asked.

"We were waiting for you," I replied and served him a plate, then passed another over to Korry.

"You should've started without me. Korry told me he was famished as we were leaving the pub."

"Quit it already and eat," I teased, shoving a mouthful of surprisingly tender beef between my lips.

Reed gave me his best finger in response.

"Save that for dessert," I warned him.

His face flushed and he bit his lower lip. Fuck, I loved to see him like this. He was always so smooth and effortless with other men.

But not with me.

"Fecking hell, this is good stuff, Tate," Korry remarked as he ate with gusto.

"Thanks. I do okay in the kitchen."

"I live on takeaway," Korry grunted. "Can't cook for shite."

Then our chatter silenced as the three of us focused on our food. The best part was the Yorkshire puddings. They were light and chewy, like a popover, soaking up every bit of the remaining gravy.

"You still want to go out this weekend, Reed? Hit a club with me and have some sexy fun?" Korry asked.

The fork I was holding slipped out of my hand and onto my now empty plate with a loud clang.

Reed nodded. "Definitely. This one here hates to go dancing."

"I don't hate dancing. I hate club music," I corrected him.

Reed rolled his eyes.

"Same thing."

Then he turned to Korry. "How about Saturday? We've got the next day off."

"It's a date." Korry smiled at Reed. "I can meet you here and we'll walk over together."

"I'm coming with you," I interrupted.

"Come on, Tay," Reed scoffed. "You hate clubs. You'll get there and five minutes later, you'll be grumbling about leaving."

"I'm going. End of."

There was no fucking way this handsome Irishman was going out with Reed alone.

Korry glanced my way, and there was a challenge in his eyes that I recognized.

Fuck him. I was never one to back down.

Korry turned to Reed. "Save me the first dance."

First dance my ass. He was not going to get his hands on Reed.

At all.

"I'm looking forward to it already," Reed replied with a flirty wink.

"We have to be on set early tomorrow," I blurted out, reaching over to collect the empty plates. "Not to give you the bum's rush or anything, Korry, but it's been a long day."

"Don't be so fucking rude, Tay," Reed snapped back and then glanced at Korry. "You don't need to go. He's just being a grumpy ass. As usual."

"We have a six AM wakeup call and it's after ten already," I countered.

"Then you go to bed," Reed offered. "Korry and I will be fine down here."

I headed for the kitchen, my hands gripping the plates so hard I'm surprised they didn't shatter. I opened the dishwasher and began to load it, making a god-awful racket in the process.

If Korry so much as flirted with Reed one more fucking time…

Reed's familiar peal of husky laughter rang out and I slammed the dishwasher shut.

When I walked back out, Reed and Korry were sitting on the sofa in the living room, in front of the fire.

Don't make a scene.

I was calm. I was fine.

Until Korry touched Reed's face.

CHAPTER 21

REED

"Got a spot of gravy on your cheek," Korry teased as he swiped at my face. "Yer supposed to eat it, not wear it."

I followed his hand and felt the crusty smear on my cheekbone. Rubbing my face, I managed to, I hope, wipe it all off.

"Still pretty," he quipped.

Korry was great company. Friendly and funny.

Bolder than his twin, Kiernan.

His work required him to remain inconspicuous, but Korry, like his twin Kiernan, was still a standout.

He was handsome and flirty. And that Irish accent didn't hurt either.

A couple of years ago, I would've taken him up on his flirtation and enjoyed a no strings hook up.

But now?

All I could think about was…

"Get your hands off him."

Tate's thunderous voice snapped me back into reality.

Next thing I knew, Tate was looming over the two of us. Until Korry stood up to him, eye to eye.

"Easy, boyo," Korry held up his hands. "I was just—"

"I know what you were doing," Tate hissed. "Don't touch him."

"Tay," I warned and reached out to grab his arm. "What the hell is wrong with you?"

Korry glanced at me. "He thought I was making a move. Ain't that right, Tate?"

Tate stepped in front of me, blocking me from Korry.

"You have ten seconds to get out of this house."

"I can't believe this is happening," I gasped and tried to push Tate aside. He wouldn't budge. "Korry, I'm so sorry."

"It's all right, Reed. I have to get going anyway." Korry stepped around Tate and gave me a nod. "You two enjoy the rest of your night."

He headed for the front door, and I walked after him.

"I'm so embarrassed. I don't know what's gotten into him, Kor. Please, don't go."

The bodyguard grabbed his jacket and threw it on, giving me a quick grin before he reached for the door handle. "You've nothing to apologize for. And I knew exactly what I was doing. Go calm your man down."

"He's not mine," I muttered, shaking my head.

"Coulda fooled me. He was the only thing you talked about at the pub. And seeing him tonight, the way he looks at you? I've only got one other thing to say: you're welcome."

Shocked and bemused, I was left standing there, while Korry gave a final wave and headed out into the rainy night.

I closed the door and took a deep breath before I stalked back down the hallway.

"You are, without a doubt, the biggest prick I've ever known," I pronounced.

Tate was sitting in the chair closest to the fireplace, leaning forward, elbows on his thighs, head in his hands. He didn't look up, so I walked right up to him.

"Did you hear me?" I bellowed.

"I did. And that's not an insult, Reed," Tate replied as he finally looked at me. "Try again."

"Fine! You're the biggest asshole to ever ass."

Tate shook his head and bit his lower lip. It looked like he was trying not to laugh. Which made my temper ratchet up another notch.

Then I noticed that his hands were shaking.

"What's really going on?" I demanded.

"Is this real?" Tate asked as he stood up in front of me. The fierce look in his eyes had my own hands trembling in response. "Please tell me I'm not the only one, here."

"What?"

"Don't 'what' me. Come on. You and me. And don't fucking pretend you don't know what I'm talking about. And don't lie. I know you."

"If you know me, then you know the answer."

"No games, Ree," Tate muttered as he took a step closer. "Tell me."

"You first."

I took a step back, my heart beating wildly.

I wasn't stupid. I recognized Tate's jealousy. And though a part of me was angry at his behavior with Korry, I had to admit that possessive Tate was hot as hell.

No one had claimed me like that before.

Ever.

He didn't relent, taking one step closer to me.

"It's not just a want, Ree. It's bigger than that," Tate whispered, looking at me with a hunger that was unmistakable. "I need you. More than... fuck, I can't even begin to explain how much. It's time we both stopped running."

"I know," I barely managed to whisper, my throat closing over. "But I'm scared."

"Of me?" he asked, his horrified expression causing me to reach up and cup his face.

I ran my fingers through his soft beard.

"No. Never you. Of this. Us. Once we cross that line, we can't go back. I can't. Not with you. Not with my best friend," I paused, my pulse racing so fast I was out of breath. "And you can't wake up tomorrow and act like nothing happened. Or leave, or—"

"Shut up already so I can kiss you," Tate quipped.

"God, you're such a—"

Any other words were silenced by Tate's lips taking mine.

There were no cameras rolling. There was no script to guide us.

It was only me and him.

And a kiss that was long overdue, but strangely enough, right on time.

Tate's lips were demanding, not giving me any room to pause. To question.

His mouth mauled mine, our tongues tangling, teasing, the pleasure so intense that I gripped his hair tightly and angled his head for a deeper connection. His tongue snaked around mine, playfully at first.

Then he full-on fucked my mouth, and his lusty aggression sparked mine.

A decade's worth of want had me desperate for more. Tate kissed me like he owned me, and I couldn't get enough.

"No more flirting with sexy bodyguards," Tate growled in between mauling kisses as he slid his hands down to cup my ass, walking me backwards.

"No more random fuckboys," I countered, nipping his lower lip.

His answering groan had me wrapping my legs around his waist.

Suddenly, Tate turned around and sat down on the couch, and I straddled his lap.

Perfect. I needed him. Now.

As soon as my knees hit the cushion, I reached for his jeans, unzipping them with shaky hands.

"Faster," Tate grunted and pushed my hands aside, taking over like the bossy shit he was.

I pulled off my t-shirt and threw it aside.

"No patience," I whispered and leaned down to lick his neck while he hooked one finger in my beltloop and pulled me closer.

"I ran out of patience a long time ago," he murmured as he quickly unzipped my jeans. "Oh shit, no fucking underwear. You goddamn tease."

I let out a dirty chuckle and bit down on his neck, sucking the skin and reveling in Tate's throaty grunts and moans, his body writhing, reaching for mine.

Next thing I knew, he had both our hard cocks in his warm, rough hand, and I could only groan and punch my hips forward. I stared down at him, at us, and my mouth watered as I took in the sight of his cut, veiny cock sliding against mine, the heads red and slick with precum.

Fucking hell, I couldn't wait to have that beautiful dick inside me. But I needed to see him. All of him.

Without pause, I grabbed the edges of his button down and ripped that fucker apart.

I attacked Tate's mouth, each kiss more desperate than the last.

He tormented me, stroking my cock faster and faster, as I rutted against him. The sight of him, the naked desire in his eyes, it was my total undoing. Pleasure sparked in my balls, and I pumped my hips faster, chasing my orgasm.

"Tate, oh God, I'm sorry," I whispered as I fucked his hand.

I was so close. I wasn't going to last.

"What?" he asked and stopped moving.

I nearly screamed in frustration.

"Don't stop!" I hissed and gave him another mauling kiss to make my point.

"What—" Tate managed to whisper when I let him come up for air.

"I said I'm sorry because I'm going to come. Like right now," I moaned and thrust my hips.

"Baby, I'm right there with you," he confessed. "Ten years of edging can only end this way."

A shiver wracked my body when he called me 'baby'.

Tate spat in his hand and began jacking us off again. Between that and all the precum we were leaking, there was no need for lube. Not for this.

My balls drew up tight, every stroke of his hand a pleasure that kept building and building. Sweat rolled down my face, my chest, my skin hot, every nerve ending in my body on fire.

Reaching down, I slid my hands over his hairy pecs and tweaked his nipples.

The resulting jolt of his body and the deep groan that rumbled up from his throat told me I was on the right track.

His hand frantically pumped up and down, our cocks rubbing together, the heat, the friction, it was so fucking good.

And knowing that I was going to come on Tate? With Tate?

My mind was blown and my load not far behind.

He licked his other hand and pushed it down the back of my jeans, teasing my ass. When one thick finger slid down between my cheeks, I pushed back, encouraging him.

"Yes! Touch me there."

"Ree," Tate growled.

"Now," I demanded.

I could be a bossy shit too. Especially in bed.

And I loved ass play. I was vers but I preferred to bottom.

Tate tapped my hole, then gently pushed that spit-slicked finger inside, and I pushed back, eagerly taking him in. The fine line between pleasure and pain was heady, and I wanted it, I needed it.

"More. Finger fuck me like this. I love it."

"Jesus Christ," Tate panted, his face flushed. "Next time it's going to be my cock. I'm gonna fuck this perfect ass of yours. Fill you with my cum so every time you move on set, you know: you're mine. You belong only to me."

"Yes!" I shouted, Tate's words making my dick jerk and my asshole clench hard.

I swiveled my hips back and forth, chasing the pleasure in my ass, on my dick, not knowing which I wanted more.

I wanted it all.

"I'm so close," Tate bit out. "Baby, you have to come for me. I need you to come."

I lost all control at his raspy demand, my body locking up tight.

I shattered, coming hard in a heated rush. The pleasure was so intense that I was shaking, rocking my hips back and forth as I shot my load all over Tate's hand, his stomach, his cock, my asshole clenching tight around his finger.

What would it be like next time when I finally had his cock in my ass? I shivered at the thought, not sure I'd survive another orgasm like this one.

Tate lost all rhythm as he moaned my name and came undone. He was so fucking beautiful like this; head thrown back, face flushed, lips swollen from my kisses, his cum joining mine.

I couldn't stop staring at Tate.

His eyes locked on mine, looking at me like he couldn't quite believe what just happened.

"Neither can I," I panted as I shook my head. "Neither can I."

Tate nodded.

He knew exactly what I meant.

CHAPTER 22

TATE

Reed and I were sweating, panting, unable to move.

Unable to let go of each other.

Even though we both blew our loads, the air was still thick with tension, with the primal urge to fuck.

I couldn't look away and he was the same. Taking in every fucking detail. Like we couldn't quite believe what just happened.

I took in his full, pink lips, and licked my own, tasting the two of us.

His green eyes were bright, feverish.

His cheeks and neck, normally so smooth and pale, were now covered in my beard burn.

No one was more beautiful to me than Reed, but when he climaxed? When he shouted *my* name? Fucking hell, I'd never been more turned on in my life.

And normally once I come, I'm done.

It's like this switch inside of me. I want to shove off and just be alone. Don't touch me.

But I didn't feel that way with him.

Fuck, my finger was still lodged in the snug heat of his ass and I was thinking it wanted to stay there forever. But I only used spit and it's not exactly the best lube. And when I lost it at the end, I wasn't all that gentle.

Slowly, I pulled my finger out, Reed's thighs quivering in response.

I ran my hand over his ass cheek, lingering there. His skin was so soft and smooth.

All fucking mine.

But the real shock came when he smiled at me.

Pretty sure my heart was never going to beat the same way again.

"Kiss me," I demanded.

I needed another taste.

"What'll you give me?" he asked with a flirty smirk.

"How about I haul you upstairs, bury my face in your delectable ass, and eat you out until you come again?"

I barely finished my sentence, and I was mauled in the very best way.

We couldn't get enough—licking, nipping, sucking—consuming each other like our lives depended on this kiss. Without pause, I ran my cum-soaked hand up his back until I reached his neck, while the other kept kneading his ass.

"Upstairs," Reed finally whispered when we came up for air. "This couch isn't big enough for all the incredibly dirty things I want to do with you."

I stood up, taking Reed with me, his legs wrapping around my waist like a snake.

I felt like a fucking god in that moment, invincible; at the same time, lightheaded, like I was dead-ass drunk.

My legs were shaking but I managed to make it to the stairs, with Reed still holding tight.

We started up the first step and then his lips latched on to my neck.

"Fuck, baby, don't do that. I don't want to risk dropping you."

Reed let out a filthy chuckle and continued to torment my

skin, licking under my ear until my eyes rolled back in my head. I stumbled, grabbing the bannister with one hand, while the other was firmly lodged under his ass.

"Shit."

We made it to the second landing, but Reed rubbed his cock against my abs, and sucked on my neck, and I was rock hard again.

I couldn't wait.

Dropping to my knees, I set him down on the stairs in front of me and flipped him over, his ass in my face. My knees burned, and I just knew that I was gonna have bruises there tomorrow.

Given my desperation, it was worth it.

I yanked down his jeans to reveal his gorgeous ass, and my mouth watered.

Spreading his cheeks, I wasted no time, leaning forward and licking him from taint to tailbone.

"Oh fuck, oh God," Reed chanted, his voice barely a whisper.

Spitting on his tight pink hole, I teased him with quick flicks of my tongue, then pushed my face in and rubbed my beard all over his sensitive skin.

"Oh God, Tay. Fuck me like this. Please."

"No lube," I whispered against his skin.

Sliding my tongue around his puckered hole, I wiggled the tip inside.

"Shit, fuck," Reed moaned. "I… wait… my back pocket."

Don't ask me how, but I managed to tear myself away from the temptation that was Reed's ass and fumbled around in his jeans, now bunched around his thighs. Reaching into one pocket, I pulled out a small packet of lube and ripped it open with my teeth.

Then a realization broke through my lusty trance.

"Were you hoping to get lucky at the pub tonight?" I bit out, my possessive streak running as hot as my desire. "Is that why you're prepared? You were gonna fuck some rando?"

"No condom, just lube," Reed explained. "So, no rando. I was hoping, wishing, that you and me... that we'd end up here. I haven't been with anyone for months. And I know you haven't either."

A wave of relief washed over me.

"Because it's me. I'm the only one you want."

"Yes," Reed declared as he looked over his shoulder, his eyes locked on mine. "It's always been you, Tate. Now hurry up and fuck me before I take care of this myself."

I poured the lube in my hand and slicked up my cock, so damn hard it's near painful. Since when was my turnaround time so fucking fast? I had no idea.

And then I couldn't think at all.

Because I was about to fuck Reed.

I lined the head of my dick to his hole and the enormity of what was happening hit me. Christ, my heart was beating so hard I thought for sure it was about to burst wide open.

I tilted my hips, pushing inside of him. The sight of Reed taking my cock, nothing between us, was erotic, mesmerizing.

"So... fucking... good," Reed moaned.

Good didn't begin to describe it. I've never fucked without a condom.

And the heat of his sexy ass surrounding my dick was the greatest goddamn pleasure I've ever known.

He was moaning, writhing, pushing back for more and I was fighting to go slow. To savor this incredible feeling.

Until I was all the way in and my heavy balls slapped his ass.

Reed was finally mine and I made sure he knew it.

I snapped my hips and the slap of our skin making contact was delicious.

As was the picture of Reed before me, on his knees, on the

stairs, his jeans bunched around his taut thighs, his pale ass and lithe back undulating with every touch.

"You are so fucking beautiful, Ree. I can't—"

Words failed me.

But thankfully, my body didn't.

I rutted into him, all finesse gone, taking what I've wanted for so long, fucking into my best friend with a primal need to claim him.

The fact that we couldn't even make it up the stairs was so telling.

So… us.

"Right there," Reed panted. "Harder. More."

My knees ached and my thighs burned, but it was all good because I couldn't get enough of Reed. And I gave him exactly what he asked for. What he needed, what we both needed.

Harder. More.

The intense pleasure rolled through me, one wave after another, and suddenly I was floating.

Higher than any drug I've ever taken.

The intensity hit me hard. And so too did the emotions.

Which was a first.

We were fucking, but it was so much more than that.

Because this wasn't just any man.

This was Reed. My best friend. The man I could never, ever let go of.

Even when we hated each other, we couldn't let go.

"Reed," I moaned. "Need you."

I was so far gone, the words barely left my throat. Leaning over, I sucked on the tender skin of his shoulder. Salt and a taste that was pure Reed hit me, and I couldn't help the loud groan that erupted out of my chest. Taking his cock in hand, I jacked him off with rapid strokes, his moans getting louder.

Sweat slipped down my face, into my eyes, but I blinked it away as I pumped my hips harder, faster, needing to be as deep inside Reed as I could get. His skin was slick against mine as we moved together in a frantic rhythm, like we'd been doing this forever.

"Fuck, Tay, just like that. Don't stop!"

Christ, the way Reed felt in my arms. The way he sounded, the way he tasted…

I picked up the pace, fucking into him in short, hard strokes, every thrust bringing me one step closer to climax. Desperate to hold on until Reed came first, I quickened my pace—on his dick, in his ass.

"I'm so close," he whispered.

"I'm right there with you," I panted, pumping my hips harder, faster. "You ready for my cum?"

Reed's loud 'yes' was followed by the filthiest moan I'd ever heard.

My grip on his cock tightened and his body jolted.

"Tate!" Reed shouted, painting the stairs with his cum.

Watching and feeling Reed come undone in my arms had my own orgasm unleashing.

Panting hard, I fucked into him with one, two more strokes, my balls tightening, my dick twitching.

I came long and hard, moaning Reed's name so loud I'm pretty sure you could hear it through the walls of this row house.

And when I looked down and watched my cum leaking out of Reed's hole? Holy fucking hell. Marking him was so sexy.

Still lost in the haze of my orgasm, my hips kept moving. I didn't want to stop. Or let go. I held on to him, wrapping my arms around his waist.

Reed turned his face to me, and I leaned in to take his offered lips. I was still out of breath but I didn't care.

Kissing him was more important than breathing.

He hummed, and I recognized his happy sound. I smiled against his lips, unable to do anything else.

Until I glanced down at the sweaty, messy state of our bodies and the cum on the stairs underneath us. And as usual, my sarcastic side couldn't be contained.

"I don't think we're getting our damage deposit back."

Reed's booming laughter was the second best sound of the night.

CHAPTER 23

REED

Once Tate and I finally managed to catch our breath, he gently eased out of me.

Slowly, we got to our feet.

I was trembling, my legs like jelly, my heart still pounding away.

"Come here," Tate whispered.

I turned around and reached for him, face to face.

His cum was leaking out of my hole, down my thighs, and I still couldn't believe it.

I'd fantasized about having sex with him for years, but nothing, and I mean nothing, prepared me for what just happened.

For whatever that was. Sex was always good and fun, but that?

We were needy, desperate, voracious.

Even after two orgasms, I didn't want to stop touching him.

I was overwhelmed, so happy I couldn't form words.

Without warning, a sudden urge to cry had me burying my face in Tate's shoulder. I was raw and vulnerable, and I didn't want him to see. Which was all kinds of strange, since he'd seen me in every possible mood, and me, him. Tears wouldn't push him away. This was, after all, Tate.

I'd fucked my best friend.

"Look at me," Tate demanded as he gently rubbed my back.

"No," I mumbled against his skin. I blinked away my tears and then playfully licked his shoulder.

"Don't try distraction, Ree. Look at me."

Of course, I couldn't deny him.

I raised my head and looked him in the eye. One tear escaped down my cheek, and he kissed it away.

This sensitive side of him knocked the remaining breath right out of my body.

"Don't be afraid, baby. I know we've got a lot to talk about, but let's go upstairs, have a shower—"

"Bath," I offered.

"Okay, a bath," Tate continued. "And then it's off to bed."

"The same bed?"

His thunderous expression told me everything I needed to know.

"Of course, the same damn bed," he groused.

I couldn't help but chuckle at his pouty tone. "Just making sure we're on the same page."

"Same page, same line, same fucking bed."

I smiled at his declaration and Tate leaned down to kiss me. My nerves finally settled.

"Good. But I need you to help me," I replied. "You fucked out my ability to walk. I don't think I can make it up those stairs."

Tate nodded and gave me a kiss. "Then we need to refuel first. Snack, then shower—"

"Bath—"

"That's what I said," Tate interrupted and pinched my ass. "Then bed. Our bed."

I shivered at his words.

"You like that, huh?"

I had no reason to deny it.

"Yes."

But I didn't just like it. I loved it.

I always worried about the potential for awkwardness if Tate and I did cross the friendship line. I felt anything but. In fact, it was the most natural thing in the world to stand around naked with him and admire the many bites and marks I'd left on his body.

After one last kiss, we finally managed to separate from each other and headed down to the bathroom. We washed up quickly, and then Tate guided me into the kitchen.

He rummaged in the fridge for cheese and fruit, while I grabbed paper towels and whatever detergent I could find and attempted to clean the carpet on the stairs.

Ten minutes later, and the stains were still there.

Although the smell of our cum was now replaced by citrus cleaner. So, it wasn't that bad. Sort of.

Tate met me on the landing, carrying a tray with our snacks and a couple of mugs of tea.

"Leave it," he motioned to the stairs. "I'll call a cleaning service tomorrow."

I shook my head.

"Maybe wait to make that call."

"What?"

I glanced at him with one eyebrow raised. "Cause we're here for another few weeks. Pretty sure we're going to make a mess in every room of this house."

Tate's chuckle was downright dirty. "You like fucking bareback, eh?"

"I like fucking you bareback."

"First time for me," he admitted.

"Me too."

My cock took interest in our conversation, but Tate shook his head. "Oh no. I need a break after two monster orgasms.

Get your delectable ass up those stairs and into that bathtub."

I slapped his butt on the way by.

"Are you going to feed me while I'm soaking in the tub?"

"We're going to feed each other. It's a tub built for two."

"I didn't take you for the romantic type."

"You don't know everything about me," Tate insisted.

That made me pause. I thought I knew everything, but maybe I didn't. And now I damn well wanted to find out.

I climbed the stairs, Tate following. The ache in my knees and thighs intensified, not to mention my ass. A-fucking-mazing.

I glanced over my shoulder as I hit the last step. The heat in Tate's gaze was undeniable.

But this time, we finally made it up to the third floor.

I headed straight for the bathroom and the white clawfoot tub that sat under the skylight. Pillar candles were littered throughout the space, in every nook, so I went about lighting them, turning off the overhead chandelier.

While the bath filled, I glanced at the full-length mirror that sat opposite it. I hardly recognized myself.

It had been so long, not just since I'd had sex, but since I'd been happy.

And that's what I saw.

Not the beard burns, or the love bites that Tate gave me, but happiness.

Casting agents have told me that my eyes are my most unique feature. Not just the color, but how expressive they are. I thought it was them blowing smoke up my ass, but in this moment, I believed it.

I'd never admitted out loud that I was in love with Tate, but if anyone looked at me now, they'd know the truth.

And that rush of emotion took over again.

Just as Tate walked in, I leaned against the counter to hold myself up.

I took my time looking him over, noticing the differences between us. His body was bigger than mine, broad, where I was lean. He rocked the hairy chest better than any man I've met, while I was smooth all over. Not to mention, Tate had the defined pecs, biceps, and abs that come from all the swimming and weight training he liked to do.

And then I finally got another good look at his long, thick cock and hairy balls, and yeah, he was a beautiful man.

And all mine.

For now.

That niggling doubt at the back of my mind was a bitch to get rid of. I couldn't really blame myself. Tate and I had been up, down, and spinning around each other for ten years. God only knew what would happen next.

But one thing I did know. We were older, and hopefully wiser.

And despite my fear, I wasn't running away.

He walked up to me, and without saying a word, pulled me into his arms and planted a claiming kiss on my lips. As possessive as his earlier words.

Every nerve ending in my body sparked to life.

I kissed him back and started to doubt that we would make it into that tub at all.

Demanding Tate was an incredible turn on. Not that I'd always give in, but, you know, him going alpha male on me was sexy as fuck. Past lovers, ones who weren't in the biz, were sometimes hesitant, given my Hollywood persona. I was often the one who made the first move. Which was fine.

But deep down, I wanted more. I wanted to be seen, to be needed, just I was, not for my celebrity.

No one ever made me feel like that.

Only Tate.

"Feel free to manhandle me anytime you want," I whispered.

When he finally let me come up for air, that is.

He smiled and swatted my ass. "Get in the tub, gorgeous."

I slid in first, and the water was just shy of painfully hot. Tate followed, sitting behind me.

I leaned back, leaning on him, letting out the biggest, most satisfying sigh.

A hot bath and a hotter man.

"Pinch me."

Tate laughed and wrapped me up in his arms instead.

"That'll do, too," I replied.

He gently kissed my head and I held on to him tighter.

"You all right?" he murmured against my hair.

"More than. You?"

"Oh, yes," he sighed. "I didn't hurt you, did I?"

I turned my head, surprised at Tate's concern.

"No, of course not. It was everything I wanted."

"Just checking. Sometimes, I don't know my own strength. I got—" Tate paused and cleared his throat. "I got so turned on, I went a little wild."

"A little? Holy shit, Tate, I'm surprised we didn't set those stairs on fire."

"That'll be next. Then we'll have to buy this house, never mind rent it."

"No doubt," I chuckled as I ran my hands along his forearms. "I've never felt… I mean, that was…Christ. I have no words."

"I feel the same."

Tate rubbed his beard against my neck, and I shivered, goosebumps popping up all over my skin despite the heat of the water.

"I'm sure I'm not the first man to tell you, but that was the most incredible sex of my life. And no condom. That's a huge deal for me. I trust in that. In you."

"I trust in that too," he squeezed me tighter. "And you're the first man to ever give me that kind of compliment. But the sex wasn't incredible because of me. It's because it's *us*."

"Tay," I turned my head and gave him a languid kiss.

"You know it's true. In the past, it was just fucking. I got off, that was it. I didn't really give a shit about how the other guy felt. As soon as it was over, I was done. A lot of that was my fear of being found out. I wanted it and at the same time, I wanted to hide. I hated myself. That fucks with your head. Makes it impossible to let anyone in. Or for sex to mean anything more than a dirty secret. But not with you."

I kissed him again.

"I never had a friend like you. Someone who saw through my shit and wanted me anyway," Tate kissed my temple. "You, Ree, have always been the exception to my rule."

"And what happens next?" I asked, voicing the fear that I was trying to suppress.

"We keep it private. For now, but not forever. I've never been in a relationship before so you're going to have to have a lot of patience, because I have no idea what the fuck I'm doing. I'm relying on you to guide me."

"I think you're doing pretty good so far."

Suddenly Tate wrapped his legs around me like an octopus, water splashing everywhere. I let out a loud squeak.

"Only pretty good?" he taunted.

"Well, the sex is amazing. And this, right here, is nice too."

"Pretty good and nice?" he laughed and pinched my ass.

I squirmed but I had no desire to go anywhere, happily trapped in his arms.

"The best, all right? You and me? It's the best."

"Now that's more like it."

CHAPTER 24

TATE

Sex is one thing.

Sleeping in the same bed with another person was a whole other matter.

And something that I'd never done with a lover. At least, not consciously. Maybe when I was in the grips of my coke addiction. But passing out after sex because I was high, and choosing to stay in bed with someone when I was sober, were two different things.

With Reed? There was no place else I wanted to be. In fact, you'd have to drag me out of this bed because spooning him tight to my body and listening to his gentle snores was so freaking perfect. It was everything I never knew I needed.

After our soak in the tub, we ate our snacks in bed, watching a movie. By the time the show ended, we were both yawning and unable to move.

I was adamant that we sleep together in the same bed, but I also worried that it might freak me out. But I should have known better.

I was so damn happy. And proud.

I wanted to take Reed by the hand and parade him around

in front of everyone, every fucking camera, and shout out loud that this man right here was mine.

For someone who'd been hiding in the closet for years, it was a heady realization.

And when my alarm sounded at five the next morning, part of me still couldn't believe what had happened.

I gently eased myself from Reed. When I stretched, I felt the aches in my body, especially my knees.

Oh yeah, this was real.

"Morning," Reed murmured as he turned over.

A lock of his blond hair fell over his forehead, and I gently brushed it back.

"Morning," I replied and kissed his pouty lips. "Time to get up. We have to be on set in an hour."

"Fuck that. I hate early wake ups," Reed grumbled, eyes still closed, and I couldn't help but smile at his grumpy tone.

"Me too. But you need to get your fine butt outta this bed."

"What are you going do if I don't?" Reed asked, blinking away his sleep.

"I'm going to use up all the hot water in the shower."

"Mean."

"That's me," I laughed and kissed him again.

This time Reed teased me with his wicked tongue and pushed me flat on my back. I forgot all about morning breath and why we needed to be up so early to begin with.

Until my phone buzzed again and rudely interrupted us.

We both groaned and pulled apart.

"You shower first, I'll go fix breakfast," I offered.

An hour later, both of us were clean, fed, and ready to go, so we took a rideshare to the set location, one of Oxford's famous university buildings.

It was strange to get out of the car and not reach for Reed's hand. What I'd carefully avoided in the past I now wanted more than anything.

It was going to take time to get used to this reality.

We made our way through security, and I jolted when I spotted a familiar figure talking to Jared.

"Korry!" Reed called out and walked over to give the bodyguard a hug.

Feeling all kinds of foolish given my behavior last night, I followed Reed.

Korry turned and gave me a slow once over. The smirk was unmistakable.

My face heated.

"Sorry about my horrible behavior last night," I said as I offered my hand. "I was rude, and I hope you can accept my apology."

Korry shook my hand readily.

"No worries," he replied with a big grin. "Like I told Reed, I knew what I was doing. Did you guys have a good night?"

Good?

That was the understatement of the year. Of the decade.

"Very good. Thanks."

My face was on fire.

I glanced at Reed, and he was as flushed as me. No, wait, that was beard burn. Then I noticed Jared staring at us.

"You okay, boss?" I quipped.

"Uh, yeah," Jared nodded, thankfully saying nothing else. "Hair and makeup are expecting you."

Reed and I hurried off down the narrow corridor of the building.

"Do you think Jared knows?" he whispered.

I glanced at Reed. "I'd be shocked if he didn't. The fact that I turned bright red would've been the first clue. The fact that you have beard burn on your face is the second."

"We can do this, right? Pretend we're still just friends. I mean, we're actors for fuck's sake."

"Definitely."

Definitely not, as it turned out.

The scene we were filming today was the first time our characters meet after the funeral. A conversation turns into dinner and a walk by the Thames.

Despite repeating the mantra that I was my character and not me, every moment of last night flashed through my mind like a movie reel.

And I wondered, how was this new relationship with my oldest friend going to play out?

Was I going to fuck it up like I had in the past?

Stepping into the restaurant scene, I felt the other actors' stares on us, and I had a strange sense of déjà vu.

Could they tell how I felt about Reed? Did they know?

Suddenly my skin was too tight, and I kept flubbing my lines.

When Jared called for a break, I headed for the catering room, in need of water and something to eat.

Reed didn't follow. Instead, I left him discussing the next shot with Jared.

I guess I wasn't as ready as I thought.

Whenever anxiety reared its ugly head, the urge to get high wasn't far behind.

I grabbed a protein bar and downed a whole bottle of water, then went for a walk around the grounds.

Exercise helped in calming my nerves, and some of my urge. I texted my sponsor back home and we agreed to a call once I was done shooting for the day.

A half hour later, I returned to the dressing room where I found Reed alone, getting changed into his next outfit.

"You okay?" he asked.

"Yeah, just nerves. I felt like everyone could, you know, tell about us."

"Except for Jared and Korry, they can't. And if they do see something, it'll be the characters we're playing."

"I hope so. I mean, I just want to keep this between us. Until we're ready."

There was no one else around, so I took his hand in mine, pulled him in close and gave him a soft kiss. His touch soothed me and at the same time, set my heart racing again.

There was a sudden knock on the door, and we quickly parted.

"Come in!" Reed yelled out.

I sat down in one of the chairs and pulled out my phone. Pretending to look busy.

I relaxed when I realized it was just the hair and makeup crew.

Once our touch ups were done, we were ready to film again.

I remembered Reed's comment and got my head in the game. We were playing characters falling in love. So, if anyone saw anything, they'd see that.

Usually, I slipped into the role of another person to escape myself. But this time, my character was taking cues from me.

Falling in love was happening in real time.

Reed

"Hey, are you okay?"

Jared's question during our break surprised me. We'd completed our scene with only a few takes, and everything was good. I wasn't stressed or anything.

The morning couldn't have gone better. The one at work, too.

"I'm great. Didn't our performance meet your expectations?"

"That, yes, for sure. Everything flowed naturally. I just—"

Jared looked around and then motioned to the dressing room.

I followed him and he closed the door behind us.

"Feel free to tell me it's none of my business but are you and Tate—" Jared started.

"It's none of your business," I snapped.

I was protective of Tate and the change in our relationship. We were brand new lovers but that didn't mean we didn't know what we were doing. Or that I needed anyone else's opinion on whether this was a good idea or not.

The heart always wants what it wants. For me, anyway.

I tended to push logic and reason to the back burner when my feelings were involved.

"Sorry, I don't mean to be bitchy," I continued. "And yes, me and Tate. I'm really fucking happy, and also protective. And distracted. Shit, Jared, be thankful I remembered any of my lines today because I'm so far gone, I'm still floating somewhere in outer space. But despite all that, I know what I'm doing. Tate does too."

Jared bit his lower lip, and ran one hand through his long hair. "I care about both of you. Not just as colleagues, but friends. And I'm concerned. Given your your recent grief, and the fact that he's not out yet, can you blame me?"

I couldn't, so instead I switched tactics.

"Don't you think this thing between me and him is a long time coming?" I asked.

Few things surprised Jared. But I did.

The director was momentarily speechless.

"I—" Jared paused and nodded. "Well, yeah, I do. Of course, I do. I mean, I've known you for years and watched you two together. The teasing, the bickering, the chemistry you have, it's all real."

"Well, then?"

Jared sighed and sat down on one of the leather chairs. "If you're happy, I'm happy for you. But I won't lie and say I'm not worried. Given your volatile history, you can't deny that this is a big risk."

"And you taking on two men as life partners isn't risky?" I asked him.

"Okay, fair point," Jared conceded. "But becoming lovers

adds a whole new dimension to your previous relationship. The stakes are higher."

"They are. But Tate and I need to figure this thing out in our own time. And no matter what happens with me and him personally, we always do our jobs."

Jared shook his head. "For once, I'm not concerned about the work."

I walked over and sat down beside him. "And your concern is appreciated."

"I'm always here if you need to talk. Alex and Aiden too," he nodded. "In fact, I just realized that Tate's a lot like them. Their brusque manner is a just a shield they use to protect themselves from being hurt. They rarely let anyone see who they really are, but if you're that lucky person? There's nothing like it."

"Oh, I know."

"And I'm proof that it's possible to have a great relationship, despite being under a media microscope."

"It hasn't stopped you."

"No fucking way. Aiden and Alex mean everything to me."

I nodded at his response.

"Then you know exactly how I feel."

CHAPTER 25

TATE

The rest of the day's filming went off without a hitch.

Save for the sudden, unrelenting downpour that caused us to move inside.

Other than that, it went well.

But unlike my usual time on set, I couldn't wait for this day to be over. So Reed and I could finally be alone again.

It didn't escape my attention that he was quieter this afternoon, even on our break. Doubts and fears pushed to the forefront of my mind, but I pushed back.

Reed wouldn't change his mind. I believed that.

Maybe he was just overwhelmed by the newness of everything. Nothing prepares you for the reality of fucking your best friend.

But it turned out that alone time would have to wait a bit longer. We were invited by the crew to another pub night. Reed couldn't drink and I didn't care to be around other people, but he wanted to go, so I went along.

Jared and Korry convinced Reed and I to play darts. I won and then bragged about it non-stop, of course, and Reed swore he was never playing with me again. Right. His competitive nature would draw him back.

Then we settled into a cozy corner booth and stuffed in huge platters of fish and chips with mushy peas.

Around nine, we said our goodbyes and decided to walk home.

The rain was softly falling and fog was rolling in, blanketing everything around us. Reed thought it was spooky, but I liked it.

I reached out and took his hand and he startled.

"Tay, what are you doing?"

"There's no one around. It's dark, it's foggy. Come on, relax."

Sure, there was a chance someone might see us, but I wasn't worried. And when he interlocked his fingers with mine, all my earlier doubts receded.

"You were quiet this afternoon, anything you want to talk about?" I asked.

"Jared knows. Well, he suspected, and I confirmed. He's concerned but I assured him that there's nothing to worry about. And he also wanted us to know that if we ever need to talk to someone, he's there. Him and his partners."

"That's very kind of him. And I'm relieved that he knows."

"Are you? I wasn't sure what your reaction might be."

"He's not just our director, but our friend. In fact, that's a good place for us to start."

Reed nodded. "How about you?"

"What about me?"

Reed stopped walking and I stared at him. The damp air caused his wavy hair to curl, and I brushed a lock of it behind his ear.

"I could tell you were nervous today," he whispered.

"I was. That first shot? It felt like everyone was staring at us. Well, you know what I mean. While I was out for a break, I texted my sponsor. The urge to numb myself always hits hard when my anxiety rears up."

"I'm sorry."

"There's nothing for you to be sorry about, Ree. But it's something you need to consider."

"What do you mean?"

"I'm an addict. I'll always deal with this. For the rest of my life. It's not going away."

"I'm the same. Our situation's no different."

"Bad enough for one of us, but both?" I sighed and stepped closer. "See, this is the type of thing I never think about, because I've never had anyone else to consider. But now… I don't want to hurt you."

"It's too late."

"What?"

"We've already hurt each other throughout the years. Plenty of times. Especially after our big blow out, when I walked away. But we're here now. Older, stronger, and smarter. Please, fuck, let us be smarter."

I chuckled and pulled him into my arms.

"What I'm trying to say is, we're honest with each other in all things now," Reed added. "No more hiding, no more secrets."

There were still a few.

"Like what I said to make you walk out on me that day?"

"You still don't remember?"

I shook my head. "No."

Reed sighed. "You said that I was living in denial about my feelings for you. But it wasn't just the words, it was how you said it. You taunted me, like you found the whole thing amusing, and that really fucking hurt."

I stared at him, and seeing the pain in his eyes made my chest hurt.

"I'm so sorry I did that. I… I guess it was easier for me to hurt you than to face my own feelings. Do you forgive me?"

Reed nodded. "You were right about my denial, though.

But I was too angry and hurt, and you were too high to make sense of what was going on to do anything about it."

"And now?"

"Now it's different," Reed looked around, and then back up at me. "We'll probably stumble around in the dark at times, but that's okay. We're not perfect. Our story doesn't end when the credits roll."

"I'm gonna fuck up."

"I will too. And then we'll figure out how to make it right."

Reed squeezed my waist.

"Come, let's get going," Reed smiled at me. "We have a damage deposit to add to."

Reed

I wanted to attack Tate the moment we stepped foot in the door, but then I remembered the call with his sponsor.

That came first.

I headed upstairs to have a bath while Tate made his call.

When I walked out of the bathroom a half hour later, Tate was already lying in bed, on his laptop, wearing... reading glasses?

"When did you get those?" I pointed to his face.

"A few months ago. I keep forgetting to bring them with me to set."

"Is that why you're constantly squinting at the script? I thought you were contemplating the scene. You know, thinking hard about your character's motivation."

"Hardly thinking is more like it," Tate quipped and lowered his black-frame glasses.

"I doubt that," I chuckled. "And by the way, you're sexy as fuck in those glasses."

He gave me a wicked grin and my cock took notice.

Closing the laptop, he placed it on the nightstand and then crooked a finger at me.

"Come here," he commanded.

Then I remembered his call. "Did you talk to your sponsor?"

"I did. I told him all about me and you, about my anxiety today, and what's ahead. It's almost painful for me to talk about my feelings but once it's done, I always feel calmer. The urge subsides."

"I'm so fucking proud of you."

Tate's face flushed and it looked so good on him.

"I want to be a better man," he confessed. "For me. And for you."

"It works both ways. I want to be that for you, too."

I undid my bathrobe and let it slide to the floor. My skin was burning up, my dick now rock hard.

"Christ, Reed. I'm going to tell you this every goddamn day: you are so fucking beautiful."

God, my heart nearly stopped when he talked to me like that. "No, love. That's you."

"I'm not just talking about the outside. I'm talking about everything."

I stalked over to the bed and slid onto it, straddling his waist. Tate was still dressed in jeans and a t-shirt. Judging by the bulge in his pants, he was as far gone as I was.

"Take your clothes off," I demanded. "But leave the glasses."

"You got a Clark Kent thing?" he smirked.

"I got a *you* thing," I whispered and leaned down to give him a devouring kiss. "Less talking, more fucking."

Tate flipped me over and my back hit the mattress.

Yes. Finally.

This time, he straddled me.

He set his glasses aside, removed his shirt, then slid the frames back on his face.

I reached for his jeans, popping open the top button. Taking my time, teasing him, I slowly opened one button after the other, revealing the hairy trail that disappeared into his navy briefs. My eyes caught on the four-leaf clover tattoo, the one that matched mine, sitting low on his hip. I traced my finger over it, then glanced up at him.

"You didn't consider getting rid of it?" I asked.

"I did, but I couldn't do it. Never."

"Same."

Tate pushed my hands away and shoved his jeans and underwear down. His cock was already hard and furiously leaking precum.

"Crawl up the bed," I demanded. "Feed it to me."

Letting out a frustrated groan, Tate shifted off me, off the bed, removing his clothes completely, leaving them on the floor.

"I've got a better idea. Scoot down the bed and tilt your head back," he directed.

I was only too happy to obey.

When he slipped back on the bed, he positioned himself behind me, one knee on either side of my head. At this angle, I could take him deeper and fuck, even before his cock touched my tongue, I was starving for him.

"Fuck, yes," he moaned and feed me his cock.

I breathed through my nose and relaxed my jaw as he filled me, one torturous inch at a time.

"That's it," Tate encouraged, his voice gravelly, needy. "Baby, take it all."

His salty precum hit my tastebuds and I hummed in pleasure.

"Fucking hell, Ree," Tate whispered and slid one hand around my throat.

He pumped his hips, slowly at first and then with increasing urgency.

I grabbed onto his thighs, holding on for the ride, ignoring my own dick.

"Oh fuck," Tate groaned, and I felt him shudder. "That's so good, too good. Shit."

My cock jerked, begging for attention, but I stayed focused on Tate.

His thighs were shaking as he slid his cock in and out of my mouth, faster now.

And all I could do was lie there and take it.

I was lightheaded, and shivered when he gently squeezed my neck, feeling his cock in my throat.

"Jesus," Tate groaned loudly. "I have no control around you. Fuck, I'm going to come. Tap my thigh if you need me to pull out."

Instead, I gripped his thighs tighter. He kept fucking my throat, his pace unrelenting.

My mouth was sore, my throat was on fire, but I couldn't stop. I wanted everything Tate could give me.

Knowing that *I* was the reason he was about to lose control was so fucking satisfying.

"Reed!" Tate yelled out as his dick twitched.

Cum flooded my throat and I kept swallowing, trying not to choke.

As Tate's cock softened, he pulled out, leaving me gasping and my mouth covered in his cum.

I lay on the mattress, panting hard, desperate for air.

And my dick was so hard it hurt, but I could take care of that later.

Until Tate leaned over, crawling over me.

With one hand around the base of my dick and the other on the bed for leverage, he sucked me off.

Tate couldn't take me deep, but it didn't matter. I was blissed out just knowing he had my cock in his mouth.

"Tate," I whispered, my voice hoarse. "Fuck."

Then I decided to play dirty. His balls and dick were back

in my face again. I licked one ball and sucked on it, then took the other in my mouth, giving it the same love.

Tate's suction faltered.

He moved his hand to my balls and tugged them gently. My entire body locked up tight.

And then I forgot what I was doing.

Tate was sucking and jacking me off.

My balls drew up tight, and everything in my body narrowed to one perfect point of pleasure.

"I'm right there. Oh God!"

I fucked into his mouth as I came apart, the vibration of his moans around my cock the hottest thing ever.

Wave after wave of white-hot pleasure rolled through me.

When Tate finally eased off, I could barely move.

I looked down the bed to find him in a similar position, staring back at me. His brown hair was mussed, his lips were swollen, and his eyes were wide with shock.

"What the fuck was that?" Tate asked, panting.

"I don't know. But give me a few minutes to recuperate and we'll do it again."

CHAPTER 26
TATE

Ten minutes later, Reed was still splayed out on our bed like a starfish.

"I'm too fucked out to move. Can you get me a glass of water?"

His voice was barely a whisper and no wonder.

Fucking his throat like that was hot as hell but I hope I didn't hurt him.

Anytime we touched each other, though, we couldn't stop. But I didn't want him to think that hard and fast was the only way I wanted him.

After giving him a soft kiss, I headed for the bathroom and returned with two glasses of water.

We quenched our thirst—one of them—and then I pulled him into my arms, spooning him.

Reed held my hand to his chest. I rubbed one nipple, gently at first, and then rolled it between my fingers, tugging.

"Hmm, feels so good," he purred.

My mouth sought out his neck, kissing, sucking, tasting every delectable inch of his skin.

My dick went from semi to fully hard, and I gyrated on Reed's ass, letting him feel exactly how much I wanted him.

"Grab the lube in the nightstand," I ordered.

Reed leaned over and yanked on the drawer, then threw the tube of lube over his shoulder.

"Is this alright? I mean, do you want to bottom? I should ask, and not assume."

He looked over his shoulder. "I love bottoming. I'm vers, but this is what I like best. Is that okay?"

"More than," I groaned out and reached for the lube.

"Just like this?" he asked.

"Yes."

On our sides, slow and easy.

My hands were trembling, and I nearly dropped the lube.

Once I finally got the tube opened, I poured a generous amount in my hand, and slid one slick finger down his crease.

Reed pushed his ass back, greedy for me.

I tapped on his hole, and he moaned.

"Pull your knee to your chest," I whispered.

He did exactly as I asked. Now I could see his perfect pink hole. I pushed one finger inside, slow but steady, and watched him take me in.

"More," Reed whimpered. "Please."

I added a second finger and scissored them gently, stretching him.

"Stop torturing me, Tay, and get your cock inside me," he growled.

I let out a chuckle and leaned down to bite and suck on his shoulder.

"Ahh, fuck, Tate."

"Fuck is right. Don't rush me. This time will be long and slow, and so fucking good. Just lie there and let me worship you."

Reed turned his face into his pillow and let out a strangled moan.

I added a third finger, getting him good and prepped.

Because once I got inside his body, I was going to stay there for as long as I could.

Once I was sure he was ready, I slicked up my cock and slowly pushed inside him.

Sliding one hand over his stomach, and up to his chest, I felt his muscles quiver and tense.

Once my cock was all the way in, our bodies plastered together, I inhaled a shaky breath.

Reed was in my arms, in my bed, with nothing between us.

"You feel so fucking good," I moaned and pumped my hips, fucking into him in short, tight strokes. "This is where you belong, understand? Only here, only with me."

"Yes."

My hand moved lower, teasing his abs, until I reached his cock. Timing my thrusts and my hand, I rocked slow and steady, keeping my promise. This time, I wanted the buildup to be long and heady, and our climax the same.

Reed turned his head towards me and I leaned down, capturing his lips.

Our kiss was like everything between us—possessive, demanding, unrelenting.

Fuck, this man made me feel… everything.

"Tay," he whispered my name. "Only with me. Mine."

Reed was just as feral for me as I was for him.

We were far beyond sex.

This was us declaring what we both wanted but were still too scared to voice.

I loved him.

And I sure as fuck knew that he loved me.

The words lived inside of me, but I couldn't speak them. I was still struggling to accept that I was capable of this depth of feeling.

But I knew that I'd do anything to protect him, and us.

I tightened my grip, showing him everything I was feeling but unable to express with words.

And the longer I fucked him, the louder he moaned. I was sweating and snarling, trying to hold onto my control but I was losing that too.

My control, my body, my heart. It was all his.

Our bodies undulated together in a rhythm that I was guiding, getting faster, and frantic now.

Suddenly, I needed more.

I pulled out and Reed hissed in protest.

"Tate, what the h—?"

Pushing him to his back, I slid my knees under his thighs, pulled his legs over my shoulders, and entered him in one thrust.

"Yes," I moaned loudly.

Now I could see every expression on his pretty face as I moved inside him.

"I need to see all of you. Need to you to know that I—"

The words lodged in my throat. I punched my hips forward, hard, fast, all my promises of slow and easy gone.

But Reed was right there with me, thrusting his hips to meet mine.

"Right there!" he cried out. "Oh fuck, don't stop."

I grabbed hold of those taut ass cheeks and made good on my promise. My hips pistoned hard and the sound of our bodies merging together was so fucking sexy.

The heat of his ass surrounding my bare dick was unreal. I'd discovered my newest addiction. But this one, I was never giving up.

I watched Reed's face as we reached for each other, every expression more telling than the last. The pale green of his eyes was all but gone, his pupils blown, and all I saw were dark pools of want.

"Need you," I growled and continued thrusting, all pretense of slow and easy, gone.

"You have no idea," Reed moaned. "God, Tay. I'm almost there."

I grabbed hold of his cock, jerking him in time to my thrusts, harder, faster, nearing the end of my control. Pleasure sparked in my blood, racing through my body.

"Ree!" I shouted as my balls pulled up tight.

I came hard, my body jerking as the incredible force of my orgasm obliterated me.

Reed let out a filthy moan and then he was right there with me, hot cum lashing my hand, and his stomach.

When I managed to catch a breath, I glanced down and watched my cum leaking out of his hole.

Knowing that I'd marked him like that, did me in.

I gently lowered his legs to wrap around my waist. He was still shaking, and I leaned down to give him a languid kiss.

It was achingly sweet and sexy as hell. I couldn't get enough.

"Fuck, we're good at that," Reed chuckled.

As it was, I could barely manage a grunt.

"Is that a yes?" Reed quipped.

"Give me a second, my brain is still offline."

Reed gently wiped my sweat-soaked hair from my forehead and cupped my face.

The serious intent in his eyes captured my entire attention. I was tempted to look away, to hide my vulnerability, but I fought my fear.

The luminous smile on his face told me he could read my cue.

This time, when I reached for him, the kiss was mauling. I slid my tongue around his, sucking on it greedily.

Our lips were feverish, frantic. I couldn't get enough. It would never be enough.

Reed gripped my hair so tight I was sure I was about to lose a handful of it.

When we finally came up for air, he stared at me with a teasing glint in his eye.

"Let's call in sick tomorrow," he suggested, his voice hoarse.

"We can't do that," I countered as I kissed his flushed cheeks and then the tip of his nose. "But as soon as filming wraps for the day, I'm yours. And we have Saturday off."

"I'm going out with Korry, remember?"

Reed's playful smirk has me reaching down to pinch his ass.

"Ow," he jolted. "As his wingman, that's all. I swear."

"Really?" I grumbled.

"Yes. Are you going to join us?"

"Can I take you to dinner first?"

"You mean, like a date?"

I kissed his forehead, his eyelids. "Yes."

His sharp inhale was so fucking satisfying.

"I'd love to," Reed whispered, "And then we can meet up with Korry and go dancing."

"You can dance, I'll sit and watch."

"Who doesn't like to dance?"

"It's not a matter of like, but can't. I had to use a body double in that western movie I did three years ago."

"No way."

"It's true. I couldn't line dance to save my life."

"They've should've hired Dylan instead of you."

As payback for his teasing, I kissed him longer and harder, silencing any further conversation.

"You may not know how to dance but you have moves," Reed whispered as he tilted his hips, rubbing against mine. I thrust my hips, meeting him touch for touch.

One kiss led to another and another...

"Thanks," I murmured against his lips, "But I still need a lot of practice."

"I'm happy to help you in any way I can."

"So selfless."

"No, selfish," Reed corrected.

I shook my head. "Impossible."

"I'll be your dedicated teacher."

"I like the sound of that," I moaned as my cock begins to fill again.

At this rate, I was going to run out of cum.

"And tonight, we're going to work on our rhythm."

I couldn't help but smile.

"I'm all for that."

CHAPTER 27

TATE

THE NEXT MORNING

I got a wakeup call in the form of an actual phone call, not my alarm.

Rolling away from Reed, I picked up my phone.

Henn calling.

I slipped out of bed to leave Reed in peace and padded into the bathroom.

"Hey, Henn, what's up?" I answered as I closed the door.

"I've been messaging you and Reed for two hours. Where the fuck are you?"

"At the rental. We had our notifications turned off last night. What's going on?"

"Have you checked your phone at all?"

The serious tone of her voice made me tense.

"No, not until you called. Why? What's going on?"

Henn sighed. "I'm afraid you're not going to have the luxury of coming out in your own time. I was flagged on a news article doing the rounds. It comes from a tabloid site, and it claims you and Reed are lovers. That you've been a couple for years. I've sent you the links."

All the blood in my body went cold.

"There's also a picture of the two of you together," Henn continued. "Holding hands. Nothing else is going on but the way you're looking at each other is telling. From what I can see, I think the picture was taken when you were filming a scene. Either that, or just before or after."

"How do you know that?"

"Reed has a mustache and we both know he can't grow enough facial hair for that."

"Christ, who would do that to us?"

"Is the set closed?"

"Pretty much. There was only one scene we shot where we were walking the grounds."

Had I reached for Reed's hands when we stopped filming? Without realizing?

"I've got a call with Jared in five minutes. I want to know who took that fucking picture. If it's one of the crew, it's a violation that will have legal consequences," Henn paused. "How do you want to handle this? Deny and deflect or do you want to move up your timeline?"

I cleared my throat.

The shock had worn off and I was surprisingly steady. "I don't see any point in denying the truth any longer. Even if I am pissed at how this happened."

"Also, your socials are very active. There are a lot of supportive comments but be warned, there are hateful ones too. Your following has dropped about ten percent since the story broke."

My stomach flipped over at her comment. This was what I was dreading.

Not coming out, but not being in control of when and how. And all the 'what-ifs' when it came to my career from here on out.

Would the riptide I was about to swim into sweep me under or was I strong enough to stay calm and ride it out?

"Me and Reed," I started, my throat suddenly tight. "It's real, Henn. I was going to tell you this week—"

"It only took you ten years," Henn grumbled.

Despite my shock, I laughed at her put out tone.

"Seriously, I'm happy for both of you," she assured me, "Even if I think two actors in a relationship is just asking for trouble. But we need to talk about how you want to handle this."

"I need to discuss it with Reed first."

"Do that."

"I'll call you back before we have to report to set."

"Don't go until I talk to Jared."

"And delay filming?"

"If you have to, yes. Call me back in half an hour," Henn demanded and hung up.

My hands were shaking as I turned on my notifications. The incessant buzzing that unleashed made my anxiety spike.

I turned around and looked at myself in the mirror.

I expected to see devastation but all I saw was me.

Tired, but happy.

Worried, but not completely freaked out.

Everything was going to be different from now on.

That nasty voice in my head began to whisper to me that my career was over, and no one would want to work with me.

"That's bullshit," I said out loud to myself, fighting the urge to give in to the fear. "Things are not over. They're just changing direction."

I wasn't as confident as my pep talk, but sometimes you have to fake it to make it.

After brushing my teeth and splashing my face with cold water, I headed back out to the bedroom. Reed was already awake and sitting up. He was perusing his phone, which was now buzzing almost as much as mine.

"I just read the article Henn sent and saw the picture," he

stated, putting his phone aside and reaching for me. "Are you okay?"

I sat down on the bed and took his free hand in mind. "Not sure I can answer how I'm feeling right now."

"You're in shock."

"A tabloid story isn't the way I wanted to come out."

"What do you want to do?"

"Are you okay if I confirm that we're in a relationship?" I asked.

"I'm more than okay with it. Are you?"

I hesitated for a split second. But Reed didn't let go of my hand.

Just the opposite. He leaned over and kissed me.

"I am, but I'm not gonna lie," I gazed at him. "I'm worried."

"I know. You have every right to be. But I'm not going anywhere."

I let out a sigh and pulled him closer. "I wanted to stay in our private bubble a while longer."

"Should we call Henn back?"

"Let's give her a bit. She's reaching out to Jared. She doesn't want us to report on set yet."

"That makes sense. I can tell from our costumes that the pic was taken sometime over the past two days when we were filming. In the meantime, several of our friends have reached out. I think you should read their messages."

He showed me his phone.

I reached over and grabbed my glasses, slipping them on.

Then I took a deep breath, my heart racing, and started reading.

Reed

I was so angry on Tate's behalf.

And to think that it might be someone on set who sold him out? So much for non-disclosure agreements.

Having your personal life posted for the entire world to see and comment on, was unnerving, especially when the speculation was about your sexuality. Which, in a perfect world, was none of anyone's business.

More than anything, I was concerned for Tate. His mental health, his sobriety.

I came out before I came to Hollywood. That wasn't easy either, but my family and friends supported me. Most of them.

A lot had changed from ten years ago.

But the fact that queer people still had to come out at all, that we had to announce who we were and who we loved, instead of just going about our daily lives like cis het people, was telling.

But judging by all the texts and messages from our friends and colleagues, Tate was going to get all the support he needed.

The question was, would he accept it?

And how would he deal with the inevitable backlash?

Nasty comments, insidious threats. Plus, there was the inability to travel to certain countries.

Tate's life, his career… it was all about to shift forever.

His career wasn't over, far from that. But it wouldn't be the same.

And for someone who was as ambitious as Tate—single-minded in his pursuit of his goals—it was going to be a shock.

I stared at him as he read, watching every nuance of the rugged face I'd never get tired of studying.

And when tears welled up and spilled down his cheeks, I did the only thing I could. I wrapped my arm around his shoulder, and I held onto him.

"Can you get Henn on the phone?" Tate whispered as he continued to scroll.

I took his phone and tapped Henn's number and speaker.

"That was fast," Henn replied.

"Henn," I greeted her.

"Reed, is Tate okay?"

"Yes, we're both here."

"Jared is livid on your behalf. He's shutting down production for the day while he looks into whoever might have done this."

"If they do it once and don't get caught—"

"Exactly," Henn replied. "So, how do you want to handle this?"

I turned to Tate and with my free hand, swiped at his tears. His answering smile made my heart stutter. It was hopeful and heartbreaking in the same breath.

Tate cleared his throat. "Like I said earlier, I want to issue a statement confirming my relationship with Reed."

I trembled at his words. He was shaking too.

No going back now.

"I'll get working on it. You're going to be inundated with requests for interviews. You know the drill, I'll deal with it and if anyone tries to approach you, refer them to me. It also might be a good idea to think about private protection for the next while. Just to be safe."

"Jared knows someone," Tate added. "He used to work for his fiancé, Alex. His name is Korry Doyle. We met him this week and he has availability."

"Great. Set it up. I'm going to write up the press release and send it off for your input."

"We'll be waiting," Tate replied.

"Talk soon."

Tate tapped end and took the phone from my hand.

"It's really happening."

"Do you want me to call Korry?" I offered.

"I'll do it."

Tate's phone rang again, but this time, it was Jared.

"Hey, Jared," Tate answered.

"Tate, are you okay? I'm so sorry about that leaked picture. I don't know who would've done this."

"I'm fine, we're fine," Tate replied calmly. "I mean, I was going to come out anyway, but this just speeds things up."

"I'll have extra security on hand tomorrow. I can't believe one of my crew would violate their NDA."

"Is Korry with you?"

"Yeah, he's helping me look at the photo to see if we can source it. But you know chaotic sets. There's so many people on site at any given moment. I don't know for sure if I'll be able to figure out who took the photo."

"Can you get Korry to call me or stop by the house? We need a protective detail."

"Of course," Jared offered. "And if we do find out who took that picture, I'll get Aiden on it."

"Suing won't turn back the clock," he sighed, "But can Aiden contact me anyway? With this news, I'm pretty sure Henn will be fielding calls from my brand deals in no time."

"I'm on it."

"Thanks Jared."

"No need to thank me. I feel awful that your privacy, and Reed's, was violated."

"Given my experience in this business, I can't say I'm surprised."

"Call me later, okay? And let me know if you need anything. Even if it's just to talk."

"I will, stay in touch."

Tate tapped end and threw the phone beside us.

"I'm already exhausted and it's only eight in the morning."

His phone buzzed again, and Tate began to visibly shake.

"Why don't you give me your phone for a while," I requested and held out my hand.

Tate passed it over to me. I typed out a message to Korry, asking him to drop by as soon as possible. Thankfully, he texted back right away and said yes, he was on his way.

"Korry's coming over."

Tate was silent, staring up at the ceiling.

"Come on, shower time," I urged him.

I got off the bed and held out my hand to him. Tate took it and slowly got to his feet. I stepped into his arms, holding on tight, reassuring him in the only way I could.

"Tate?"

"Yeah?" he stared at me with anxious eyes.

"I have to tell you something."

He cupped my face, his hands cold and sweaty.

"I'm not sure I can take any more surprises this morning," he whispered.

"This isn't a surprise."

"Then what is it?"

I leaned up and kissed his soft lips, taking my time, slow and easy.

"I have to tell you that I—" I took a deep breath and went for it. "I love you. I've been in love with you ever since we lived together in that shitty apartment in North Hollywood. Ten years. Ten fucking years, Tay. I should've told you ages ago, but—"

Tate placed a finger to my lips, cutting off any further words.

"You knew, just like I did, that I wasn't ready to hear them," Tate acknowledged.

Then he gave me a wide smile. The one that showcased his rare, but irresistible dimples.

The smile that set my heart off running.

"But I am now. And Reed, baby, I've never loved anybody but you."

CHAPTER 28

TATE

Reed loved me.

Me.

A part of me recognized his feelings a long time ago, even though I always chose to ignore them. And I fought like hell against mine.

Until fighting became futile.

And to hear him finally admit what I'd suspected for years?

The power of those three words shook me to my core.

We kissed for ages, feverish, until our mouths were sore and our lungs breathless.

But the interruption of our phones ringing was a reminder that the real world outside this bedroom was calling.

Even though it pissed me off to let him go, I gave him one last kiss and stepped back.

"We'll continue this later," Reed assured me.

"I'm holding you to that."

I was tempted to turn my notifications off, but I couldn't miss any important calls from my agent.

Reed and I reluctantly got dressed and called Henn back. We reviewed the statement that she prepared. Once the final version was approved, I dialed in Aiden so he and Henn could map out a plan for contacting my corporate brand deals.

An hour later, there was a knock at the front door.

I headed downstairs cautiously, but when I glanced through the peephole, I was relieved to see it was Korry.

"Come on in," I greeted, ushering him inside.

"How you holding up, Tate?"

I shrugged and motioned for him to enter the living area. "I honestly don't know yet. I think I'm fine. But then again, I haven't left the house yet, so—"

Korry nodded, then ran a hand through his hair. "Yeah. That'll be different. Especially given your public profile."

"I'm trying not to freak out about all the what ifs. But apparently I need a bodyguard for a while."

"It's a good idea. Better to be safe."

"Have a seat. Coffee or tea?" I asked.

"Tea, please. Milk, one sugar."

"I'll be right back."

I heard Reed coming down the stairs as I made my way into the kitchen.

By the time I got the tea ready and headed back out to join them, Reed and Korry were already deep in discussion.

But unlike the other night, when I made a total ass of myself, I wasn't jealous.

Okay, maybe I was still a bit jealous. Possessive as hell is more like it.

And with good reason.

Because Reed loved me. He loved *me*.

Holy fucking shit.

It was going to take a while for that to sink in.

My hands were anything but steady and the tray I was carrying rattled until I set it down on the table. I glanced at Reed, and he was staring back at me with a lusty gaze, like he wanted to get naked right now. Fuck, I did not need to pop a boner in front of our guest.

Glancing away, I offered Reed and Korry each a cup, then took my own and tried to get my brain to focus.

"I've never had a bodyguard before. I mean, occasionally as an escort to awards and things, but not full time. Does this mean you're going to move in with us?" I asked.

"I can. If you want. But I don't think it's necessary. Not while we're here. But I will be on hand any time you need to go out during the day—to the set, dinner, shopping. Just in case you run into a fan who's less than thrilled at the latest news that you're in a relationship with a man."

"I can't believe I need to do this," I grumbled.

"It's temporary. And a precaution."

"We're here in the UK for another few weeks then back to L.A. How long do you think I'll need you?" I asked.

"I'd recommend that I travel back to the U.S. and stay a few weeks. If everything is quiet, then I'm done."

"I'd hate for you to travel all that way for nothing."

"It's not a problem. I have another job in the U.S. that starts in three months, so the timing is perfect."

"Another celebrity?" Reed asked.

"Can't say. But sort of." Korry leaned forward. "Between you and me, it's a gig in the sporting world. Race cars."

"That sounds much more exciting than following me around," I quipped.

Korry laughed. "I'm pretty chuffed about it. I gotta thing for fast cars."

"Adrenaline junkie?" Reed asked.

"Sometimes."

Korry's wicked grin told me it was more than that.

"I texted you Henn's number. She'll set up the contract."

"Cool. You guys have any other questions?"

I reached for Reed's hand.

"Baby?"

"I'm good," Reed whispered in response.

But he was looking at me, not at Korry.

"Can I just say that you two are fucking hot together," Korry commented with a sigh. "You're making me wish I had a special guy."

Reed turned to him. "No prospects?"

"Nope. The guys I meet just wanna fuck. Which is fine. My schedule's all over the place. It's not exactly great for relationships."

I thought about my own schedule and Reed's. We were lucky to be working together now but that wouldn't always be the case. Weeks, sometimes months, apart was a reality in our business.

A warning slithered through my brain, but I ruthlessly ignored it.

My phone pinged and I picked it up, reading Henn's latest message.

"The official press release just came out," I announced. "And me along with it."

Despite Henn's advice to stay away from social media, I gave in and looked.

I was sweating, my palms damp, my heart about to fly right out of my chest.

Tapping on one account, I noticed dozens and dozens of comments.

Reed sat closer to me and Korry on my other side. I held the phone up so we could all read.

Most of the comments were supportive, some angry on my behalf that I was outed by the tabloid.

Many were insanely happy that Reed and I were together, calling us Hollywood's newest "it" couple.

And then there were others, calling us slurs I'd heard many times from my sadistic stepfather. Hateful names I never, ever wanted to hear or in this case, read, again. It wasn't the first time, nor would it be the last, but the vitriolic evidence was still jarring. I blocked and deleted as many as I could. Then I realized Henn was going to ream me out if she knew I was even looking at this.

"I expected that," I finally managed to speak. "Trolls."

My right knee began to bounce, and Reed placed a comforting hand on my thigh.

"Unfortunate but true," Korry stated. "We're always going to face people who can't accept us for who we are. But that's their problem, not ours."

I nodded.

"Are you guys sticking around here today, laying low?" Korry asked.

"That's the plan. Not that there's a shitload of media here in Oxford about to descend upon us."

"No, but London's less than two hours away," he replied. "Don't be surprised if you find the paps camped outside tomorrow morning."

"They won't find us here. I hope." Reed looked at me. "How would they find out where we're staying?"

"Have you seen any neighbors?" Korry asked.

"Um, yeah, I think the day we arrived," I replied. "Shit."

"Don't worry about it. I'll be here bright and early, just in case."

I grimaced. "How early?"

"Five."

"Can I give you a key so you can let yourself in? Cause I sure as fuck won't be up by then," I snarked.

Korry nodded. "That's a lot of trust. Are you sure?"

"Yes."

"Just don't venture upstairs unannounced," Reed added with a grin.

"That's a given." Korry stood up. "Well, I best be off. I've got to extend my hotel stay. Text or call any time. If you need me to stay over, I will. A couch is fine."

"There's two bedrooms on the second floor so there's plenty of room. We'll consider that plan B."

Korry nodded. "Fair enough."

"I'll get the spare key and walk out with you," Reed offered.

Reed got up and followed Korry to the door.

I sat back down on the couch.

My phone rang but I didn't recognize the number, so I ignored it.

The notifications kept coming in. I made the mistake of looking at my socials again and reading more comments.

The hateful ones. Ones I shouldn't be looking at but did.

I closed my eyes but that didn't help matters.

Suddenly, I was back in that shithole I grew up in.

It an unusually warm October day.

I was fifteen.

I told Mama I was going to try out for a part in our high school play.

All I wanted was to be on stage. To be someone else. To escape the reality of home.

I didn't hate her, but I hated our life. And the feeling of being trapped. I couldn't tell anyone our secret. No one would believe us.

I was always told to keep my mouth shut, no matter what. And today was no exception.

Mama told me to keep quiet about the audition, but it was too late. Kenny overheard us talking.

Then he was cursing at us both, the angry shouts followed by the shrill echo of my mother's screams as he punched her in the face. I tried to stop him, but I was no match for his size and strength. Mama passed out on the floor of the kitchen, blood flowing out of her mouth, her long brown hair soaked in it.

I had no one to protect me now. I was alone.

Kenny yanked on my hair and dragged me away from her, into the hallway. I was punching and screaming, trying my best to get free, but it only enraged him. I was no match for his strength.

"You cocksucking little shit! No son of mine is gonna be a pansy-ass actor. You're a piece of trash, just like your mama!"

He pushed me to the floor and kicked me in the back, over and over. By the fifth blow, I couldn't move. I was balled up, my hands covering my head, screaming in agony.

Not that anyone could hear me. Our house was surrounded by miles of countryside.

When would it stop? Please make it stop...

Just when I thought I was going to pass out, Kenny stepped away. And kicked the wall beside me so hard that pieces of plaster rained down over me, covering me in dust.

His footsteps got farther away until I heard a door slam...

The door slammed. I opened my eyes.

I recognized Reed's footsteps, but I was already in full blown panic.

My body was shaking. The acid in my stomach churned full force and I bent over, holding my head in my hands.

I couldn't take a breath. Fucking hell, I couldn't breathe.

All I heard was that bastard, the slurs, the anger, the horrible sound of his hand hitting my mother's face, his foot hitting my back.

I tasted bile in my mouth and then it was too late.

Tears blurred my vision as I lost control and vomited all over the floor.

Why does it have to be this way?

I had Reed now, the best thing in my life.

All at once, I was terrified. Scared to love him and terrified about losing him.

I needed something, anything to calm down. To give me control.

The last thing I heard was Reed calling out my name.

CHAPTER 29

TATE

I opened my eyes and for a moment, wondered where I was.

Then it all flooded back.

I was in the UK. With Reed.

And I was out.

I remembered Henn's call and reading all the hateful comments on my social media.

The flashback to my childhood. Puking my guts out after that.

You know what makes the pain go away.

Just one line and like magic, you're high and bright.

All the bad memories are gone and you're on top of the world.

And there it was. No matter how long I'd been off the coke, there was no escaping its temptation. It was a toxin that lived in my marrow, feeding off my fear. Something I couldn't ever get rid of.

As I sat up, the vile taste in my mouth overwhelmed me. I sniffed the air but there was nothing around me but the scent of lemon. Not like the mornings during the worst of my addiction. Waking up in my own vomit was gross but not uncommon.

I glanced around and spotted Reed sitting in one of the leather chairs near the fireplace, staring down at his clasped hands.

The firelight illuminated his face. A profile that, if I was an artist, I could sketch from memory alone.

He looked devastated.

Or was I just seeing myself in him?

"Reed," I called out his name in a hoarse whisper.

He shot up out of the chair and rushed over to my side.

I shook my head, dizzy and lightheaded.

"Jesus, Tate, you scared the shit out of me," he replied and offered me a glass of water.

I gratefully accepted it and washed away the bitter taste of bile.

"Sorry," I croaked out, then took another long gulp of water. "How long have I been out?"

"Not long. I was going to call an ambulance, but Korry checked you over and said that you'd be okay."

"He's a doctor as well as a bodyguard?" I griped, my jealous flare igniting.

"No, he was in the military and has seen a lot of medical emergencies."

"I need to call my sponsor," I blurted out. "While you were saying goodbye to Korry, I... I had a horrible flashback about my stepdad, Kenny. Fuck, I want a hit. I want it so bad. I'm so fucking sorry."

The tears came again, and the full body shakes along with them.

There was so much to lose now. Too much.

"It's all right, love, it's okay," Reed murmured and pulled me into his arms.

His familiar scent and his soothing touch made me cry harder.

"I'm not going anywhere. We're going to get through this together, just like everything else."

"Why? Why are you even with me?" I muttered against his shoulder. "You could do so much fucking better."

"No! And don't say that again."

Reed pulled back and his gaze burned into mine.

"It's true," I implored. "I act like I have it together, but the truth is, I'm a fucking mess. It's taken me so goddamn long to come to terms with my sexuality. I don't know if I'll ever be the confident person that I play. Don't you get it, Ree? I don't know who I am. I've spent most of my life wishing I was someone else or pretending to be someone else. Tate Aduma is a character I created. He's not real."

Reed sighed but didn't let go.

"No, love, you've got that all wrong. You—" He paused and cupped my face. "You are the only real thing. Look at everything you've accomplished, despite the horrible shit you've been through. You, Tate Aduma, are a stubborn, ambitious, infuriating, smart, beautiful, talented man."

"Ree—"

"I'm not finished," Reed continued, "You're the man that I love. And I see you very clearly, the good and the bad. I see it all."

"Baby, I—"

"You told me you loved me. Was that a line?"

"What? No!" I nearly shouted. "I love you more than anything."

"Then?"

"I don't want to drag you down with me."

"You're not dragging me anywhere. I'm holding your hand, and you're holding mine. We're going to walk through this together. You and me."

I was overwhelmed by his words. By his love.

"Finish your water and call your sponsor." Reed gave me a kiss on the cheek and stood up. "I'm going to make us something to eat."

Reed headed off to the kitchen.

My phone was sitting on the coffee table, but I looked at it like it was a bomb about to detonate.

Taking a deep breath, I reached for it and tapped on the home screen, realizing that Reed had silenced the notifications. Thank fuck. There were more than forty text messages, but I ignored all of them.

I tapped on a number I knew by heart and waited for a response.

"Tate, I saw the news and I just messaged you. Are you all right?"

My sponsor, Dare, answered in his rumbling voice.

"I'm not sure how I'm doing to be honest. I finally told Reed that I love him. We're together. For real. And now I'm out. Part of me still can't believe it," I sighed. "On the other, I just had a massive panic attack, a flashback from my childhood. Well, you know all about that. It was so bad, I puked my guts out. And you know my history with anxiety, that's when my urge to get high goes into overdrive."

"I know all too well," Dare replied. "But drugs are just a band-aid, they're not going to heal your wounds."

I sighed. The lure of being high was that I didn't give a shit about what anyone thought of me. And it dimmed the memories that haunted me.

If only for a little while.

"Coke gave me the kind of confidence I've never had on my own. It made me forget the past and worries about the future."

"You know that's not true," Dare implored. "Coke, booze, pills—none of them give you confidence. All they do is temporarily numb the pain and fool you into thinking you're invincible. But none of us are. That's why we gotta talk about what's going on inside us. Hiding our fears, our pain, just makes the urge to use that much stronger. And numbing yourself isn't a long-term solution."

"Easy for you to say. You're not going to be judged by millions of people."

"No, I'm not. But like you, I know what's it like to struggle with identity. I grew up in an ultra-conservative household and there wasn't a day that went by that I didn't know that being gay was not acceptable. Being disowned by my family is a trauma I carry to this day. And for most of my adult life, alcohol was my solution to dealing with that pain. I used it for everything—to numb the devastation at losing my family, to deal with bad relationships, you name it. Because I didn't want to talk about what I'd been through. It was easier to get drunk and forget, even if for a little while."

"Exactly. And I'm so fucking scared I'm going to slip up again. The last thing I want to do now is hurt Reed. I think that's why my craving is hitting hard. I have so much more to lose now if things between us don't work out. I've never... I've never loved anyone like this. He's everything to me."

"It's a heady thing. All you can do is talk it out with him. You told me he's got his own battle with alcohol."

"He does."

"Then he understands exactly what you're going through. Be honest and tell him what's going on in your mind. And reach out to me whenever you need to talk."

"Thanks, Dare," I replied. "I feel calmer now."

The need was still there, whispering to me, but I felt like I could manage it.

"No thanks necessary. Talking to you helps me as much as it helps you."

"I'll probably call again later, if that's okay?" I asked.

"I'll be here."

I tapped *end* and placed the phone back on the table.

Feeling better, I made my way upstairs. I brushed my teeth, gargled with mouthwash, and then hopped in the shower.

By the time I came back downstairs, Reed had lunch laid out in the living room.

"Hey," I murmured, suddenly feeling all kinds of shy.

Which was not like me at all.

I walked around and sat down beside him on the sofa.

"You don't have to tell me if you don't want to, but how did your call go?" he asked as he poured a cup of green tea.

"Good. I still have the urge but it's not as strong."

Reed smiled and leaned over to kiss me.

"Jared called while you were in the shower," Reed added. "Filming resumes tomorrow and they've added more security. Also, Aiden and Alex are driving up from London. They're going to be in town for a few days and wanted to know if we'd like to get together."

"That would be great."

The more friendly faces around me, the better.

"I know this is a huge step for you. But I'm right here and I'm not going anywhere. There will always be haters and naysayers. But they don't get to control our lives. Their opinions don't matter."

I nodded. I knew Reed was right.

But it was going to take time for me to get there.

CHAPTER 30

REED

Tate's world didn't come to an end when we walked out our front door the next day.

The complete opposite.

Korry arrived by car to escort us to set, and yes, there were several paps waiting on the street to photograph us. But they were respectful and kept their distance.

I was doing the same with Tate, unsure what kind of PDA, if any, he wanted to show. I was never big into hand holding, but then again, I'd never been public with a man that I was head over heels in love with.

Tate surprised me by taking my hand and interlocking our fingers.

Flashes popped and reporters shouted. Both of us flinched, but our hands didn't separate.

Not on the way to the car. Not on the car ride over. Not even when we arrived on set.

Jared was the first to greet us, glancing at our joined hands.

He seemed hesitant at first to say anything. Which wasn't like him.

Until Tate let go of me and reached over to hug him.

"I've been worried about you guys," Jared admitted. "And I'm still pissed that I haven't been able to identify who took that photo."

Tate waved him off. "If you find them, great. If not, whatever. I don't want to spend any more time worrying about whoever that asshole is. It's not worth our time. I have nothing to hide."

"Tate's right," I added. "We're not going to run."

Jared nodded and walked us back to the set where the crew, upon seeing us, began to clap and whistle.

Someone yelled out, "it's about fucking time!"

It turned out that the only people that Tate and I had been fooling were ourselves.

We looked at each other and tried not to smile but it was useless.

"Okay, thank you," Tate held up his free hand in mock surrender. "Now that everyone knows our business, can we let it go, and get to work?"

And we did.

The day was like any other on set.

We filmed, we flubbed, and we did it again until we got the take.

Afterwards, we headed to our favorite pub for dinner. No one paid us any particular attention. Not that I noticed. I was too busy pinching myself that me and Tate were real.

Tate seemed to relax as the day wore on, but I was still watchful.

Until we made it home that evening and Tate showed me exactly how he was feeling.

I'd barely had time to say goodbye to Korry and close the door when Tate all but pushed me inside the house.

Next thing I knew, I was stumbling into the foyer, my back hitting the wall as Tate took ownership of my mouth.

A shiver wracked my body from head to toe. Possessive Tate was hot as fuck.

"I've wanted to do that all damn day," Tate whispered in between deep, drugging kisses. "You were right there, so close, so fucking tempting. It was all I could do not to pull you into that dressing room and fuck you over the makeup table."

Desire pooled low in my belly.

"Tay."

Without hesitation, I dropped to my knees and unzipped his pants. I shoved his briefs down and pulled out his cock, already rock hard and leaking pre-cum.

His cock was long and thick, fucking gorgeous, and all mine.

"Fuck, shit, goddamn it," Tate bit out.

I chuckled. "That's a lot of swearing."

Leaning forward, I gave his cockhead one provocative lick, watching the feral expression on his face.

"It's warranted because watching you touch my dick is... fucking hell, Reed. It's the hottest thing ever."

His hands were shaking as he gripped my hair, tugging me closer.

"Then fuck my face, love. Don't hold back," I demanded.

His taste was salty, musky, so fucking good that I was ravenous, swallowing him down in one smooth glide. Thank God for no gag reflex. Plus, I was damn proud of my blowjob skills. And Tate's responding groan spurred me on.

I wanted to drive him out of his mind. I wanted to wreck his control and give him all the pleasure.

Bobbing my head, I swallowed again, sucking his dick like my life depended on it.

He was moaning now, incoherent. His hands tightened on my hair and his hips punched forward, pushing his cock down my throat.

My knees were on fire, my jaw ached, and saliva ran down the sides of my mouth. I didn't care what I looked like. The only thing I wanted was for Tate to let go, to unleash in my mouth.

Gripping the base of his dick, I sucked and swallowed faster, my rhythm faltering only when he chanted my name.

My own dick was painfully hard, throbbing, but I ignored it. There would be plenty of time for me to come later.

Sliding my other hand to cup Tate's heavy balls, I gave them a tentative tug and felt him jolt in return.

"That's it, baby, take my whole fucking cock down your throat."

I moaned around his dick.

"Fuck, fuck," Tate whispered. "I'm almost there. Are you gonna swallow my cum?"

I answered his question by sucking harder.

"Oh God, Reed, that's it. Please don't stop."

Then I felt his cock twitch.

Tate shouted my name and my mouth filled with hot, salty cum. I swallowed as much as I could, but there was so much it dripped out of my mouth and down my chin.

Tate's spent dick slipped out, and he slid down the wall until his ass hit the floor with a resounding thud.

I was panting hard, licking the cum off my sore lips until Tate reached out and pulled me in close.

Taking my mouth in another scorching kiss, I straddled his waist and pumped my hips, my own cock begging for friction. For release.

His beard teased my swollen lips and we made out until his cock hardened again, poking me in the stomach.

"Your turnaround time is impressive," I whispered.

"Only with you."

I bit his lower lip and sucked on it.

"I want to fuck you," Tate growled. "Let's go upstairs."

"No," I moaned out. "Here. Now."

I shoved one shaky hand in my jean pocket, pulled out a packet of lube and passed it to Tate.

While Tate slicked up his cock, I shoved my jeans and briefs down my legs and pulled them off.

I straddled his body again and Tate grabbed my ass cheek with one hand, tapping my hole with the other. When his long, slick finger pushed inside me, I gasped, the pain and pleasure heady. Pushing my ass back, I welcomed the fullness, the burn.

Then Tate slid a second finger inside me, slower this time, and I all but growled.

"That's enough prep," I bit out, too far gone, primed to fuck. "Shove that gorgeous cock in my ass already."

"So fucking bossy," Tate teased.

He pulled his fingers out, and when I felt the head of his dick touch my hole, I moaned loudly, the wanting so fierce I was shaking. I leaned back, taking him in, relishing the intensity and pleasure of penetration.

"Easy," Tate whispered and gripped my hips.

"I know what I want," I bit out and sat down in his lap, until he was all the way in.

I leaned back, one hand on the floor between his legs, and pumped my hips, rocking back and forth. Riding him hard and fast. At this angle, his cockhead hit my prostate with every thrust.

"Oh God, that's it love. Right fucking there," I groaned.

Tate let me set the pace, sliding his slick hand around my dick and stroking me off while I rode him fast and furious. I didn't know what I wanted more of, his hand on my cock or his dick in my ass. It was a painfully sweet tie.

"Love you," Tate admitted, his eyes locked on mine as he rocked his hips, as desperate as I was to get as close as possible.

"Love you more."

I swiveled my hips, reaching, thrusting, riding him so hard I wasn't sure I ever wanted to be separated.

"Fuck," I moaned out, the pleasure overwhelming. "I'm almost there."

Tate's hand shuttled up and down my dick, faster and faster, while he fucked into me without pause.

"Come for me," Tate urged. "Come all over me."

"Yes!" I shouted as my climax hit.

My dick jerked, and ropes of cum unleashed all over Tate's hand, his abs.

My thighs quaked as the pleasure rolled through me, one wave after another, until I was so lightheaded, I was sure I was going to pass out.

And then Tate's cock jerked in my ass, flooding it with cum. Nothing was more satisfying than knowing a part of Tate was inside of me.

We were a beautiful mess, covered in cum and sweat.

I looped my arms around his neck and leaned forward to kiss his jaw. "God, that was… that was… shit, I can't talk."

Tate chuckled, rubbing his beard against my skin.

"And at least this time, we just got cum on the hardwood."

"Never mind that," Tate panted. "I think we broke the floorboards that I'm sitting on."

He shifted and I heard a loud creak.

"You break it, you buy it," I laughed out loud.

"In that case, welcome home."

CHAPTER 31

TATE

BACK TO LA

The rest of our time in the UK went off without a hitch.

My favorite part came at the end of every day, when Reed and I went home, together.

It was simple, but there it was.

Sharing meals, waking up in the same bed, making love every spare moment we had. It was everything I didn't know I needed and more than I ever dreamed possible.

I had a boyfriend, and he was something else.

And every day, I fell a little harder, deeper.

Do best friends make the best lovers?

Fuck, yes.

And being out wasn't like I'd imagined. I kept waiting for something dramatic to happen, but it didn't. Not that it would stay that way forever. I wasn't naïve. But I felt more secure in my ability to handle whatever would come my way.

Thankfully, my urge to get high had subsided.

Would there ever come a time when I didn't want a hit? I hoped so, but I was a realist. I knew the nature of addiction. It feeds off trauma, and because of that, I'd always be susceptible.

I was more concerned about it now, being back in LA.

Under the glare of the spotlight again.

Being in the UK was different. We weren't on showcase there.

And being active in LA meant parties and such, and the temptation was always there.

For both me and Reed.

"Are we dropping Reed off first and then you or the other way around?" Korry asked, interrupting my musings.

I was grateful to have Korry on contract. He'd gotten us through LAX faster than usual, blocking aggressive paps along the way.

I was missing England already.

"Um, Reed's place. If that's okay with you?" I glanced at him.

I didn't have any of my stuff at Reed's anymore. Except Cary, since he and Grant were being taken care of by Reed's housekeeper.

The truth was, I wanted to go back to Reed's and stay there. Forever.

Would he want me to live with him now that we were together, or would he prefer going back to our separate spaces?

"I think it's only right that you to stay," Reed gazed at me. "Think about Cary and Grant."

Reed was worried about our cats?

Then I noticed the glint in his eye, which told me I was being an idiot.

Jet lag will do that to you.

"Oh yes, Cary and Grant. It wouldn't be right to separate them," I whispered back. "They love each other too much."

"That's right," Reed leaned in close, smiling at me. "Now that they're living together, they're happier than ever."

"They are," I leaned over and kissed him.

"Please, you two, you're making the single guy feel like shite," Korry quipped from the front seat.

I continued kissing Reed and offered Korry a response via my favorite finger.

"This better be a short gig," the bodyguard grumbled.

Reed kissed me one last time and leaned back. "I'm sorry, Kor. But Tate is irresistible. I can't help it."

Korry groaned. "God, please tell me the guest room I'm staying in is far, far away from yours."

"On the other side of the house," I offered.

"Speaking of which, this neighborhood is gorgeous," Korry stated as he drove up to Reed's security gate. "And all the sunshine. Feck, between this and my upcoming trip to Florida, I don't know how I'm gonna go back to living in Ireland."

"Trust me, after a few weeks in LA, you'll be ready to go back to the dampness and the clouds. The sun is the only good thing about living here. Everything else is so goddamn fake."

Reed coughed.

"With a few notable exceptions," I added.

"You're sleeping in the pool house tonight," Reed muttered.

"Hey, I said there were exceptions. And you're it."

Reed chuckled. "You're so fucking romantic."

Despite my tired brain, the sarcasm wasn't lost.

What can I say? Reed knew I was a brooding asshole at the best of times, and he still loved me.

We waved hello to the security guy, Henry, and were motioned to go on through.

Once we'd parked, Korry helped us get all our luggage inside.

Cary and Grant greeted us as we entered the house, mewling their disapproval of us being gone for so long.

Both cats looked as healthy as we left them.

"My babies," Reed cooed. "Aw, you missed us."

Of course, they ran to Reed first, rubbing against his legs and purring so loudly I could feel the vibration.

"What about me?" I mumbled and crouched down.

I reached out to give Cary a scratch on the head and was greeted with a hiss that had me standing back up again. Grant's flat glare told me he was about to do the same.

"Korry, this is my ungrateful cat, Cary. And of course, Reed's cat, Grant," I sighed. "He doesn't like me either."

Korry tempted fate and crouched down, reaching his hand out.

"I wouldn't do that if I were you, they don't like—"

My sentence was cut short by my cat traipsing over and flopping down in front of Korry, showing off his furry belly. Korry ran his hand along the cat and the purring got louder.

"—strangers," I finished. "What the hell is this? I'm the one who pays for your special food, and the cat sitter, and I get nothing?"

Korry laughed out loud, and Reed shook his head.

"Come on, Tay, let's give Korry the tour first," Reed implored. "You can lecture the kids later."

Korry snorted and picked up both cats.

Just like that.

I glared at all three of them. Not that it had any effect.

We stepped into the sunny living room, and I let out a huge sigh. It was good to be home.

"Help yourself to whatever we have in the fridge and cupboard. If you have special requests, let us know. We get a food delivery every Tuesday," Reed remarked. "Outdoor pool and hot tub. Tate does laps in the morning but other than that, it's all yours. Laundry is just off the pantry. Your room is to the left of that. The cats usually sleep in their beds, but they might wander into your room. If you don't want them in there, best to keep the door shut."

"I don't mind at all," Korry stated as he walked around, both cats still in tow, clinging to his biceps.

Show off.

"In terms of our schedule," I added. "Reed and I have a press party tomorrow night, and three interviews the following day."

"Cool. I'm going to unpack and take a quick nap," Korry replied and set the beasts down on the sofa. "Yell if you need me."

He wandered off, Cary and Grant following.

"Can you believe that?" I asked Reed.

"That our cats just fell in love with Korry? Absolutely. I mean, come on, look at him."

I pulled Reed into my arms and kissed away his smirk.

"You like playing with fire, huh?"

"I like playing with your dick, is that close enough?" he quipped.

"Show me," I chuckled and punched my hips forward, making my point.

"We should do like Korry and get unpacked before anything else."

Reed slid his hands down around to cup my ass, contradicting his words.

"Dirty laundry can wait," I whispered hoarsely. "Dirty fucking on the other hand—"

Our luggage went unpacked for two days.

Reed

The next night

Tate and I were dressed up in our finest suits, waiting for Henn to pick us up for tonight's national press event.

The who's who of Hollywood would be in attendance.

Our first public outing as a couple.

Strangely enough, I was more nervous than Tate. At least, it appeared that way.

He was dressed before me and sitting patiently in the living room while I paced in front of the window, glued to my phone.

"Reed, I love you, but you're acting like Cary when he got into the cupboard and ate that entire box of cookies. You need to relax. She'll be here shortly."

I was a pro at these events, and why was I the only one panicking?

"Are you sure you're ready for this?" I asked, pivoting to face him.

Instead of replying, Tate stood up, buttoned his navy suit jacket, and walked towards me.

He took my goddamn breath away. Every fucking time.

The effect this man had on me was insane. We met ten years ago but it felt like ten seconds.

"What's really going on?" Tate asked as he took my phone, threw it on the sofa, and turned back to me. "I've already told you a dozen or more times that I'm fine."

"What if it's too much? What if the press hates us? I don't want you to have regrets."

Tate shook his head and leaned forward to kiss me.

He knew how to distract me, but he couldn't kiss me forever.

Could he?

"Reed, baby, the only regret I have is not telling you sooner about my feelings. That's it," he punctuated his words with another kiss. Some of my nerves calmed, but not all of them. "And the press doesn't hate us. You just watch, they're gonna be eating out of the palms of our hands. Hell, they're already eager for every detail about our relationship."

"And what are we going to tell them?"

"I think the love bites speak for themselves," Tate teased.

"I'm serious."

"So am I."

I shook my head. "Well?"

"We tell them the truth. You're mine, hands off. Simple as that."

I snorted at his response. "You know, you're a lot better at this boyfriend stuff than you give yourself credit for. Are you sure this is your first time?"

"Damn right. You popped my relationship cherry."

I leaned up to kiss him again, but the doorbell rang and both of our phones chimed at the same time.

"That's our ride," Tate offered and squeezed my hand before letting go.

He reached for my phone, passed it back to me, and checked his own.

Korry walked into the room, dressed in a grey check suit, complete with a vest. It fit him perfectly, his massive arms and shoulders barely restrained by the expensive looking fabric.

"Looking sharp," I commented.

"Thanks. I got it before we left the UK, but I was concerned about the fit. Does it look too tight?" he asked.

"Yes," Tate replied at the same time I said, "No."

Korry chuckled and pulled a pair of sunglasses out of his pocket. "Are we ready?"

I nodded and turned to Tate. "Last chance to back out?"

"No chance. You're stuck with me."

CHAPTER 32

REED

We opened the front door to find Henn and Charlene waiting for us on the other side.

Holding hands.

"Wait, what's going on here?" I asked, looking at them.

"If you don't know, Reed, then I have to wonder about your ability to read cues," Charlene replied with her typical snark.

Henn cleared her throat. "What my girlfriend is trying to say, is that we're dating. Surprise!"

"For real?" Tate asked, his eyes wide.

"Yes, for real," Charlene snapped. "I may be sixty, but I still have a social life. A very active one."

"That's scary AF," Tate muttered under his breath.

Charlene used her free hand to gesture at Tate and let him know exactly what she thought of his comment.

"Well, congratulations!" I exclaimed. "When did this happen?"

"A few months ago. We didn't want to say anything until we decided to be exclusive," Henn replied, her face flushed.

She looked at Charlene and I was shocked to see Charlene smiling in return.

"Congrats," Tate repeated. "I've never seen Charlene look happy before. It must be love."

"It is. And we thought you guys could use the added support tonight. For you, and for us," Charlene paused and gifted us with her rare smile. "I've been out for years but this is new for Henn."

I was so moved by their gesture of support. Tate too, judging by the way he swallowed hard.

I squeezed his hand and he glanced at me, his eyes filled with warmth.

Korry stepped up beside me and his sudden appearance jolted me out of my musings.

"Oh, sorry, this is our bodyguard, Korry Doyle," I offered. "Korry, our agent Henn, and her girlfriend, our favorite casting director, Charlene."

After the introductions were done, we hopped in the limo and headed to the event.

The closer we got to the venue, the bigger the traffic jam.

When we finally arrived, there was the usual wall of photographers and fans lining the street.

No matter how many junkets, premiers, and award shows I'd been to, the first flash was always jarring.

And you think one is bad? Try fifty or more going off at the same time. Even for experienced actors, it took a lot of practice not to flinch.

Tate and I stepped out of the limo and waved to the crowd. Cheers and hollers rang out.

So far, so good.

When Tate took my hand, the volume of shouts and call outs increased exponentially.

Then he stepped closer, wrapping his right arm around my waist, and pulling me in tight. His claiming gesture made my heart pound so fast and wild that I thought for sure I might faint.

Swelling with pride, I wrapped my arm around him in turn.

No space in between us.

With one embrace, and without saying a word, Tate and I said it all.

More flashes, more shouts, more smiles. I turned my head to face him, our noses almost touching.

There was no mistaking how we looked at each other.

Our love was there for everyone to see.

It was surreal but so fucking right.

And for once, I was going to track down every single photo from tonight's event so we would have a memory of this moment.

"You and me, baby," Tate reminded me with an intimate smile.

"I'm so fucking proud of you. I love you."

"I love you more."

Korry, Henn, and Charlene stepped up beside us and ushered us down the line for more photos and the start of interviews.

The first reporter didn't waste any time.

"Tate, how are you dealing with being outed by the tabloids?"

Tate leaned into the mic. "While I think it's reprehensible that anyone should be pressured into revealing their sexuality, I'm not going to deny the truth any longer. Reed is mine."

The reporter nodded. "How long have the two of you been together?"

"Not long enough," Tate replied and guided me on, ignoring most of the shout outs.

"One more and let's head inside," Henn said to us.

We bypassed several eager journalists and landed on one at the end of the row, just before the entrance.

I glanced at Henn, and she nodded, waving the reporter to step forward.

"You guys are being called the hottest Hollywood power couple on the red carpet tonight. How do you feel about that?"

I bit my lip and then glanced at Tate. "Being here with Tate feels pretty damn amazing. But I don't know that I'd use the term 'power couple'. We're two people in love."

"Two of the biggest stars in this town. That's pretty powerful."

"No, powerful is how this man makes me feel," Tate replied and squeezed my waist. "And despite our celebrity, we're like any other couple. Making great movies together is just a bonus."

"What do you say to the reports that claim your relationship is purely a PR stunt for your next release?"

Tate raised his eyebrows and leaned into the mic. "I'd say they haven't been paying attention for the past decade."

And with that, Henn motioned for us to keep moving.

We waved to the crowd one last time.

"How about we *really* get the press going?" Tate asked me just before we stepped inside.

I looked at him, puzzled, until he pulled me in tight and laid a kiss on my lips.

Flashes popped like fireworks all around us.

But the only thing I saw was Tate.

Tate

Stepping into the Hollywood spotlight as a gay man was not at all what I imagined it would be.

When I looked around the venue, I recognized several openly queer actors and executives, some alone, some with their partners.

Back when I was just starting to make a name for myself, queer actors rarely commented on their personal life or showed up to events with their significant other. It was the big secret that no one talked about, but everyone knew.

But times had changed.

I'd changed too. It had taken a long time, but I had finally arrived.

And I was right. The press were eager for all the news about my relationship with Reed.

Now that walking the carpet was done, I could relax. Cocktail hour was well underway, and the room was filling up.

"I'm going to grab some water, you want anything?" I asked our entourage.

"Sparkling water and lime for me, please," Reed replied.

"I'm fine," Charlene said. "Henn?"

"A glass of champagne, thanks."

I nodded and stepped over to the makeshift bar, leaving Reed to walk the room.

Once I placed the order, I leaned against the bar top, and perused the glamorous scene.

I spotted so many familiar faces, many of whom came up to say hi and to offer their support.

A few passed by without returning my acknowledgement, including my former mentor, Neal Lockwin. Not to be ignored, I offered a wave and a wink, which got me his trademark sneer.

It made me smile that much harder.

Cranky fucker.

I didn't give a shit anyway. The old guard in this town was going to be replaced with new blood. It was happening already with progressive artists like Jared and other young filmmakers.

One of whom, Leah Garwick, an up-and-coming director, was talking to my boyfriend. Female directors in this town were still a rarity, which didn't say much about our business either.

I was pretty sure Leah was busy convincing Reed to star in her next film.

"Hey, stranger."

I whirled around to find Dylan standing behind me. In a dark green suit and brown cowboy boots, I almost didn't recognize him without his hat.

"Hey! I didn't know you'd be here tonight," I leaned forward and gave Dylan a hug. "Where's Max?"

"I decided to come at the last minute. And Max had to stay home, but he sends his best."

"It's so good to see a friendly face."

"You and me both. I spotted Neal Lockwin passing by. Holy shit, if looks could kill, eh?" Dylan whistled, running one hand through his undercut. "What a dickbag. You know, he once told me that I was a better actor when I was drunk."

"He's a grade-A asshole," I replied and then shook my head. "But enough about him. What do you think of the event so far? Did you walk the carpet?"

"I did, but far behind you guys," Dylan gave me a knowing smile and a dimple popped out. "You and Reed are the talk of the party. And both of you look really fucking happy."

"We are," I said, my voice hoarse. "I wake up every day and wonder what the fuck he's doing with me."

Suddenly, I was jostled and nearly lost my balance. Thank fuck for Dylan grabbing hold of my arm to steady me. And the fact that I didn't have any glasses yet in hand.

"I'm so sorry, are you okay?"

I followed the raspy southern voice to find a young man, in his early twenties, staring at me. With sleek copper hair and big blue eyes, he looked like he walked the fashion runways, not just the carpeted ones.

"I'm fine. No harm done," I replied to the stranger and offered my hand. "Tate Aduma, nice to meet you."

"Oh my God, it's an honor to meet you, sir. I just loved

your performance in *Jagged Edge*," the man replied, his cheeks flushed. "I'm Colm McDade. I'm a guest of Kendrick Sloan."

"Cool. I haven't seen Kendrick yet. Where is he?"

"He's doing interviews."

"Are you in the biz?"

"I'm an actor. And a model. Well, I model to pay for my acting classes, but my first love is acting—" he paused and ran a nervous hand through his hair. "Shit, I'm rambling. Sorry."

"It's okay," I reassured him. "Are you new to LA?"

Colm nodded.

"Have you met Dylan Aylmer?"

"Holy shit! Pardon me, I mean, wow," Colm reached out his hand to Dylan in slow motion, like he couldn't quite believe this was all real. "Nice to meet you. I'm a huge fan."

"Thank you. How long you been in town?" Dylan asked.

"Two months. It's been interesting. Not sure I've found my footing yet."

I knew that well. "Any roles yet?"

"One, but we haven't started production yet. And I've had a ton of auditions. My rep introduced me to Kendrick, who told me this might be a good event for networking. But so far, I've been too nervous to talk to anyone. And I'm starting to wonder what the hell I'm doing here."

Colm reminded me of myself ten years ago.

Right down to the southern accent. Except, I had all but banished mine by the time I arrived in LA.

"Do you have a business card?" I asked. "Or the name of your rep?"

Colm checked his pockets, searching frantically.

"Yes!" he pulled out a card and passed it over. "My rep's contact details are on that."

"I can't promise anything, but I know one particular casting agent that's always looking for new talent. She's here tonight. I'd be happy to introduce you."

"Oh my God! That would be amazing," Colm gushed and gripped my forearm. "Wait until I tell my boyfriend."

"Kendrick?"

"No. Kendrick is purely business," Colm explained. "My boyfriend, Ace, lives in Nashville. He works as a sound engineer for a rock band."

"That sounds fucking cool."

"It is. But unfortunately, long distance isn't," Colm sighed. "He's on the road a lot. I'm from Louisiana, so it was easier to visit him back in the winter. Now that I've moved here, though, we're doing the bi-coastal, sometimes international, visits."

"I can't even imagine."

If Reed moved, I'd follow him. No question.

But that was me. I was possessive as hell when it came to him. And just thinking about being separated reminded me of the time when we weren't talking. I didn't ever want to be there again.

"You're a lot stronger than I am," I confessed.

"Me too," Dylan added. "I did the east coast, west coast thing for a bit with Max until he moved out here. Longest fucking days of my life."

"Ugh, you guys aren't making me feel any better," Colm confessed. "I mean, sorry, I shouldn't have said that. I'm acting like we're actually friends or something. Shit, that sounded weird... and, I'm just going to go and hide in a corner somewhere."

Colm's face reddened as he started to move away. I gripped his arm.

"Stay. I can't tell you how nice it is to meet someone who isn't kissing our ass or asking us for a selfie. Right, Dylan?"

"Speak for yourself."

CHAPTER 33

REED

I was only partially paying attention to what director Leah Garwick was saying to me.

Which was so fucking rude, I know.

But to be fair, my concentration was already screwed. Walking that red carpet with Tate was something I was never going to forget.

And when I spotted Dylan talking to Tate, I made my excuses to Leah, promising to get in touch about her next project.

But as I made my way through the crowd, I spotted a man, one I didn't recognize, in conversation with my boyfriend. The guy in question looked to be in his twenties, handsome in a classic way, with cut cheekbones and big eyes. His pouty lips were curved in a smile aimed at Tate.

And then it hit me.

Now that Tate was out, he was going to get approached.

A lot.

A sliver of doubt toyed with my heart, telling me that he'd have so many options now. He wasn't hiding anymore. He could have any man he wanted.

Why the fuck would he want to stay with me?

I shook off the feeling but the longer the guy chatted with him, the louder Tate's laugh. And by the time I reached them, my inner caveman was ready to erupt.

Tate wasn't the only one who had a possessive streak.

I looked around and reminded myself about all the press in attendance. I wasn't going to make a scene in front of that kind of audience.

"Hey," I muttered when I walked up to them.

Tate smiled at me. "Hey! Reed, I'd like you to meet Colm McDade, he's a—"

"I'm going to head in and grab my seat," I interrupted and then stormed off.

Tate called my name, but I didn't want to be near him right now. Around anyone. My temper was about to unleash, however unwarranted.

I entered the main salon and located our table near the stage. Once I sat down, I realized that only a handful of other attendees were in the room. It was calm and quiet, unlike my mind and my gut.

Then I noticed the bottle of champagne that sat on each table.

The temptation to numb my insecurities was right there in front of me. My hand itched to grab that bottle.

Take it. Open it.

Enjoy it.

Fuck.

"Reed."

I startled, looking up to find Tate standing beside me, Korry not far behind.

"Why did you run off like that? What's wrong?"

"Nothing," I snapped. "Nothing's wrong."

I didn't want to explain my jealousy. My fear that I wasn't enough for him. I'd never felt vulnerable like this in any previous relationship.

But then, I'd had nothing to lose.

"I'm the rude and surly one, not you. Now tell me what's going on," Tate implored as he took hold of my left hand and sat down beside me. "Are you upset that I kissed you in front of everyone?"

"No," I turned to him. "Never. I just... I don't know if I can say it. It's dumb."

"Doubtful. Now spit it out."

Korry was standing near the stage, not far away, but enough to give us privacy.

"It's just that when I saw you talking to that guy—"

"Colm. He's an actor. Well, a model and an actor."

"Of course, he is."

Tate chuckled. "He's so green. Reminds me of me back in the day. Except, he's way nicer."

"And really fucking gorgeous too," I added, then let out a big sigh. "Watching him talk to you, I realized that you're going to get approached like that all the time now. You can have any man you want. A different one every night. More than that."

Tate shook his head, his expression darkening. "No."

"No?"

"I don't want that. I screwed around plenty in the past. It was all fast, meaningless fucks. But that's all it was, a release," Tate explained. "And during all that time, with all those hookups, there was always one man I couldn't stop thinking about. One guy I wanted to be with. You."

"Tate—"

"Listen to me and listen good: I don't want anyone but you. I don't love anyone but you."

"But now—"

"Then, now, next week, next year, it doesn't fucking matter. Baby, it's always been you."

His words made my pulse quicken and my breath catch. And the way he gazed at me was so telling.

"I got so damn jealous," I admitted. "And then when I sat

down here, I saw that champagne bottle and for a moment… for a moment, I wanted to drown out the doubt in my head."

"But you didn't."

I shook my head. "There's no guarantees."

"All we can do is try our best."

Tate pulled my hands up to his chest.

"Do you feel that?" he asked.

I swallowed hard as the rapid beat of his heart vibrated against my palm, pounding fast and furious, mirroring mine.

I nodded.

"You do that to me. No one else. And I'm going to tell you every goddamn day if I have to, until you believe me."

"I do," I sighed. "And I'm sorry for ruining our night."

"You didn't ruin anything. Fuck's sake, Reed, we're brand new at this. It's only natural that we feel protective of each other. And you wanting me all to yourself is fucking hot."

He leaned forward and took my lips in a heated kiss.

Not a polite one fit for the public, but a deliciously dirty one, tongue and all.

Screw this event, I wanted to head back home.

"Just promise me, if you're upset, you tell me," he whispered against my lips. "We talk about it. No silent treatment."

"That's my line."

"Well, then take your own advice."

I laughed at that. "You just had to ruin a sexy moment, didn't you?"

"Hey, you like my direct manner."

"I do," I admitted. "And how's this for direct: let's check into one of the rooms here in the hotel and fuck until someone complains about the noise."

A throat cleared.

Tate and I turned to find Dylan and Colm standing behind us. And Korry was there too. All three of them looked highly amused. Well, Dylan and Korry did. Colm looked like he was embarrassed more than amused, his cheeks matching his red hair.

"Um, can we sit down and join you or are we about to interrupt a really raunchy version of your red-carpet PDA?" Dylan teased.

"Sit at your own risk," Tate quipped as he gave me one last kiss.

When I looked around, I realized that attendees had begun to filter into the salon, and almost half the room was now filled.

Tate leaned in and whispered in my ear. "We'll stay for a bit. But I'm taking you up on your offer."

I nodded and squeezed his hand.

Colm sat down on Tate's other side. I had an apology to make.

I leaned over and offered my hand to Colm. "Reed Larkin, nice to meet you. I'm sorry I ran off earlier."

"No problem. I was tempted to do the same thing given how nervous I am. This is my first major event. I don't even know if I'll be able to eat."

"You'll be fine," I reassured him. "This is a great event to get your feet wet. It's more about the business side of film-making, the role of the press, than it is about individual achievement. It should be great networking for you."

Dylan sat down beside me, and Korry followed. We got into a conversation about our favorite roles, movies, and people we wanted to work with. Korry chimed in with a funny tale about one of his famous clients, also a fellow actor. Not naming names, of course.

Leah stopped by our table to say hi to everyone and Colm nearly fainted after shaking her hand.

Then Kendrick finally joined us, along with Henn, Char-lene, and two other guests, journalists, who were seated at our table of ten.

Four courses later, we were still laughing and having a

great time. Colm managed to eat everything on his plate, despite all the talk about his nerves. His phone chimed and he proudly showed us all a picture of his boyfriend.

Tate was right. Colm was a down to earth guy, and really fucking smart. He knew what he wanted for his career, and I could tell that his natural charm was going to get him a lot of call backs. Some people had that 'it' factor. They walked into a room, and you immediately wanted to get to know them.

When the awards portion of the evening finally got underway, I realized that Neal Lockwin was sitting at the table beside us.

The dirty looks he sent our way were bad enough, but halfway through the presentations, he leaned over and opened his ugly mouth.

"Why don't you tone it down? Bad enough you're shoving your disgusting relationship in our faces."

Everyone around us went silent. Tate made to stand up.

Korry shook his head at me.

I held his arm. "Don't. That's just what he wants. In full view of the press. We're better than that. Ignore him."

Tate nodded in agreement.

But Kendrick didn't.

"The only thing disgusting here is you, Neal. No one likes you and no one wants to work with you anymore. Why don't you take your small mind and smaller dick and get lost?"

Neal stood up and threw his napkin on the table.

For a moment, I worried he was going to stalk over and confront Kendrick. Korry got up and rounded the table.

A fistfight was the last thing any of us needed. Especially since we had reporters sitting with us, and others that were seated throughout the venue.

Instead, Neal stormed out of the room. No one from his table got up and followed him.

Kendrick smiled at us and raised his glass.

"Now it's a fucking party!"

CHAPTER 34

TATE

Reed had been far too quiet on the ride home.

He'd gotten a phone call near the end of the evening and excused himself from the table. By the time he got back, his face was ashen. I'd asked him what was wrong but the only thing he said was 'later'.

So, I let it go.

Until we got back home.

Korry said goodnight and headed for his bedroom.

My boyfriend took off for the kitchen, Cary and Grant on his heels.

Reed got out a couple of mugs and began to make tea, and I forced down a sudden urge to laugh. We were the antithesis of our younger selves, ready for bed by midnight. Most parties in LA were just getting started.

After asking him twice if he was okay and getting the same 'fine' response, I decided to poke the bear.

"My realtor has received five offers on my house."

Reed nearly dropped the mug in his hand.

"What are you talking about? Since when are you selling your house?"

"Since I'm moving in here with you."

Reed slammed the mug on the counter. "Seriously? You weren't going to ask me? You just announce it like it's no big deal, *hey Reed, I'm moving in.*"

With his hands on his hips, and a flush staining his cheeks, he was riled up. Good. Better that than stony-faced silence.

"We're almost living together as is."

"Yeah, but come on, Tate. Moving in together is a huge thing. How about making it special?"

"We lived together for two years."

"As roommates."

I held out my arms. "I love you and I want to wake up next to you every single day. How much more special can you get? What do you need?"

Reed shook his head.

"You still should have asked me first."

"Reed, do you wanna shack up together?"

"That's a half assed attempt," he snapped.

"You want the full ass? It's right here, baby. It's all yours."

I turned around and bent over to shake my butt.

Reed let out a laugh that was so loud it startled our cats. They ran out of the room and down the hallway, out of sight.

I pivoted and quickly pulled him into my arms, kissing him.

"You're ridiculous," Reed replied, his smile making a comeback. "And I should be so mad at you right now."

"But you're not," I smirked.

He shook his head.

"We've wasted enough time. I want to spend every fucking day with you," I announced.

"I think I'm okay with that," he teased.

"Okay? Just okay?" I whispered and took his lips in a punishing kiss.

"More than."

"Good. Now that we've got that out of the way—"

"Out of the way?" he said and raised one eyebrow.

"You know what I mean," I kissed him again. Harder. "Who called you earlier?"

Reed's smile vanished as quick as it came.

"It was Rissa."

"Is she okay? How's your dad?"

Reed nodded. "They're both fine. It's my mom's case. The court date has been moved up. The trial starts next Thursday. I have to head home tomorrow."

I pulled him in tightly, his body trembling.

"I'll come with you."

Reed shook his head. "No. You have auditions next week and meetings with Henn and Aiden about your corporate partnerships. Plus, selling your house. I'll be fine."

"I'll cancel. Nothing is more important than you."

Reed placed a finger over my lips.

"I appreciate your offer. I'll be okay."

My gut was telling me no. That Reed wasn't prepared for what was about to come next. Reliving the trauma of his mom's death. Facing the man who carelessly took her life.

"If you need me, you call," I added. "And I'm on the first plane out."

Reed nodded.

"I don't want to think about it tonight," he admitted and held me tighter. "Make me forget, if only for a while."

"That I can do."

Taking him by the hand, I led him to our bedroom.

"I wasn't totally joking earlier," I whispered when I shut the door behind us.

"About what?"

"About my ass being all yours." I paused, a sudden lump in my throat. "I've never... I mean... I've always, you know, topped. But I think I want to try. With you."

I was tongue tied like I never was.

Even though bottoming was something I'd been curious about, I never let anyone fuck me. I never trusted any of my hookups in that way.

"Are you sure?"

"Only one way to find out," I quipped, trying to ease my nerves.

"We go slow," Reed assured me, sliding both hands up to cup my neck.

Pulling me in for a kiss that was deep and drugging, his tongue wrapping around mine. It was so hot that I forgot why I was nervous.

"Get undressed and lie down on the bed, ass up," Reed whispered.

A shiver wracked my body. Bossy Reed was sexy as fuck. And the feverish look in his eyes told me he more than liked the idea of claiming my ass.

What started out as slow and sensual turned frantic in a heartbeat as we both raced to get our clothes off as soon as possible.

When I was finally naked, I stepped over to our bed and slid over the cover.

I looked over my shoulder to find Reed standing at the foot of the bed, staring at me.

"Fuck, Tate. I don't think I'll ever get used to the fact that you're in my bed."

"Our bed," I reminded him.

"Yes," Reed whispered and got up on the bed behind me.

He cupped my ass cheeks in his hands and then slowly bent over, his hot breath tickling my crease. Watching the look of hunger on Reed's beautiful face had me squirming, wanting him closer.

The first flick of his tongue against my sensitive skin made me moan loud and proud.

I buried my face in the duvet and panted, while Reed tormented my ass with his tongue. He undid me one teasing lick at a time, from my taint, to my hole, to the divot at the base of my spine, then back again. He didn't miss a fucking thing.

"More," I moaned, tilting my ass back.

When he pushed the tip of his tongue in my hole, fucking me with it, I nearly screamed.

"Oh God, oh shit," I chanted, spreading my legs wider, needing more.

Reed groaned and circled my hole, slower this time. The dirty, delicious pleasure had my aching cock jerking hard.

"Tate. You taste so fucking incredible."

Reed's raspy moan had goosebumps popping up all over my skin.

"Get the lube," I growled, wanting Reed inside me.

Right fucking now.

But I nearly shouted in protest when he pulled away and reached for the nightstand.

I got up on my hands and knees, my arms shaking hard.

And then Reed was back, one warm, slick finger circling my rim.

When he pushed the tip of his finger inside me, I bit down on my lower lip. The pain was intense, overwhelming.

Until he slid his other hand around my dick, jerking me off. The pleasure on my cock more than made up for the burn in my ass.

My arms trembled, then gave out as I rested on my forearms, my head hanging down.

And then his finger was gone.

"What are you—"

"Roll over."

Without pause, I did as I was told.

"Push out when I push in," Reed whispered as he kneeled

between my legs. "It's going to feel so fucking good, I promise."

He pushed his lubed finger back inside me, deeper this time. I was too overwhelmed to speak.

Until he crooked it and hit my prostate. Every part of my body lit up, as bright as the Hollywood sign.

"Holy fucking shit!" I shouted.

Reed chuckled. "Shh. I'm pretty sure Korry can hear you."

"I don't fucking care. Do it again. Holy hell."

"You've never played with your ass?"

I shook my head. "I will now."

Reed added more lube and finger fucked me until I was babbling incoherently. He eased a second finger inside, stretching me, pumping slow and easy. Then a third finger, and shit, that's when I realized that his cock was gonna split me in two.

But the burn was fading, replaced by a pleasure that was heady, exquisite.

And every time he touched my prostate I cried out, begging for more.

"I'm ready. So ready. Fuck me," I pleaded.

Reed's fingers were suddenly gone, and I was empty. Until he pushed his fat cockhead to my hole.

"Nice and slow, love," Reed murmured as he entered me.

His cock felt ten times bigger than his fingers and I had a moment of doubt that this was going to work out.

"You okay?" he asked, pausing.

A dappled flush covered his face, his neck, his chest.

"Yes. Don't stop."

Reed slowly pushed all the way in.

Knowing that he was inside me, nothing between us, and that he was going to come in my ass, had my flagging dick turning rock hard again.

He pumped his hips slowly, rocking forward, and his cock hit my pleasure point again.

"Goddamn it, right there," I moaned out. "I'm ready, Reed. Fuck me."

The pain was gone and now all I felt was pleasure.

"Are you sure?"

"Yes, I'm sure!"

His answering chuckle was followed by the swift punch of his hips.

With one hand on my hip and the other gripping my dick, Reed fucked into me into short, hard strokes that had my eyes rolling back in my head.

"Oh God, that's unreal," I moaned. "More. Harder."

Between the fullness in my ass and the friction on my dick, I was chasing *all* the pleasure.

I clutched the duvet in my hands as he nailed my prostate over and over.

"Tate," Reed groaned as he rutted into me, pummeling my ass.

My climax was building with every stroke, my balls drawing up tight. So close. I just knew that when I reached my climax, it was going to wreck me.

"Right there, baby," I pleaded. "I'm going to come."

My body locked up tight as I went over the edge. I screamed Reed's name as my orgasm imploded.

"Tate," Reed moaned as his cock jerked and my ass was flooded with his cum.

Jesus fucking Christ. I didn't know if I'd be able to speak, never mind move, after being fucked like that.

Being owned by Reed was the sexiest thing ever.

He collapsed on top of me, both of us sweaty, my cum trapped between us. We'd be stuck together in no time. I didn't care, I was too blissed out to move an inch.

"Are you okay?" Reed finally asked me, kissing my ear. "Was I too rough?"

I turned my head and met his eyes. "Are you kidding me? Every time gets better and better."

"You're going to give me a big head."

"I'd make a joke about head, but you fucked out my ability to sarcasm."

"That good, huh?"

I gave him a kiss in response.

A long one.

CHAPTER 35

REED

NEW YORK

The happiest week of my life was followed by one of the worst.

And leaving Tate at home was harder than I imagined.

But necessary.

My family needed me.

And Tate and I would have to get used to time apart. Our careers meant weeks, often months in different locations. Long-distance would become our norm.

But the thought of being separated from him for any length of time made me restless.

Still, nothing was going to stop me from attending this trial. My mother deserved justice, and I needed the man who took her life to see—and hear—exactly what he'd done to our family.

The only time I'd ever been in a courtroom was for my job, back when Tate and I played opposing attorneys.

This trial, unfortunately, was far too real.

Jeremy Saks, the man who killed my mother, stood up beside his lawyer, facing the judge.

He didn't once turn around to face us.

I'd done my research on him. He was a married, thirty-five-year-old father of three with a corporate finance job, and a house in the suburbs. On the outside, he appeared to be an upstanding member of the community.

Except for the fact that he got into his car when he was dead drunk at six AM one Tuesday morning.

The court clerk stood up and read out the charges. "People of the State of New York vs Jeremy Saks. The charges are as follows: vehicular manslaughter in the first degree."

"How does the defendant plead?" the judge asked.

Saks leaned into his lawyer then cleared his throat. "Not guilty, your honor."

Not guilty?

What a fucking load of shit. I wanted to stalk up to Saks and punch him in the goddamn face. Bad enough my mother was dead, but he was denying all responsibility?

Reigning in my impulse to get up and get in Saks' face, I gripped my sister's hand and I glanced at my dad. He was staring at a picture of my mother that he held in his hands, unable to look up.

I placed my other arm around his shoulder and held on tight. I didn't know if it would be of any comfort, but it was all I could do.

Then the first witnesses were called.

The emergency responders, the police officers on scene, the pathologist, the forensic techs...

My brain was about to explode.

And my heart ached with a pain that was as sharp as the day I found out my mom was dead.

Listening to the details of her death, her injuries, it was heartbreaking.

After three hours of testimony, the judge called a recess. Court would resume tomorrow.

Saks finally turned around and startled when he spotted us.

My stomach heaved, bile filling my mouth, but I held on. And my eyes didn't waver. He might be trying to fool the jury, but he sure as shit wasn't fooling me.

He looked gaunt, sickly and exhausted, but I didn't want to feel any sympathy for him.

Then, just as quick as he'd turned around, he was gone.

I'd noticed several reporters at the back of the gallery, but they were filing out of the room.

"Let's get out of here," Rissa sighed. "Darren's got dinner ready."

"Right."

Not that I felt like eating. Or talking.

I didn't get up to leave. I just sat there, staring at the empty courtroom.

"Reed?" Dad called out.

I looked up to find him and my sister standing, their coats already on.

"Sorry," I replied, shaking off my shock. "I'm lost in my head."

And that was a scary fucking place to be right now.

———

It went on like that for two days.

Witnesses, cross-examinations, evidence, arguments.

I could barely sleep or eat. Or speak. My dad and sister were the same.

We sat on those hard wooden benches in the courtroom for hours and listened to every minute of the proceedings. By the time we reached the end of the second day, everyone's nerves were frazzled.

The press had caught on that I was in town and the few local reporters were now outnumbered by the more aggressive media from the city.

It was bad enough that my family and I had to live through this. Having cameras shoved in our faces didn't help.

Tate had texted and called, usually first thing in the morning and last thing at night. Hearing his voice gave me the strength to walk back into that courtroom.

As much as I wanted Tate here with me, I realized that it was better that he wasn't. My celebrity was drawing enough media attention as it was, but the two of us here would have created a frenzy.

After the weekend break, we were back on Monday for the third day of the trial.

The day Saks was taking the stand.

And that's when my sanity threatened to derail.

The prosecutor had warned us that it wasn't common for the accused to take the stand. Which gave me a bad feeling. If his defense lawyers were confident enough to put him up there, they had to reason to think he might sway the jury.

"Mr. Saks, tell us what you remember about the morning of April 19?"

"Not much, unfortunately. I'd been self-medicating with alcohol, prescription pain killers, and illegal drugs since the night before."

"And why is that?"

Saks sighed and licked his lips. "I injured my head just over a year ago in a boating accident. And I became severely depressed as a result."

"So, you do admit that you were intoxicated that morning?"

"Yes."

I was confused. He was admitting to being drunk and high but he was pleading not guilty?

"And you got into your car that morning and drove into town?"

"I left the bar at two AM and checked into a nearby motel first."

"And proceeded to take drugs? Prescription painkillers and ecstasy, to be specific."

"Yes."

The prosecutor leaned on the divider, facing Saks.

"Did you sleep?"

"For a few hours. Then I woke up and checked out."

"And then you got in your car, exited onto route 6, and slammed into the vehicle driven by Rosalin Larkin."

"I don't remember anything after leaving the motel. I'm sorry."

"But you do admit to getting in your car while intoxicated?"

"Yes."

"No further questions, your honor."

Saks' defense lawyer stood up.

"What was your mental state leading up to this event?"

"The worst it's ever been. I was seeing a therapist for depression and suicidal thoughts. I swear, I didn't intentionally kill Mrs. Larkin. It was a terrible, horrible accident. One I wish more than anything that I could go back and change. But mentally, I was in a really bad place. So depressed that I wanted to take my own life."

Instead, he took someone else's. The sad irony wasn't lost on me.

"Are you stating that what happened that morning, was in fact, a suicide attempt gone horribly wrong?"

Saks nodded.

"I didn't mean to hurt anyone else. In my fucked-up brain, I got the idea to get in the car and drive to the abandoned salt quarry at the edge of town. There's a high cliff there. I thought it would be the perfect place for me to end my life.

But I guess I was still so high that I lost control of the vehicle before I could even make it to the other side of town."

I glanced at the jury, but their expressions were unreadable. If I was an outsider, I could empathize with Saks' struggle with mental illness, but given my situation, emotionally, I was unforgiving when it came to his actions. His sickness didn't absolve the fact that he got in that car and weaponized it.

"No further questions for my client, your honor."

Saks was excused and he walked back to sit beside his attorney.

The judge called a brief recess, and it was then that I noticed Saks leaning over to talk to his lawyer.

A few minutes later, the head of the defense team walked over to the lead prosecutor, Jed Maller.

We were too far away to hear what was being said.

Until Jed headed in our direction.

"A deal's been suggested, and I feel in it's in our best interest to take it. Saks pleads guilty to a lesser charge, second-degree. It means a one-to-four-year prison sentence. But he's eligible for parole after six months."

That's it? All this so Saks could get six months in jail for taking my mom's life?

"That's a shit deal, Jed," I spat out. "What kind of justice is that?"

"I know, Reed, and I'm sorry. We can take our chance with the jury, but the state of his mental health at the time might persuade them to look at the lesser charge."

"Take the deal," my father stated.

"Dad?" I turned to him, shocked.

"It's fine, Jed. Take the deal," he repeated, then turned to me. "No amount of jail time is bringing your mother back. I just want this over with so we can heal as best we can."

Rissa grabbed hold of my arm. "Dad's right. It's not fair, but we knew this going in."

I tamped down my anger and nodded in resignation.

"I'll get it done," Jed replied.

And just like that, it was over. Saks pleaded guilty to the lesser charge and was sentenced to one year in jail.

After the sentencing, we were asked to give our victim impact statements.

I walked up, hand in hand with my dad and sister, and each of us spoke in our turn.

I was the last one up, trying to keep hold of my emotions so I could get through the entire statement.

"Nothing in my life prepared me for losing my mother. She was the center of love in our family and will remain always," I paused, swallowing past the enormous lump in my throat. "The manner of her death leaves a pain that will scar us forever. I won't forgive Jeremy Saks for getting in his car that day and taking my mother from us. But I also won't let her death be the marker of her life. My mother was more than a victim. She was a loving wife, mother, sister, daughter, and aunt. She filled a room with laughter and joy. My mom didn't just give love, she was love. And that's what I will carry with me."

The tears slipped out and I brushed them away as we made our way back to the gallery. Friends and extended family gathered around us, and we quickly headed for the exit.

Reporters jammed mics in our faces as we left the building, yelling out for comments.

For once, I had nothing to say to them.

As we headed for the parking lot, my phone buzzed.

When I saw Tate's name flash, I was finally able to breathe.

CHAPTER 36

REED

I spent the next three days helping my dad go through my mom's stuff, deciding what to keep and what to let go of.

It was something we'd meant to do sooner but didn't have the heart to tackle.

But it was time.

The process was painful but necessary. And it wasn't all sad, there were happy memories too.

We did our share of laughing and crying as we sorted through pictures, letters, and cards that she'd kept stored away in their closet.

The hardest part was going through her clothes. Her rose perfume lingered over everything, like she was right there in the room with us.

I half expected her to walk through the door, singing a happy tune.

By the time Thursday rolled around, I was more than ready to go home to Tate.

I'd held up pretty good. Better than I thought.

Until I hit the airport.

Or, rather, an airport bar.

After I checked in, I wandered through the terminal,

needing the walk. I left my sunglasses and baseball cap on, and thankfully, that did the trick. No one recognized me.

I made my way over to the first-class lounge, which was one of the nicest I'd ever been in. But the place was surprisingly small and packed with too many people. I was craving a quiet spot all to myself. Not easy to find in a busy airport in New York.

So, I headed back out into the terminal, passing shops along the way.

And then I spotted a restaurant that looked like a good option.

The tables were filled but the bar only had one patron. There was plenty of room for me to sit undisturbed.

Not that I had a habit of sitting at bars anymore.

Fuck it. I can do this.

I wandered in and took the last stool at the end of the bar.

The briny smell of beer hit me first. Or maybe that was wishful thinking on my part.

Everything was fine. Until it wasn't.

Sitting there, alone, raw from a week of emotional hell, I wanted to numb myself.

And all the reasons why I shouldn't have a drink faded into the background like white noise around me.

I could order a double gin and tonic and let it burn away the ache that had lodged in my chest for days.

It's one drink. It'll help me relax.

I watched the bartender, a middle-aged guy, as he mixed drinks and poured pints. It was all so normal, so easy.

Another person sidled up to the bar, sat down, and ordered a beer.

There was no problem. I could do the same.

It's just one drink.

"What can I get you?" the bartender asked, a smile on his weathered face. "All of our wines are half-price during happy hour."

Happy sounded perfect right about now.

My mind was kinetic, haunted by the memories of this past week and unwelcome flashbacks of my mom's funeral. The aftermath. The endless cycle of booze and hangovers, the headaches, the everything-ached.

"I'm not sure yet."

He nodded. "Take your time."

My hand was shaking as I reached in my pocket for my phone.

I tapped the first name in my contact list and waited.

"Hey baby, are you still at your dad's or are you at the airport?" Tate answered.

"I'm at the airport," I whispered. "My flight's leaving on time for a change."

"That's good. I can't wait to see you."

"I'm sitting at a bar," I blurted out.

I heard Tate's sharp inhale on the other end of the line.

"Have you been—"

"I want to. I mean, it would be one drink. I could do that, right?"

Silence followed my words. Dead air hit my lungs. I couldn't breathe.

This wasn't my proudest moment and I hated myself for it.

"I can't speak for you," Tate finally responded. "You have to make that decision for yourself."

"What the hell kind of an answer is that?" I snapped.

"I can't control what you do, Ree. And it works both ways. Sobriety is a choice. One we make every fucking day."

I let out a growl of frustration and the guy seated in the middle turned his stool around.

"Tell me no. Tell me I'm being stupid. Tell me something!"

"Look, I don't want you to have that drink because I know what happens next. But I'm not going to tell you no and you're far from stupid," Tate paused. "I know the answer to this but I'm going to ask anyway. What do you think is gonna happen if you have one drink? Will it be enough, or will you want more?"

It always took a couple of drinks for me to feel the effect.

One was never, ever enough. It was always that way with me.

All or nothing.

"One is never enough. I want to fucking drown out this past week."

"That's understandable. But is the booze going to make you feel better about what happened?"

"I… in the here and now, yes," I confessed. "Later? Tomorrow? No. I always feel worse."

"So, what do you want to do?"

My brain finally kicked online.

"I want to go find another place to wait until my flight is called."

I got up, grabbed my carry on, and walked out of the restaurant.

"Stay on the phone with me?" I asked.

"For as long as you need."

I made my way through the terminal, searching for a coffee shop.

"Just when I think I've got it under control, it fucks with me again," I said as I walked past several souvenir shops.

"I know, baby, believe me. I know."

"I should've called my sponsor first but I… I had to hear your voice."

"Even if you don't like what I have to say?"

"You don't bullshit. That's one of things I love about you," I replied, my stomach finally unclenching. "And you were right. It is my choice. I just… I don't want to make the wrong one. I don't want to let you down."

"You could never."

"Even if I slipped?"

"I accept that it might happen. For you, for me. It wouldn't change how I feel. I'm not going anywhere."

"I'm stuck with you?" I teased.

"For-fucking-ever."

Tate

I hung up the phone, my hands clammy, cold.

I was shivering.

Reed's admission, and the fact that he was so far away, had all my fears churning overtime.

There was nothing I could do. Except listen to him.

And listening to him, I was scared. Worried that all the hard work he'd done to stay sober was going to unravel.

The only bit of positive news was that his mom's case was over. Reed was upset, but at least he and his family could start to slowly heal.

"Tate? You all right, boyo?" Korry called out.

I looked up and spotted him standing in the hallway near the kitchen, staring at me.

I nodded. "I'm fine. Just worried about Reed."

Korry walked into the living room and sat down beside me on the sectional.

"I can't even imagine what he's going through right now, losing his Ma like that and then having to relive it all."

I nodded.

"But he's got you and his family and friends. He'll be okay."

I sighed. "I'm not always sure that I'm good for him in these kinds of circumstances."

"What do you mean?"

"I've got a lot of baggage. I mean, a lot. Growing up, I had no role models for good relationships. And I run my mouth. Also, a lot. We're both still figuring things out as we go along."

Korry leaned forward. "I've been around you guys for a while now. You two are just like my brother and his boyfriend. So in love it's nauseating. No offense."

I smiled despite my mood. "None taken."

"Are relationships easy? Feck no. Is Reed worth it? Judging by the way you look at him, I'd say yes."

"You ever been in love?" I asked.

Korry rubbed his beard. "I thought so, once. When I was twenty-one. But the guy I fell for was straight, so I was stuck in the friend zone."

"Did you ever tell him?"

"No. But years later I realized that it wasn't love, it was limerence."

"I have no idea what that means."

Korry cocked his head. "Like when you're infatuated or obsessed with someone, but they don't reciprocate."

"Ah, okay."

"I was fixated on the idea of being in a relationship, and of course, hoping that this guy would somehow miraculously fall for me. But it was never gonna happen. So, no, I haven't been in love. Thought I was, but nope."

"But you're open to it?"

"Yeah. I'd like to have a family of me own someday. But for now, I'm happy being single. Or at least I was," Korry paused and smiled at me. "Until I started working for you two."

"Sorry, not sorry."

"Yeah, yeah. You might consider soundproofing your bedroom though, for future guests."

"Jesus Christ."

"Yeah, I heard that too. Even on the other side of the house," Korry chuckled. "I'm teasing. In my job, I see and hear it all, it's no big deal."

My cheeks were flaming red. "I can imagine."

"The trickiest ones are the clients who want my services to extend to the bedroom."

It was none of my business but now I was curious.

"And no, I haven't stepped over that line. That's a shite-hole I never want to fall into."

"But look at Alex, Aiden, and Jared," I countered.

"Risking your job for love is one thing, for a casual screw is another."

"Speaking of jobs, any more news about your next one?"

Korry nodded. "Well, it's not news but keep this on the down low: the hotshot racecar driver I'm going to be shadowing? It's Charlie's brother, Travis."

"Really? Charlie's great. I'm sure his brother's the same."

"I hope so. But from what Charlie told me, Travis is kind of a lone wolf. He doesn't like anyone telling him what to do. I can't imagine he's gonna take my security advice seriously."

"I'm sure it'll be fine. And hey, even if he's an asshole, you get to be around all those incredible cars, and watch races. That's exciting."

"That's the only reason I said yes," Korry replied, and stood up. "You okay now?"

I smiled up at him. "Better, thanks. I was all up in my head when I got off the phone. Thanks for the talk."

"That's what I'm here for."

"Not to guard my body?"

"That too."

CHAPTER 37

TATE

t turned out, Reed's flight wasn't on time.

It was delayed. By three fucking hours.

I'd offered to pick him up, but Reed texted and told me to stay home, he had a driver arranged.

Guilt gnawed at my gut. I should've gone to the airport. I couldn't sleep anyway.

While Reed was in New York, I'd spent the week getting my brand deals sorted, auditioning for two movies, and most important of all, getting my stuff moved into his house.

Our home.

Mine was on the market.

With Korry's help, I'd packed up most of my belongings and moved them over, boxes now littering every room.

And now, at one in the morning, unable to sleep and needing distraction, I finished unpacking my clothes.

Something as simple as hanging my shirts up next to Reed's in the walk-in closet gave me goosebumps. If I had any remaining doubts, they were silent now as the truth stared back at me.

His. Mine. Ours.

Despite everything we'd been through, time and again, we chose each other.

We couldn't change the past and the future was uncertain.

There was only here and now.

I reached for one of his white dress shirts and slipped it on. It was tight on me, but I left it unbuttoned.

Then I continued my unpacking efforts until I was interrupted by my phone buzzing.

> Reed: I'm five minutes out, are you still awake?

> Tate: Silly question. I've hardly slept all week.

> Reed: Tell me about it. I've been dreaming about curling up next to you.

> Tate: Don't forget our cats. They've been seriously displeased with only having me around.

> Reed: Obvi LOL. The only thing I want is you and our bed. And a bath. Exciting, right?

> Tate: Just wait

My heart was pounding hard and fast.

I headed for the front door, waiting, and watching. Finally, a few minutes later, the car pulled into the driveway.

In Reed's shirt, my ratty old shorts, and a pair of flip flops, I walked outside. The driver opened his door.

"I got it from here," I announced. "Thanks."

The driver nodded and got back in.

I opened the back door and held out my hand. Reed all but tumbled out of the car and into my arms.

"Fuck, I've missed you," I confessed. "Welcome home."

I felt him tremble, and I held on tighter.

"You don't know how happy I am right now," Reed replied, his voice muffled against my shoulder. "I missed you so much."

"Before you kiss me and I forget what day it is, where's your luggage?" I asked.

"Back seat," he whispered, and kissed my cheek.

I reluctantly let go of him and bent down to retrieve his suitcase, pulling it out and then slamming the door shut.

With Reed's hand in my right, and his carry-on in my left, we headed inside.

"I don't want to damper our reunion, but I'm fucking exhausted," Reed admitted.

"Sleep first," I replied as I put the bag down. "You, me, and our California king."

Reed's eyes suddenly welled up.

"Baby, it's going to be okay, I promise," I whispered, cupping his face. "You still feeling anxious?"

"No, I'm better," he shook his head. "I'm just really fucking glad to be home."

I smiled at him. "All my stuff is here."

"That's great, but that's not what I meant. When I say home, I mean being with you."

Now I was the one in danger of crying.

We reached for each other, my lips devouring his.

I pushed him against the wall and laid claim to him, showing him what his words meant to me.

This beautiful, incredible man that was all mine.

I slid one hand down over his hip and he wrapped his denim-covered leg around my waist.

We rocked together, grinding our hips, our kisses desperate, needy.

"Bedroom," Reed whispered when we finally came up for air.

He took my hand and we stumbled past the living room,

kissing, grappling, bumping into furniture, and making a god-awful racket in the process.

"What the—" I heard Korry call out. "Oh, I should have known. Night."

I waved at Korry, or rather, in the direction of his voice. Reed and I were too caught up in each other to separate.

When we finally made it to our bedroom, we were both panting and sweating. I wanted to strip him down and devour him.

Until I got a good look at my boyfriend's face, and the dark smudges underneath his eyes.

My needs would have to wait. Reed came first.

I licked my lips, tasting him. "Get in bed, I'll join you in a sec."

Reed nodded. I watched as he stripped down and slid under the covers.

I shut the door tight and then turned off the lamp in the corner of the room, the darkness settling around us.

By the time I slipped my shorts and shirt off and joined him in bed, Reed was already asleep.

I spooned his body tight and everything in my world was right again.

Sleep, which had all but eluded me for the past week, finally came.

Reed

I woke up surrounded by bright sunlight and strong arms.

And Tate's hard cock pressed against my ass.

Fuck, it was good to be home.

I traced a path down his forearm with my finger, then pulled his hand up and kissed his palm.

"Did you have a good sleep?"

Tate's gravelly voice in my ear was the best thing I'd heard all week.

"Out like a light. You?"

"Same," he kissed my neck. "You wanna talk about your trip?"

I shook my head. "Later. Right now, I just want you to touch me."

"Your wish is my command," he replied as he rolled on top of me. "And now that you're rested, I can do dirty, dirty things to you."

I was all for that.

Our lips met in a heated kiss that was long and languid.

The perfect wake up call.

Until there was a knock on our bedroom door.

"Sorry to interrupt, but Henn is here!" Korry called out.

"Fuck," Tate grunted and slowly rolled off me. "We'll be out in five minutes!"

I reached out and cupped his jaw, rubbing his beard.

"Later," he promised me, taking hold of my hand and kissing my fingers.

By the time we got dressed and headed out to see Henn, I was fully awake but still tired, emotionally wrung out.

Henn was sitting at the island talking to Korry and sipping on a cup of tea. I gave her a hug and sat down beside her.

Korry clapped his hands together. "Well, I'm off to pack."

"Thanks for the tea, Kor," Henn replied.

"Ta." He nodded and left the three of us in the kitchen.

"Henn, I hope there's a very good reason why you're in our house so early in the morning," Tate grumbled as he headed for the coffee machine.

"Our house?" she repeated with one eyebrow raised.

"You didn't notice all the boxes?" I replied.

"Oh, I noticed. I just wanted to hear Tate confirm it," she smiled. "And I'm here because I had to drop off updated contracts for you to sign. I also wanted to let you know that we finally figured out who took that photo. It was one of the makeup crew, some guy named Landon Barnes. Turns out, his brother-in-law works for the tabloid that ran the story."

"I wish I could say I'm surprised," Tate scoffed. "But I'm not."

Henn nodded. "Jared's production company is taking legal action since he violated his contract. Do you want to join the suit?"

Tate looked at me. "Baby, what do you think?"

I sighed. "I don't know if it's the right time to ask me that question."

Not after the week I'd had.

"Oh shit, Reed, I'm so sorry. I didn't think—" Henn started and placed her hand on mine.

"It's okay," I squeezed her hand. "Really, I'm fine. Now that the criminal trial is done, we're taking Saks to civil court, so I'll have to prepare myself for that. And yeah, I've been down the lawsuit road before. It takes a long time. It's a lot of expense too, but sometimes you have to take a stand."

Tate finished making his coffee and took the first sip, nodding. "We're in. If only to make a point. And I better not see that guy in or around a movie set ever again."

"You and Jared both," Henn replied and reached for her purse. She pulled out a thick envelope and left it on the counter. "Your movie contract offers."

Tate nodded. "I'll look them over and drop them off this week."

Tate put his cup down and walked around the island to stand beside me. I slid my arm around his waist.

"Or I could wait, there's only—" Henn started and then paused when she glanced at us. "Yes. Later this week is fine."

"Now, if you'll excuse us," Tate cleared his throat. "We would like to be alone."

"That's a lot less rude than I expected, love," I quipped. "In the past, you would've just told Henn to get out."

"That too," he added with a smirk.

"I'm outta here, my girlfriend is waiting for me. I'll call you guys tomorrow," Henn replied as she made her way to the door.

"Add another day to that," Tate yelled out. "Make it two."

With a final wave, she was gone.

"Eggs, pancakes, sausage?" Tate asked.

"I thought we were going to fuck first?"

"You need a lot of calories for what I have in mind," Tate chuckled.

I glanced at him, or rather, at the white shirt he was wearing. Or not wearing, since it was unbuttoned, showing off his tight pecs and abs. Then I noticed the monogram on the cuff.

Tate was wearing my shirt.

A shiver ran through my body. Fuck, I liked it. I loved it.

"Nice button down," I commented. "A little tight around the biceps, though."

"I think I look pretty good," Tate smiled, and those dimples did me in. "You don't mind?"

"That you're wearing my clothes? Fuck, no. It's sexy as hell. What brought that on?"

Tate pulled me off the stool and into his arms, giving me a resounding kiss. I forgot all about breakfast and contracts and lawsuits.

"I had a realization last night, at one in the morning."

"And?" I asked, curious.

Tate smiled and licked his lips.

"I'm better at show than tell."

CHAPTER 38

REED

THREE MONTHS LATER

glanced at my phone and the last message Tate sent me.

> Tate: Meet me at 11. 3561 St. Sierra Blvd.

He'd left the house early this morning, telling me that he had an errand to run, but not what or where. Which wasn't like him. Not just being up and out the door by six AM, but the way he nearly vaulted out of our bed.

After three months of living together, I knew my man. And an early wakeup call, unless it was about work, was rare.

I wracked my brain about his upcoming auditions, but nothing came to mind. He had one role booked but filming didn't start for another month.

So why the rush to leave home today? And why the sudden meeting at an unfamiliar address?

Something was going on.

As I sat in my car, in our driveway, I texted him.

Reed: What's going on?

He replied in typical Tate fashion.

Tate: Just get your sexy ass over here.

How could I say no to that?

So, I drove out of our neighborhood and headed for the highway, southbound.

When I exited the traffic gridlock a half hour later, I drove along Sierra boulevard. The area started to feel a bit more familiar to me. Too bad I couldn't recall exactly why.

This was the older, industrial section of LA, where former warehouses were now being converted to condos. I'm sure one day it would be filled with bustling restaurants and coffee shops, but for now, it was pretty much a construction zone.

Once I spotted the building with the correct address, I parked on the street and got out. Looking up at the warehouse, I noticed there was a sign that indicated it was set to be redeveloped. Maybe Tate wanted to buy in? I was curious since he didn't mention that he wanted to buy an investment property.

Besides, we'd already discussed it, and our first purchase together was going to be an apartment in Europe, some place where we could escape the chaos of our LA life.

A flicker of déjà vu echoed in my brain as I walked up the stairs and opened the front door.

Oddly enough, I heard music. Or was that my imagination?

Then I glanced at the exposed brick walls and the wide-plank wood floors.

The dimly lit hallway.

The flashback hit me fast and hard.

This was the building that Charlene rented once upon a time for her auditions.

The place where I'd first met Tate.

Then I glanced at my phone again and realized what day it was. The date and time, it was the same.

I began to tremble, but I kept walking, my heart pounding so hard it drowned out the music.

And yes, there was music.

The song was a decade old, but I knew all the words by heart. Tate had teased me relentlessly about the fact that I used to sing it, off-key, in the shower, in that apartment we first shared.

By the time I finally entered the last room on the right, the audition room, I was shaking all over.

Tate was sitting in the same exact chair Charlene used, with a camera set up and everything.

"What's all this?" I asked.

"Do you remember this place?"

"Not until I stepped foot inside it again, but yes. I do. Of course, I do. It's where we met."

Tate got up and slowly walked towards me.

"I came out of that audition, pumped up but so fucking nervous," he admitted as he licked his lips. "And there you were, standing in the hallway, chatting up those guys, all relaxed and easy."

I wasn't relaxed. Not when I spotted Tate.

I remembered the swarm of butterflies that sat in my stomach.

They'd taken flight that day and hadn't settled since.

"When you came up to me, I couldn't help but stare at your unforgettable eyes. Then you laughed," Tate continued, clearing his throat. "And even though I swore to myself that I didn't want to talk to you, when you laughed, I couldn't help but lean into it."

"I was nervous too," I admitted. "Not for the audition but when I saw you walking down the hallway. And it wasn't because you were handsome, because you were that. It was the look in your eyes, a fierce determination that I'd never seen in anyone before. I just knew I had to talk to you. I just knew that you were someone I wanted to know."

Tate took my hands in his. We were both shaking.

"You don't know how grateful I am, and always will be, that you came up and talked to me that day. You, Reed, changed my life. And here we are."

"Why are we here?"

Even though my heart knew the answer, I needed to ask the question.

To make sure this was real.

"You know damn well why we're here," he replied with a wink.

He shoved a shaky hand in his pocket and dropped to one knee in front of me.

Then I remembered the camera.

"Oh my God, are you really recording this?"

"Yes, but this time, I'm the only one who's auditioning. And if you find me worthy," he paused, his voice hoarse. "If you find me worthy of the biggest and best role of my life, to be your husband, then I will be the happiest man alive."

"Tay," I whispered, tears spilling over my cheeks.

"Give me your hand, baby."

I held out my left hand and he took it gently in his right. When he placed the diamond eternity band at the tip of my finger, I choked on a sob.

"Will you, Reed Anthony Larkin, be my husband?"

"Yes, yes, yes," I chanted, my heart so full and near to bursting.

"You sure you don't need more time to think about it?" he teased me.

"Put the gorgeous ring on my finger, Tate!"

Tate laughed out loud at my demand and finally pushed the ring on my finger.

It fit perfectly. I was never taking it off.

He stood back up and drew me into his arms. "Are you ready to make it official?"

I leaned up and kissed him.

"It's about fucking time."

Tate

I was smiling so wide my face hurt, tears welling up and sliding down my cheeks without warning.

Only Reed could make me laugh and cry at the same time.

Suddenly, it wasn't just the two of us. The room was bursting with noise.

Our family and friends, hidden in the room next to us and watching the proposal via my video, came barreling in and crowded around us. Reed's dad, sister, brother-in-law, and his niece and nephews had all flown out, as well as Dylan, Max and their daughter, Blake. Charlene and Henn, of course. I'd also invited Jared, Alex, and Aiden, but they were traveling in Italy. Jared confirmed they'd be heading to LA next week, so Reed and I would have another, smaller celebration with them at our house.

I still couldn't believe I'd managed to pull off this surprise without a hitch.

"How did you do all this?" he asked me.

"With a lot of help from me," Henn piped up.

"Did you pick out the ring too?" Reed asked her.

"No," I proudly declared. "I did it myself."

"That's a lot of diamonds, Tate."

"I need everyone to know you're taken. This way, even from afar, they'll spot your ring."

After we'd hugged everyone, and took a thousand photos, I pulled Reed aside for a quiet moment.

"Are you sure you like it? I could always—"

Reed silenced me with a kiss.

"It's beautiful, love. I'm never taking it off."

"Next week we can go and pick out my ring."

"It's a date."

"Speaking of dates, when *do* you want to get married?" I asked him.

"Um, we just got engaged," he whispered. "Don't you want to take your time?"

"I'm ready now. I don't want to wait."

Reed stared at me and smiled. "In that case, why don't we pick your ring sooner rather than later and go to the courthouse next week?"

"Just the two of us?" I asked.

"I'm sure we can convince my family to stay a few more days."

"Let's do it."

I pulled Reed back into the chaos of the party and whistled to get everyone's attention.

When the chatter finally quieted, I raised my hand. "We have another announcement to make—"

"You're pregnant!" Rissa called out.

"Not yet," I clapped back. "We're getting married next week, and everyone's invited!"

More shouts, claps, and hollers rang out around us.

"You know what this means?" Dylan added. "Bachelor party!"

"Oh no," I said at the same time Reed called out, "Yes!"

"I know just the place," Dylan winked. "Leave it with me."

I glanced at Dylan and shook my head. I could only imagine the kind of debauchery that he had in store for us.

I was about to reply when Reed tugged my hand and pulled me into the hallway again.

Alone, just the two of us.

He leaned against the wall and offered his hand to me.

"Reed Larkin. I've never seen you here before. You new in town?"

"What—" I startled, and then clued in to what he was doing.

Re-enacting our first conversation.

I turned and stood beside him, leaning up against the wall, our shoulders brushing.

"Tate Aduma," I replied. "You got another audition after this?"

"Nope," Reed glanced up at me. "Just lick me."

I fought back a laugh at that line. "Excuse me?"

Reed nudged my shoulder. "I'm heading to a club called Lick Me. You wanna come?"

"Baby, that club is long gone," I replied and turned to face him. "But to answer your question, yes, I want to lick you and I definitely want to come. But there's something I want even more than that."

"Really? What?"

"To love you. Every damn day for the rest of our lives."

Reed's resulting smile lit up the hallway.

I leaned down to kiss him, tasting his happiness. And mine.

"It only took you ten years to admit it."

"Was it worth the wait?" I asked.

"No question."

EPILOGUE

TATE

FIVE YEARS LATER

"Reed!" I called out as I entered our house. "Baby, are you home?"

My question was met with silence.

That was odd. Our home was anything but.

I wandered through the living area and noticed that the patio doors were open to the backyard.

When I finally spotted him, my heart began to flutter.

Every fucking time.

Reed was sitting on a lounger under the umbrella, our three-year-old daughter, Kylie Rose, fast asleep in his arms. She was my husband's twin—from her curly blonde hair to her green eyes, to her sunny personality.

She was a happy baby and now a talkative toddler who had everyone who met her, smiling.

Even her grumpy-assed Papa (that's me).

Doing my stealthiest walk and trying not to wake her, I wandered outside and joined them.

My family.

Something I never, ever thought I'd have, was now the only thing in the world that mattered to me.

And after spending many years chasing my dreams, I finally realized that he was standing right in front of me.

Now I had two of them.

Movie roles and awards were all well and good, but they didn't fill up all my empty places. Only the love of my husband and my daughter did that.

"Hey," I whispered as I leaned down to kiss my husband on the head.

"Hey, she fell asleep ten minutes ago. She was exhausted after her playdate."

"Did you manage to get a nap in yourself?"

Reed snorted. "Nope. I had last minute stuff to organize since Dad and Rissa will be here in a few hours."

"About that—"

"Let's order in tonight, I'm too tired to cook."

"We can do that, but you and I aren't staying for dinner."

"What?"

I leaned over and gave his lips a soft kiss.

"Your dad and sister have agreed to look after Kylie. You and I are heading to Big Sur for a weekend away, just the two of us."

Reed's shocked face was worth all the planning.

"Are you sure?"

"It's all booked," I explained. "We've been going non-stop for the past few months, and we've barely said more than ten words to each other in passing. It's time for an adults-only weekend. I'm stealing you away. Tonight."

Reed's luminous smile made my pulse pound hard and fast.

"Thank you, love. I can't wait."

I kissed him again, longer, harder, and everything was right in my world.

But our intimate moment was interrupted by our daughter's sudden squeal.

"Papa!"

She wiggled out of Reed's arms and held them out to me.

"Uppa!"

I picked her up and stood up.

"Guess who's going to be here soon? Grandpa and Auntie Rissa!" I told her.

"Yay!"

She squealed louder and I blew a raspberry on her neck. Her infectious giggle had Reed and I laughing right along with her.

It had taken a lot of therapy and a lot of love to get here.

When you grow up in a family that's anything but, the fear of letting anyone get close to you, of anyone knowing your truth, weighs heavy. So too does the anxiety of repeating painful patterns. Not that I was anything like my stepfather, but I still had a lot of anger about my past that needed to be let out. And it took a few years of tackling the subject head on for me to reconcile with it.

I'd never forget the abuse I endured, but it wasn't going to define the rest of my life.

Both Reed and I faced our trauma and addictions head on and learned healthier ways to cope.

No matter what came our way, we always turned to each other.

Our life wasn't perfect, but it was perfect for us.

A lot had changed, and we'd grown, together.

For the past two years I'd been working with Max, trying my hand at screenwriting. Reed always said I had a special way with words. At first, I thought my husband was being sarcastic, but it turned out, he was right.

Writing was something I never imagined I would love doing, but did. It was cathartic in a way that was not all that different from acting. And it gave me the opportunity to work from home most of the week. Between that and a few select acting roles here and there, I was busy and fulfilled.

When Kylie was born, Reed became a stay-at-home dad, and he was loving it. Not that he was completely out of the business either. Once a month he worked with Charlene at her casting agency, scouting for new talent. Following in his mother's footsteps, Reed had a gift for mentoring fellow actors.

We still got calls to star in movies together, but we were holding off. Until the right opportunity came along.

Or, until my latest screenplay was finalized. Which happened to be today.

I had another surprise for my husband this weekend.

Some people buy their spouse flowers, I was giving Reed a script.

Hey, it worked for us.

"And guess who else is coming to visit next week?" Reed announced.

I stopped and turned to stare at him.

"Who?"

"Max and Dylan and the kids as well as Jared, Aiden, and Alex. And their kids."

"You know what that means?" I said to Kylie.

"Pool patty!" she giggled.

"That's right, a pool party," I repeated and kissed her temple.

Reed stepped up to me and slid his arm around my waist, the other around our daughter.

Staring into his eyes, I saw the truth.

I used to chase the Hollywood spotlight. Never satisfied, always hungering for something more.

But this right here, the family that Reed and I had created together?

It *was* the light.

And I was so damn happy that it was our life.

———

THANK YOU for reading Co-Star!

You can read Dylan and Max's story here: Starboard

And Jared, Aiden, & Alex: Endeavor

Get ready for 4-EVER, Book 3 in my Wayward Lane MM rockstar romance series!

ABOUT THE AUTHOR

I write steamy and dreamy MM romances full of heartwarming characters, cheeky banter, and swoony moments.

Read my **Wayward Lane MM rockstar romance** series: **PUNK-IN, B-MINE and 4-EVER**

And check out my **Voyagers series**: everyone who boards the superyacht *Now, Voyager*, will meet their match!

Sign up for my newsletter for the latest updates, cover reveals, and bonus scenes:

http://avaolsenauthor.com

OTHER TITLES BY AVA OLSEN

Wayward Lane: Rockstar Romance

PUNK-IN

B-MINE

4-EVER

Voyagers Series

Oh Buoy

Starboard

The Cockpit

Endeavor

NY Nights

Novel Affair

Troublemaker

Unforgettable You

NY Nights Bodyguard Edition

Hate to Love You

Love Like Yours

Never Knew Love

Made in United States
North Haven, CT
22 March 2024

50312456R00182